PENGUIN BOOKS

A Victim Must Be Found

Howard Engel was born in Toronto but raised in St. Catharines, Ontario. He later lived in Nicosia, London and Paris, where he worked as a journalist and broadcaster. Back in Canada he became a distinguished producer of programs at the CBC, where he stayed for many years. He has now published six Benny Cooperman novels: *The Suicide Murders, The Ransom Game, Murder on Location, Murder Sees the Light, A City Called July* and *A Victim Must Be Found*. His endearing private eye, Benny Cooperman, has been described as a cherished national institution. He is rapidly also becoming known internationally through the many foreign editions of his adventures. Both *The Suicide Murders* and *Murder Sees the Light* were recently made into TV films. Engel is a member of the Mystery Writers of America, the British Crime Writers' Association and a founding member of the Crime Writers' Association of Canada. He was 1984 winner of the Arthur Ellis Award for crime fiction. He lives with his wife, the writer Janet Hamilton, his son, Jacob and his two cats in Toronto.

A
Victim Must
Be Found

Howard Engel

Penguin Books

PENGUIN BOOKS

Published by the Penguin Group
Penguin Books Canada Ltd, 2801 John Street, Markham, Ontario L3R 1B4
Penguin Books Ltd, 27 Wrights Lane, London W8 5TZ, England
Viking Penguin Inc., 40 West 23rd Street, New York, New York 10010, USA
Penguin Books Australia Ltd, Ringwood, Victoria, Australia
Penguin Books (NZ) Ltd, 182-190 Wairau Road, Auckland 10, New Zealand

Penguin Books Ltd, Registered Offices: Harmondsworth, Middlesex, England

First published in Viking by Penguin Books Canada Limited, 1988

Published in Penguin Books, 1989

1 3 5 7 9 10 8 6 4 2

*Publisher's note: This book is a work of fiction. Names, characters, places and incidents
either are the product of the author's imagination or are used fictitiously,
and any resemblance to actual persons living or dead, events,
or locales is entirely coincidental.*

Manufactured in Canada

Canadian Cataloguing in Publication Data

Engel, Howard, 1931–
  A victim must be found

ISBN 0-14-011205-7

I. Title.

PS8559.N49V53 1989   C813'.54   C88-093790-4
PR9199.3.E54V53 1989

*For Bill Roberts
and in memory of two friends:
Gwendolyn MacEwen, the Shadow-Maker,
and the mercurial Patrick Hynan*

*The idea for this story
came from a conversation with
my friend Harry Barberian,
to whom I am indebted*

As some day it may happen that a victim must be found,
I've got a little list — I've got a little list.

W.S. Gilbert

A
Victim Must
Be Found

Chapter One

It is only a couple of days from the 28th of March to the beginning of April, yet there seems to be a lost month in there this year that I'm only starting to account for. I'm sure that there is no perceptible difference in the temperature today and what it was last Monday, but Monday appears to be already backing into the clouds of history. Last week I heard that the United Cigar Store on St Andrew Street is closing down, that Ella Beames, my friend at the library, is being retired and after ten years I've had to leave my room at the City House. Everything is in flux with a vengeance. It's all I can do to keep my head above water.

It would be easier if change could be blamed on someone. Maybe municipalities should elect an ombudsman on the understanding that on leaving office he'll become the public whipping boy for a year, the person to blame for everything from ingrown toe-nails to the untimely death of a good friend. Life would be simpler that way. All you have to do is find the right person.

Of course I wasn't thinking of any of this last Monday. On Monday, last week and a thousand years ago, I had other things on my mind.

I was surrounded by boxes. They rose around me like ungainly towers of cardboard. In one of them were my cuff links and my toothbrush. In another I had a list of all my belongings and a key for finding each obj___ in its numbered box. "If I had this to do ag___ the half-formed thought that kept kicking me in the ear. But moving again was out. I was sure of that much. I had given up the simplicity and familiarity of my old room at the City House on King Street. If I had to do it all over again I would keep the master list on my person and put the numbers on the sides of the boxes and not the top. As it was, I couldn't see a single number, they were all hidden by the boxes on top, and the top box stood above my sight line.

I sat in the middle of this mess, trying to get a handle on it. At least the room had a carpet. I'd never owned a carpet before. I thought, one day I might even own a tree. For the last hour, ever since the moving man had taken his tip and my last cigarette, I'd been trying to put some order in my life by moving the packed boxes from one wall to another. Whenever I opened one of the cartons, it was the wrong one. What was I going to do with LPs when I couldn't locate the stereo? I needed a place to put the records. It was on my "must buy" list, wherever that was.

I stood on a chair and looked down on the number of the top box. It didn't mean anything to me. I raised the flaps and saw the buff colour of office files. That box wasn't even supposed to come here. I tried to readjust the lid. I was getting good at closing cardboard cartons. At first I had a devil of a time getting the flaps to lock. It was like trying to tie a reef knot and always coming up with a granny. It took a long time to sort out the over and under technique of getting the tops to b   Naturally, the mover could do it blindfolded. Fu   demonstrated an assortment of skills: slid-
            ts through tight corners with a blanket
                ne awkward package through the
                  cape.

                  nd remembered the depart-
                 t in the pack, but had let

me know it wasn't his usual brand. He had also let me
know that he didn't think much of my new apartment.
Looking around at the towers of cardboard, I was inclined to agree with him. The place wasn't huge. It was
a lot bigger than my room at the City House, but it
didn't present a vista of rooms melting away through
vast corridors to the vanishing point. It was a room for
sleeping, sitting and eating. There was a kitchenette
behind a curtain and a three-piece bathroom. Outside
the window on one side was a schoolyard with a metal
geodesic structure for the kids to climb on at recess.
From the other windows I could see a streetscape of
parked cars and damp trees. What had started as a
Scotch mist had degenerated into a cold, wet drizzle.
The window-panes of the apartment shook in the
wind. Parallel rain tracks were diverted by the blasts
as they moved down the soot-stained glass.

I pinned a note on my door for the telephone man
and left both my apartment door and the downstairs
door unlocked. It was time to buy cigarettes and to
rethink a few things.

The wind blowing across Court Street wasn't exactly
strong, but it cut into me. It made the fierce winter we'd
just come through a lot closer than the calendar indicated. Last week we were forgetting our jackets and rolling down the car windows. And now the puddles
looked like they'd freeze if the thermometer dropped
a notch. In the corners of the alley, the detritus of the
winter was still showing; the pile of garbage that had
collected in the snowdrifts during February still clung
to the walls and gutters. Fragmented newspaper pulp
and scraps of plastic wrap stuck to the brick. The wet
chill made my feet feel the thinness of my shoes as I
hurried to the United Cigar Store for a cup of coffee.

The United wasn't the same. For the last couple of
months I'd been hearing that they were goin

it down. I took my usual place at the dark marbletop counter and accepted the coffee as my due when Irene slid a cup in my direction with neither a greeting nor a glance. I was part of her day and needed no more recognition than another full ashtray or empty ketchup bottle. I sipped in silence, thinking of my boxes.

"Benny? Can I talk to you?" I turned around and it was Pambos Kiriakis moving in on me from five stools away. I said hello to the little guy and took my coat off the stool next to me. Shoving his coffee mug along the green marble counter, he left a wet trail of heavily creamed coffee behind him. He frowned at that. I wondered whether that was because he used to be a waiter. Anyway, he let Irene do the honours with her damp cloth. A nod from him initiated another fill-up from her Silex, a smile brought a handful of plastic cream containers.

The first time I met Pambos Kiriakis, he was flipping steaks in the steakhouse which briefly occupied the store under my new apartment. It had been a launderette and a typewriter repair store before that. Now it was having a fling as a Mexican restaurant specializing in refried beans. Death was written on its menu. I didn't give it another three months before it gave up the ghost. Where do people get the idea that you can make a buck from refried beans in Grantham, Ontario? I tried to think of other sure-fire misses: a store specializing in coloured paper-clips, a boutique dealing in designer luggage, a head shop, a rare-book store. Since he took off his white apron and chef's bonnet, I'd seen little of Pambos except at the United or the Diana where most of the town filters the day through a sort of community dialysis. Sitting there I can see all of the kids I went to school with and half of my teachers. Here deals are made and marriages ruined. I've seen a couple leaning across a table so close that their heads touched as they held hands over a banana split. Later I saw the same couple working on a separation agreement. I knew it was a separation agreement, because the boy had asked me to follow his young wife when she was supposed to be going to her choir practice. But that was in the days when there was a buck to be made in divorce work. Right now an honest private investigator has a hard time not reading the want ads. It's the nearest thing to being unemployed in the whole Niagara Peninsula.

I'd heard that Pambos had done well. I remembered that he was managing the Stephenson House, a small exclusive hotel overlooking the old canal. "Benny, I think I need your help. I mean, I think I need your professional help. Can you sit a minute?"

"Sure, Pambos. What's on your mind?"

The little guy stroked his chin, reaching for a place to begin and not finding it. I tried to make it easier for him. "I just moved into that apartment over the steakhouse where you used to work," I said. "It's a Mexican place now."

"Yeah, Tacos Heaven. It's run by a Hungarian from Niagara Falls. I give it three more weeks before it's empty again." He was still groping for a starting place. He took a stab. "You still do private investigations, don't you, Benny?"

"Specialty of the house."

"That's what I thought. I should have come to your office, Benny, but seeing as how I saw you sitting here by yourself, I thought, what the hell? What can he do to me?" I gave him a grin to show that he wasn't stepping on my corns. He smiled too, but then asked in a quieter voice:

"You want me to wait and come to the office, Benny? I can take a hint."

"Pambos, if you want to talk to me about it here in the privacy of the United Cigar Store, that's your privilege. What can I do for you?"

"It's a question of stolen property."

"Pambos, I'm not a fence. I'm an investigator."

"I know that! I'm just having trouble getting the story started. Something that belongs to me is missing. It's not where it should be."

"You're talking about an expensive object?"

"I want to talk to you about a list." He looked into my face like I was about to tell him he'd won the lottery. If he saw a shadow pass over my features it was a brief recollection of my own list in one of the twenty or so boxes in my apartment.

"What sort of list?"

"A piece of paper. It was in my office and now it's gone."

"I take it this list is valuable, eh?" I always try to let my clients see into the workings of a professional investigator's mind. Little scraps of deduction or expert knowledge always help. I once tried to get an intimate grasp of the map of the city so I could without looking recall that Binder's Drug Store is right next to the wooden building with a barbershop on the ground floor. On the other side's a gas station. But I was always mixing up Chestnut Street with Maple and Hillcrest with Glenridge. Pambos was looking at me.

"It is and it isn't," he said. "To some it would have value, but it's not valuable in a general way. I mean, it's not money or stocks. It's just a list of names." We both took a sip of coffee. I couldn't help imagining Pambos's list in the last of the boxes at my place, in the bottom. I thought of trying to put off the rest of the interview until after I'd moved in and gone back to my office on St Andrew Street. But I didn't. I did something that's routine with me, in this case I meant it.

"Why don't you go to the police about it, Pambos? The cops have a great reputation for finding things."

Pambos's smile went in out of the rain. "Look, I got nothing against the cops. Some of my best friends are cops. You know Christophoros Savas? He comes from Cyprus, like me."

"Sure, I know Sergeant Savas. He's a good cop. Why don't you tell him about it?" I thought I'd found an out. In spite of the fact that I needed the business in a general way, what I needed right now was a few snappy stories to help lighten the load of moving-day confusion. I felt like I was a gymnast doing the splits. I was still more than half living at the City House and not safe and dry in my new home yet. I wasn't sure if I had a bed to sleep on for the night. I had the makings of a bed, but that was a mile short of comfort. I thought, what the hell, I might as well come clean. I told Pambos about my problem. He'd just started to give me the usual list of ten reasons why he couldn't go to the cops when I stopped him. He pulled at his chin again. It had been getting bluer as we'd been talking. Pambos needed to shave every half hour.

"Okay," he said. "Why don't we go back to your place? I can help you unpack and tell you about the rest of this stuff. What do you say? I'm very good at organizing things," he said with a touch of pride. "It's because I'm not sentimental. I got a lot of true sentiment in me, but I don't get sentimental, if you catch my meaning. There's a difference."

I paid the check and we went out into the chilly March weather. At least it had stopped raining.

Chapter Two

An hour later my bed was assembled and made up for the night, several of the boxes had been flattened and tied with twine, their contents given to the closets and cupboards of the apartment. Numbers for the remaining boxes were written clearly on four sides and the ever-important list of contents lay on the coffee-table in the middle of the room. Pambos and I sat in our sweaty shirtsleeves drinking the first cups of tea of the first day of the new regime.

Pambos Kiriakis was a little dishevelled, but he looked relaxed, balancing his saucer on his knee like an ancient spinster, and raising his cup to his lips.

"Pambos, I'll never be able to thank you for all this," I said. He brushed it aside with a broad gesture. "I'll never be able to repay your kindness." Here, the gesture was less sweeping. It felt feeble compared to the last sweeping movement of his hand. By this I saw that while I needn't try to thank him, there was a way to repay the kindness. I got up and returned from the kitchen counter with the teapot. "This list," I said, pouring Pambos another cup, "the one that was taken from your office. Tell me about it."

I sat down and eased myself into a situation that couldn't be altered. I had taken the case when I accepted Pambos's help with my boxes. It was one of those quid pro quo something or others you read about. Now that I was all attention and tuned to hear, Pambos began by looking at my ceiling and then out through the white inside shutters with brass catches. He cleared his throat. "Well, let me see. You suggested that I talk to Chris Savas about it. I can't. It's a delicate matter, you see." I smiled in spite of myself. Hell, who ever talks to a private investigator about things that aren't delicate? The cops would be surprised too to be brought in on a case of no delicacy whatsoever.

"Maybe the time for Savas will come later," I suggested, and he bought that for the time being. Pambos began looking lost again, so I reminded him. "The list," I prompted from where I was sitting on the corner of the bed.

"Yes. The names on the list aren't pulled out of the phonebook, Benny. Most of them, as a matter of fact, are unlisted. I'm talking about names that are well known from Grantham all the way to Toronto. I don't want to embarrass anybody. You know what I mean?" I nodded as I sipped tea.

"You can't get a new list?"

"No." He gave me a look that said I hadn't been listening. But I had. I put it down to Pambos knowing his story too well. He couldn't imagine that I didn't have all the tidy details tucked away already. I tried to look even more concentrated. I felt cross-eyed, but he didn't get up and walk out.

"You said back at the United that this list of yours would be valuable to some people but not to everybody. Can you explain?"

"Look, Benny, before we go on with this, I want to put things on a businesslike basis. You know what I mean?" This was my cue to make a grand gesture. But I held my hands on my teacup. Somewhere inside me a voice was saying "Remember your rent!" It was right, moving from the hotel had moved me into a whole new debt bracket.

"Is this going to be worth a hundred a day plus

expenses, Pambos? You have to decide that."

"Well, Benny, I guess money is only money. You know I own a piece of the Stephenson House, don't you? I'm no millionaire, but I'm comfortable enough, if you know what I mean."

"Sure."

Pambos Kiriakis owned a piece of the Stephenson House! That surprised me. I thought he was just the manager. The hotel, one of the oldest and most traditional institutions in Grantham, had been established when the old canal town was at the height of its career. It had started as a health spa when the smelly open sewer that now ran behind St Andrew Street was a forest of tall masts making their way up to Lake Erie or downstream towards Lake Ontario. That heyday lasted until the third Welland Canal was opened just over one hundred years ago. This canal bypassed Grantham's centre of gravity and the town began to look elsewhere for a reason for being. Somehow, some called it a miracle, the Stephenson House was spared in the general rethinking that slowly went on following the close of the Hitler war. No longer a spa noted for its healing waters, the hotel put out feelers to social clubs and Grantham's most exclusive circles. When the private boys' school named after the martyred Bishop Cranmer held a public dance off its Western Hill campus, the location was invariably the Stephenson House. In fact, when a fire put part of Cranmer's lower school out of service, classes were held at the hotel until the damage had been repaired. When the mayor held a function that required a hotel's amenities, the Stephenson was booked and the proprietors of other local hostelries didn't even begin to question the choice. The Stephenson House was a hotel that was out of its category, a find in a small city like Grantham.

From the fifties to the seventies the hotel had been

owned by the Lawder family, one of the oldest families in the district. I went to school with one of the Lawder girls, who impressed all of us when she passed around a photograph of her horse, Pegleas. I remember it with jealousy unabated over these many years. During the last decade, the hotel had changed hands at least twice that I heard about. But, then I'm not the first to hear about the wheeling and dealing among the powerbrokers of the city, even when the power is losing its steam and the broking is largely trying to pay off an incrustation of mortgages deposited along the classical lines of the ancient brick main building.

So, Pambos Kiriakis had a piece of it. Good for him. Some of the old blood around these parts is getting thin. It was time for some transfusion to come along and take a fresh look at the old place. Kiriakis had caused some local eyebrows to be raised when he began managing the hotel. I remember the gossip from St Andrew Street about this Greek coming along and pushing old Phin Lawder off to pensionland. A day earlier the same people had been trading stories about Phin's wasteful and intemperate ways. Phin was a drunk and a spendthrift, but he came from a good family. At least it was a good one back in 1813. Pambos's family didn't arrive on the scene until at least a century and a half later. His father, so he told me, became a shoeshine man in a narrow store near Queen and St Andrew in the early 1960s. Pambos's older brother fell in with some unpleasant characters in Malham, south of Grantham, and ended up as a sacrifice to appease some god of the wars between the mobs. While he was still alive, Pambos said, it was hard not to get a ticket for going through a green light. The cops took their responsibilities more broadly back then. But Pambos never showed any sign of letting his brother's failure to make a success of crime build up a resentment in him for law, order and the establishment. Quite the opposite in fact. The first time I talked to Pambos, he told me about the beginnings of his coin collection, which he figured at the time was worth several thousand dollars. He didn't get this by brother Costas's methods, but by simply culling his change at the end of the day and checking catalogues.

Now that I think about it, Pambos was always dipping into a catalogue of one kind or another. I remember him telling me about a couple of auctions that I might have taken advantage of, if I hadn't been living in a hotel room where all the furnishings were marked by matching cigarette burns. He once invited Wally Skeat from the TV station and me to look at his art collection. When we got to his apartment, we saw the usual Van Gogh prints on the walls. The art collection was in an old cardboard portfolio left over from public school. Three pencil drawings! Now what kind of art collection is that? One was a picture of old Joe Higgins, on his crutches selling balsa birds at the corner of St Andrew and James, like he always was every Saturday when he was sober. The next was a group of houses in Toronto. They were heavily outlined and simplified so that what you saw was more pattern than a lot of details. The name in the lower right read "L. Harris." It didn't mean anything to me, but it lit up Wally's face. "L. Harris" was, I gathered, somebody every civilized person should know about. The other drawing was a sketch of a Venetian street scene judging from the gondola and the flooded streets. The signature down at the bottom read "Perdix." This didn't excite Wally, so I guessed that he wasn't a household word in as many households as "L. Harris."

And that was it: three pencil drawings in a kid's portfolio. The Van Gogh sunflowers by the bathroom door were looking better and better every minute. As Pambos brought his little brass Turkish coffee-maker to a boil three times, no doubt to shake off the evil eye, he explained that Harris was a member of the Group of Seven, not one of whom I'd ever run into before, and Perdix was a fellow at Cranmer College, who was, according to Pambos, going somewhere. The sketch of Joe Higgins was by a local artist who may or may not have heard of the other two. Anyway, it wasn't my idea of a picture collection. After we sipped the thick, sweet coffee, Pambos had got going on his hobby-horse about supporting Canadian arts, which made me feel like it was twelve-thirty instead of only a quarter after nine. Wally and I got out as soon as we could after that. I was glad Pambos had a hobby, I wished I had one.

So now Pambos was comfortable, not a millionaire, but with a tidy piece of Grantham history in the form of an interest in the Stephenson House tucked into his pocket. I guess he could afford to part with whatever it took to locate the missing list.

"Pambos," I asked, "tell me more about this list. A list that has the kind of value you're putting on it isn't your average laundry list. What kind of list are we talking about? Why is it so valuable? Tell me why somebody'd want to take it from you."

"I'll get to that, Benny. Give me a chance to organize my thoughts, eh?" I didn't know he was feeling pressured. I was only trying to help, after all. Pambos took a deep breath and appeared to notice his rolled sleeves for the first time. As he spoke, he unrolled them and refastened his cuffs. "You see, Benny, I can be sure it wasn't anybody working for me that took it. Sten and Andy have been with me for five years. If they wanted to steal from me, which they do, they would take directly from the bar receipts or from the restaurant cash. The list I'm talking about wouldn't mean anything to them."

"So, who does that leave?"

"If you ask me, somebody on the list swiped it."

"Pambos, have you taken up blackmailing or some other kind of extortion?"

"Me? Hell, Benny, this is Pambos Kiriakis you're talking to! I never pinched so much as an apple off a fruit stand in my entire life! I'm clean, Benny, and so is this list."

"Pambos, you're driving me insane!" He looked at me like the shoe was on the other foot.

"What've I done? I'm bringing you some business. I've helped you unpack. What more can I do?"

"You can give me a lead that isn't missing for a start. From what you say, all we have to do to find our suspect is to find the damned list. What kind of trick is that?"

Pambos nodded. But he didn't look too worried. I was not getting a handle on this investigation. I was asking the wrong questions. Here I was at the very beginning of what might become a case, and already I was as mixed up as if it had been dragging in and out of courtrooms for three years. I knew that everything depended on getting a grip on the nature of Kiriakis's list, in order to find out why it was so valuable, but Pambos was not prepared to tell me until he was good and ready. I felt like I was trapped in a computer that had to learn the entire English language before it could tell me "yes" or "no." I tried to master my irregular breathing.

"Pambos, can you remember any part of the list that might be important? Can you remember any of the names on it?"

"I been thinking of that. That's why I came to see you back at the United. I know you keep half your office hours there."

"And?"

"And, what?"

"And do you remember names from your list?"

"Yeah. Sure I do. But, like I said, it's a delicate business. Most of the people on the list wouldn't want to be brought into this."

"Right, Pambos. Maybe I'm the undercover editor of the Grantham *Beacon* instead of a private investigator. Maybe the word private means I'm a stringer for *The Toronto Star*. Is that what you think? Either you came here to trust me—I mean apart from helping with the boxes—or you came to shoot the breeze. Which is it?"

"Benny, don't get hot at me! I'm just feeling my way through this. If it was somebody on this list that took it, I want to wipe the floor with him!"

"Good! I recognize the emotion. Tell me, Pambos, do you remember the names on the list?"

"I remember some of them. There are about twenty-five names in all. All big shots in the Niagara district. I can remember maybe half a dozen of the names. That's all."

"Okay. Have you seen any of the people who appear on the list lately?"

"I was coming to that."

"I'm glad you were coming to something!" Pambos ignored the anxiety he was building in me brick by brick.

"Three of them were in the hotel shortly before I noticed the list missing." I rooted through one of the half-emptied boxes and found a scrap of paper and a ballpoint pen.

"Now we're getting someplace," I said. "Who were they?"

"Jonah Abraham..." The whistle that came out of me was unpremeditated. It represented genuine surprise.

"I can't imagine the head of Windermere Distilleries rifling your desk, Pambos." Pambos looked wounded, like I'd interrupted a vast torrent of information.

"Will you let me finish? Another name is Peter Mac-Culloch. The other is Alex Favell. They were all at the hotel. Any of them could have taken it."

If Pambos had handed me a *Who's Who* of the Grantham élite, I couldn't have found more prestigious names. Abraham, MacCulloch and Favell, while they might never sit at the same table, have graced the best tables in town and beyond. MacCulloch was vice-president of Secord University. He'd come to academia through business. A local boy, he'd made a name for himself in the west, in oil, I think. After more than five years in the job, his face in the paper had become a second logo for Secord. As a fund-raiser, he had no match. He brought into the ivory tower some of the bottom-line philosophy he'd learned in the blitzkrieg of modern business.

Alex Favell, whose name I'd heard around town over the last few years, wasn't as well known to me. I remembered at once that he had something to do with the paper mill in Papertown, south of Grantham. I'd read or skipped through pieces about him on the business pages of the *Beacon*. I couldn't conjure up a face to fit the name. The best I could do was remember seeing the name connected to some social note about the opening of a paper-mill-endowed floral clock somewhere along the road between Niagara Falls and Queenston. The floral clock must be among the wonders of the world least included on the endangered lists.

Lists. I kept coming back to lists. I tried to imagine what kind of list would include Jonah Abraham, Alex Favell and Peter MacCulloch. Favell and MacCulloch were old Grantham, old Ontario, even old Upper Canadian names. There is no equivalent to the Mayflower in Upper Canada. If you came too early, you were

French and not in the pecking-order. If you came too late, you couldn't qualify as a United Empire Loyalist, which meant that you belonged to them foreigners who came after 1800. The UEL list was an important list for some people, but it wasn't the one I was looking for because it excluded Jonah Abraham, the well-known and well-fixed distiller of just about everything but attar of roses.

"Pambos, none of these guys are picking up butts from the gutter. And you say the others on the list are just as rich? Why do you think they would stoop to petty larceny? Now grand larceny is another matter." Pambos looked uncomfortable. He got up and paced the room, finally stopping to fix a few slats in a shutter that had fallen half out of the frame. Very tidily, he picked up the falling pieces and slipped them into their grooves. But he didn't answer my question. It gave me a moment to wonder why I had used those old-fashioned terms for theft. I took a deep breath and tried again. "Isn't Jonah Abraham sniffing around trying to get a Senate appointment?"

"The only Senate appointment he'll get is an appointment to see a senator," Pambos said, with uncharacteristic cynicism. "And since your memory is so good, you'll recall that MacCulloch is a leading candidate for a future lieutenant-governor here in Ontario."

"Noted," I said with a scowl. And when that had sunk in I added, "Which all adds up to the fact that you have more talking to do, Pambos, before I can tell you whether or not I can help you find this thing." Pambos sat down on the edge of my bed. He looked like he had avoided all of the hard questions he was capable of avoiding. From now on he would have to play with the facts or not play at all. "Tell me about the list," I said.

He sucked at something caught in his teeth for a few

moments, trying to turn the thing over in his mind sufficiently to find the best starting point. When he had it, he said, "Have you ever heard of the painter Wallace Lamb?" I thought about that and shook my head.

"No, but that doesn't mean anything. I only heard about Picasso a year ago. How does he figure?"

"His dealer gave me the list. The people on it all have pictures on loan from Tallon's collection."

"Tallon?"

"Arthur Tallon. He ran the Contemporary Gallery on Church Street."

"Oh, yeah. I've walked by it." The Contemporary Gallery, which I had actually been in, although Pambos didn't have to know how I spend my spare time, was an honest-to-goodness art gallery just like the ones in Toronto or Buffalo. To indicate sales, they used the little red dot system like all the big-league galleries. It was the only gallery in town where picture-framing wasn't the big deal. The only other large gallery was for exhibitions only. It was located in the mansion built by the man who built the Welland Canal. They didn't sell pictures at Rodman Hall, you just got to look at travelling exhibitions. The only things for sale were dainty little hasty notes which were just the thing for sending "regrets only" on.

"Why did Tallon give you the list, Pambos? Was he worried about it getting lost?"

"I was buying a Lamb from him. He gave me the list of local people he had lent a few Lambs to." I was beginning to feel more shepherd than investigator, but at least I thought, now, we are beginning to get somewhere.

"Now, we are beginning to get somewhere. All you have to do is ask Tallon to give you a duplicate list." Pambos didn't like my idea. His smile faded on his face and he began shaking his head.

"I can see you don't read the *Beacon* as thoroughly as you should. Arthur Tallon died in Grantham General four weeks ago." Light was beginning to sift through the slats in Pambos's story. If Tallon was dead, that could complicate things.

"We're still getting somewhere," I said. "Has Tallon's death got anything to do with the value of the list?"

Pambos Kiriakis looked at me like he'd been patiently teaching me the two-times-table for the last three hours and I still was stumbling over two times six. "Of course," he said, making me feel about seven-and-a-half and not too swift into the bargain. "Tallon was a terrible businessman. Disorganized. Depended on his memory or slips of paper. If I didn't force him to take my money, he would never take payment. The only receipts I ever got from him are written on torn-up pieces of cigarette packages."

Pambos was setting up Tallon as a bad businessman. I wonder whether he knew what kind of private investigator he was in the process of engaging. I thought of the ratty files in my single, disorganized stack of four filing drawers in the office. Usually I keep everything, new, old, important, sentimental, in an untidy stack in the middle of my desk. Once I start trying to sort things into categories and enter them in different files, that's when I begin to lose hold of the shape of the universe. If everything's under my nose, it can't get lost. The file drawers are good places to hide my lunch in and store my galoshes between winters. I was beginning to get a picture of Tallon in my mind. It was the only substantial thing to come along so far, so I was holding on tight.

"After Tallon died," Pambos went on, "his assistant, Patrick Miles, couldn't tell what paintings Tallon had out on loan. Tallon was always lending pictures. You know, 'Take it home, and give me a call if you decide to keep it.' That sort of thing. I'm talking about hundreds of thousands of dollars' worth of paintings, Benny. I mean, when he started out lending and selling, Tallon didn't have to trust people very much. A Lamb in those days wouldn't be worth more than a couple of hundred dollars. Now a single Lamb might be worth twenty or thirty thousand dollars."

"Tallon seems to have had a special liking for Lamb."

"Yeah. He discovered Lamb. Not that Lamb would ever admit that anybody discovered him, but you know what I mean. Tallon sold the first Lambs in Canada. When New York wanted to see what Lamb was doing, they had to go through Tallon. And Tallon was always generous with them, even though New York prices were always higher than even Toronto prices. Tallon told me he remembered when he couldn't get more than fifteen dollars each for a Lamb canvas, not a sketch, mind you, but a full canvas." I tried to look surprised. I didn't own a painting or a sketch, and the only genuine oils I saw regularly were the work of my Aunt Dora in my mother's living-room.

"So, this list is a list of the people that Tallon knew had pictures on loan from his gallery. If the list was written around the time of his death, that makes it a good inventory of his estate not actually under his roof."

"That's right. Of the Lambs anyway. He lent other pictures too, of course. Now Paddy Miles and Tallon's brother are trying to put the estate in order. As it is, a good portion is unaccounted for. Not everybody who has pictures on loan has come forward. Without the list of pictures on loan a lot of people in big houses are going to make unrecorded capital gains."

I could see the temptation. Only the closest I ever come to that kind of gain is when I get the change from my five-dollar bill *and* my five-dollar bill handed to me by the distracted cashier at the convenience store. I don't know much about rich people, but I've never met anybody who thought he was rich. Everybody always says he's just getting by, even when I'm not on the point of asking for the loan of a few hundred. Anyway, I could see people at the top of the local cultural ladder sitting on their masterpieces and waiting to hear from the executors. After all, nobody got rich by volunteering to give back borrowed property before it was asked for.

"Paddy Miles is going crazy trying to locate the missing pictures, Benny. When I told him about the list Tallon gave me, Paddy nearly kissed my feet."

I was beginning to feel strange getting mixed up in the art world, even the local art world, which might look a little parochial from the outside. Has anybody in Paris or London ever heard of Wallace Lamb, I wondered. By Grantham standards Arthur Tallon was a dealer, but by a real picture dealer, say in New York, was he a dealer? I didn't know. All I knew was that I felt I was sliding into water well over my head. To my rescue came the recollection that I had taken a few drawing lessons when I was a teenager and that Rembrandt's "Saskia" has always hung at the turn of the landing on the way to the second floor of my parents' town house. It was a reproduction glued to canvas of which I was very proud as a kid. I remember how disappointed I was when I examined it through a magnifying glass: all those little printed give-away dots of colour disillusioned me. We didn't have the only genuine Rembrandt on the street after all.

"Pambos," I asked, after I'd put my mind back to more immediately useful work, "tell me this: why are you sitting here worrying about Tallon and not Paddy Miles or Tallon's brother? What do you get out of this?"

"I gave Tallon over two thousand dollars towards a Lamb painting," Pambos said, looking down at the black marks on my off-white carpet. Damned movers!

"Until the estate is settled, I can't get my money back or collect my painting. I'm trying to do Miles and George Tallon a favour, but I'm trying to speed things up a bit on my own account. I won't go broke on this. I may even come out ahead." I couldn't figure how he could make any money by hiring me, but maybe he had some money down in bets on how little I could dig up in the week I said I'd give it before we talked again.

Pambos looked at me, expecting me to make some move that would put him out of his misery. I got up and thanked him for helping me get unpacked. I was glad he hadn't seen the pictures that I'd left on the wall back at the City House. If he had, he would have dropped the whole idea of hiring me. "Okay," I said, "I'll call on your three suspects and see what I can dig up in the way of news about your list." He looked relieved. I looked forward to having a long nap on that newly set up bed.

Chapter Three

Secord University is housed in a single building that sits on the edge of the Niagara Escarpment. If the building were less modern, less the middle of the twentieth century, one might say it beetled, but this rectangular structure of glass and cement was centuries from beetling. It was too four-square and artificial. It looked as if the architects were hedging their bets on the university authorities. "If it doesn't work as a seat of learning," they seemed to be saying, "it might make out as headquarters for an insurance company or perhaps a new post office."

I drove up the hairpin turns that lead a zigzag path up the heights of the escarpment and hung a right into the university's huge parking lot. It was hard to imagine that this one isolated highrise could inspire this much driving. I parked the car at the first vacant space reserved for visitors, about a ten-minute walk from the wing-shaped breezeway which sheltered the front door. There was more than a hint of early spring up here. The sun had come out and the tar and asphalt were beginning to warm up.

The corridors echoed with comings and goings, like a high school. I was surprised that the din of higher education should sound so familiar. The walls were striped and colour-coded to help the sub-normal find the right branch of learning: blue for English, yellow for Modern Languages, red for Geography, and so on. Administration was brown. It figured. I checked my watch. I was on time for my two-thirty appointment with Peter MacCulloch. So I followed the brown line like a trusting undergraduate until it fetched me up in front of the door marked "Office of the Vice-President." Mac-Culloch's name stood out from the wall in uncompromising block letters that made me feel like I'd discovered the vice-president of vice-presidents, the assistant large Stilton of all time. I opened the door and went in.

I told the blonde with big glasses who I was. She checked my name on a list and tried to square the name with my face, like maybe there was another Benny Cooperman who comes in all the time and who doesn't look the way I look. But I must have passed the test, because in a minute she had returned to eating small sesame-seed wafers and I was standing in front of the desk of the great man himself. Behind him I could see all the prime real estate in the whole Niagara peninsula stretched out to the even shores of Lake Ontario.

"Mr Cooperman! What can I do for you?" He got out of his chair and leaned across a desk of impressive dimensions with an outstretched hand. I shook it, and thought I detected a tennis player in his grip. MacCulloch was a tall, lean, sinewy man of middle age. He was the sort that would turn cannibals off missionary stew. His flesh seemed to have been hardened by years of keeping fit. His finely tailored business suit didn't contrive to hide a pot belly. I felt that if these were not early days in our acqaintanceship, he might slap his midsection and give a boast or two about the shape he was in. MacCulloch's face looked almost rosy-pink under his shock of white hair. The lines around his mouth and eyes were deep but friendly. He indicated a chair and I took it. I told him I was checking up on some paintings from the Tallon collection. At first he just smiled and I explained again what I'd already said, but in different words. So, I sat listening to the sound of Peter MacCulloch's tendons stretch as he flattened his palms on the desk blotter.

"Ah, I own, you know, two Lambs, which I bought from Arthur some years ago. There's no secret there. And I explained everything to Paddy Miles at the hotel last week."

"Hotel?" I asked, lifting a curious eyebrow.

"The Stephenson House, on..."

"I know the place."

"I really don't see, Mr Cooperman, what purpose is served in going into this all over again." I dodged the question with one of my own.

"Did you have any paintings on loan from the collection?"

MacCulloch coloured slightly, turning his pink skin a shade or two along the scale to bright red. "No!" he almost shouted, then, evening off and controlling himself better, "not now." He took a breath and pretended to be sweet reason itself. "I did have one, but it went back some months ago. I took it back to the gallery myself."

"Did anyone see you, Mr MacCulloch? Did you get a receipt or discharge or anything like that?"

"I'm not sure I like the inference, Mr Cooperman. Arthur took the painting from me himself."

"But you have no record on paper that the picture was returned." He was glowering at me now and not sorry to let me see it.

"If it comes to that, I have nothing on paper that says the picture was borrowed in the first place. It cuts both ways, Mr Cooperman. Now, if you have no further questions...?"

I wasn't finished asking, and I resented the push I was getting, but I never got to tell him that. For a moment I was aware of noise in the outer office: voices and a muted peal of laughter. Then suddenly there was a blonde woman in the room. She swept in wearing a fawn-coloured trenchcoat and a denim skirt. Her sweater was pink. I know she saw me sitting there, but she went into her act as though she'd found the room empty except for the man behind the large desk. "Peter, dear, I'm just off to the golf club to meet Nesta and the girls. Can you let me have…" She stopped in order to show that I had now become visible. My ectoplasm had been restored. I'm sure the secretary warned her of my existence, but she made a little red moue and said, "Oh, I'm sorry." She looked at MacCulloch like this was the latest in a long list of minor misdemeanours. "I didn't know you were busy."

"That's all right, my dear. Mr Cooperman's just leaving." The look he gave me was stronger than a stage direction. I got up, not wanting to debate the point in the presence of what might be a tender domestic moment.

The woman looked at me. She had large dark eyes for all her blondeness. "Mr Cooperman? Mr *Benny* Cooperman?" She continued to stare. I tried to recall when I had last zipped myself up. MacCulloch looked embarrassed.

"Why yes," he said, fingering a brass paperweight. "Mr Cooperman, my wife, Mary. Mr Cooperman, I think that concludes our business. Good afternoon."

MacCulloch's abrupt dismissal sounded rather school-teacherish and final. It was the first sign of the academic I'd observed. He liked using power when he needed it, I sensed, but I wondered why he chose this moment.

"Sure," I said. "Nice to meet you both."

I walked past the secretary with the big glasses. She didn't look as blonde as she had when I saw her ten minutes earlier. Her boss's wife won the contest in blondeness with no also-rans panting at her tidy heels.

Outside in the corridors, the academic buzz began again. I found it easy to glamorize the lives of students. I imagined their lives as being updated versions of life in a garret, like in *La Bohème* before things get complicated. Struggling with books that have to be read, essays that have to be finished, theses that need extensions is the stuff of the academic world of my imagination. I wasn't planning to hang around Secord University long enough to see how right I was. From where I stood—actually, I was making for the stairs as fast as I could go, bumping past youngsters with briefcases and notebooks—it looked like it would be hard to be a stranger in this community; everybody seemed so intent on his own business.

I headed back to the Olds out in the parking lot, but before I'd even cleared the wings of the marquee over the front door, I heard my name called. I looked back and saw Mrs MacCulloch running past a table where some sort of balloting was taking place. Signs posted near the ballot boxes made me begin to doubt my command of English. I could read the words, but they conveyed no meaning to the off-campus population.

"Mr Cooperman! Mr Cooperman. Just a minute!" She was walking fast, nearly running, which, considering the heels she was wearing, must have been quite a trick. She slowed down when she crossed a patch of new asphalt. For a moment she wallowed like a trapped lawn animal, but then spun free and hurried to catch up like she placed a value on my time that not even I'd suspected. The flying trenchcoat and skirt caught the light as she came nearer. It was one of those outfits women wear to the golf course to change out of. On her it looked good, but then, on her anything including a gunny sack would look good. On balance, I'm glad it was the pink sweater. She slowed down a little when I stopped and waited. It didn't take her that long to catch up.

"Thanks for waiting, Mr Cooperman, I wanted to talk to you." She fell into step with me as we continued the walk to my car.

"Sure, Mrs MacCulloch. Anything I can do?"

"My husband and I have no secrets from one another..." This was an interesting prelude, but I didn't at once see where it was leading.

"Uh-huh?"

"I, well, I frankly want to know why you saw him today?" She tidied off her question with a cock of her head and a little smile. It made her look about seven and begging for seconds from a rather starchy head mistress. At least that's the effect it had on me. After all, where had she been all my life up to this afternoon? I couldn't really take her sudden offer of friendliness seriously. But I didn't want to frighten her away either.

"I suggest, Mrs MacCulloch, that you take that up with him." Her eyes entangled with mine. She was looking for a fellow spirit, reckless like herself. She pouted.

"Yes, but he's so busy." Again she cocked her head. She was good at it. She knew her way around and how to get what she wanted. I kept on in the direction of the Olds.

The day had grown warmer. Up here on the escarpment, the parking lot was like a huge mirror. It felt more like July than March. It was clear that for the moment Mary MacCulloch had nothing better to do than tag after me. Maybe I should have taken the car in for a wash. I hadn't been expecting company like this. "You don't mind if I walk along with you, do you, Mr Cooperman?"

"Be my guest." She moved a little closer to my right side and we continued in silence for a second or two. I could feel her marshalling arguments about why I should tell her the reason for my visit to her husband.But I try not to let more people than necessary into the circle of knowing parties in a simple investigation. In a complex one, sometimes your life depends on keeping as little to yourself as you can. Secrets can be deadly treasures. The best defence is to pass them around.

"Mr Cooperman, my car is in the garage today, I wonder if you'd be very put out if I asked you to drive me up the road to the Otterpool Golf Club. It's only a mile or so." I looked doubtful. She went on talking to stifle my questions:

"It's always breaking down. It has to have its transmission out. Is that serious?"

"Is a triple bypass?" We had arrived at the car. I unlocked the door on the passenger side. The key moved like a stranger in the lock, but the door finally opened. She gave me a toothy smile as she ducked her head under the door-frame.

"You're a peach," she said. I walked around the car wondering what I was letting myself in for. Far off, over the edge of the escarpment, a black silhouette hung in the air. Through the windshield I watched it play with the wind currents as I got the motor going and found the reverse gear. I tried to remember my last passenger without coming up with either a name or a face.

"It's just a little way up the road, honestly."

"I was there once." I remembered that night. Eight years ago. It seemed like more. I'd been taken there against my will by a few people who aren't around any more. Mary MacCulloch interrupted my reverie:

"You know, Mr Cooperman, I lead a pretty raffish life for a university vice-president's wife. But I'd never dream of leaving Peter."

"Uh-huh." I didn't know why I was getting this blast of confidences from my right. Maybe it was my good, plain honest face. Maybe it was something she thought her old man was hiring me to do. I played dumb and kept my eye on the road as it crossed over the reservoir bridge. "Sorry it's so warm in here," I said, by way of getting her off her topic long enough for me to figure out what was going on. "Very unseasonal."

"Like a moderate oven. I guess you don't have air conditioning." She was looking at a button that said "air conditioning" on it in neat capitals, but the function had vanished some time before I traded in my old Olds for this not-so-old old Olds. "The least I can do, when we get to the club, is buy you a drink." She looked across at me. I kept my attention on the transport truck pulling off a minor road at slow speed. I'd learned to expect that from the local farmers going down the road a piece, but usually the trucks were more considerate. I braked hard and fell in behind the transport at a comfortable distance.

I made the turn up Otterpool Creek Road and watched for the two pillars that formed the gateway into the club. I didn't have to wait long. They loomed on my right and I slowed to turn up the lane into the parking lot. At night you can smell sulphur from the paper mills in the air. That afternoon a few golfers, with sweaters tied around their necks just in case the weather returned to the normal temperature for the time of year, pulled their carts after them to the fairway and the first tee. The wind in the bare trees reminded us that it was still March. Mary MacCulloch was looking across at me, studying my face. I could feel it without turning.

"About that drink," she said, as I found a place to leave the car. "I can't just abandon you after you brought me way out here, now can I?" There was something sad in her face that hid under the ready smile. It didn't take away from the warmth of the smile, but it was there, just detectable, like an old war wound or a rough upbringing. I smiled and shrugged, accepting her invitation, and struggled to get my door open. I ran around to the other side of the car and opened hers as well. She got out like that sort of thing happened every day. I followed Mary MacCulloch across the driveway and into the clubhouse.

The Otterpool Golf Club occupied rolling land along Otterpool Creek, which entered the Niagara River a few miles above the falls. It was choice farmland, but here the old fields had been trimmed and manicured into one of the tiny gems that local golfers neglected to mention to tourists, preferring to keep the greens free from outsiders. Unlike many clubs, the membership fee wasn't steep, but then neither were the amenities. The clubhouse consisted of a number of lean-tos that had been attached to the original squared log farmhouse. The blue-grey of the thick wooden walls could now be seen only from the inside, supporting shelves in the pro shop, and standing behind the bar in that small, unpretentious room.

I followed her to a seat by a window that looked out on the green of the eighteenth hole. It was still chilly enough for me outside to give me a sense of comfort and warmth sitting out of the wind. She wanted to buy me a rye and water, but I settled for some soda. I'm not much of a booze-hound. She ordered a double Scotch and wore out her right arm trying to pump me.

"Have you known Peter long, Mr Cooperman? Was this a friendly or a business call that brought you to Secord this afternoon?" I dodged the questions as well as I could, burying my nose in my drink when it was my turn to say something. I could see that she was losing patience with me. In her place, I would have wrung my neck.

"Mr Cooperman, why can't you be more reasonable?" she said, moving into new territory. "Peter doesn't care.

I'll pay you." She looked at me over the top of her glass, so that I started wondering about those dark eyes again.

"What was your husband doing at the Stephenson House the other day?" I thought I'd try to find the aggressive side of my personality. I watched the effect on Mary MacCulloch's face. She looked more confused than startled, as though the question wasn't among those submitted in advance by a reporter to a visiting head of state. Her mouth moved, but she wasn't able to form a response and that made her angry. She began to look like she might explode.

"I know you've been checking up on me! I know that's what he hired you to do. You've been following me, haven't you?"

"Look, Mrs MacCulloch..." I began, but she wasn't finished yet. And while she spun on, I began to listen more closely. There were always things to be learned when people talked at cross purposes.

"Admit it," she said, "Peter hired you to spy on me." I said nothing, letting her diesel on like a car that won't quit even when the ignition is turned off. Like a lot of people, she pinned her current dislike of her husband on me. Later, they'd make up, but she'd go on thinking of me as something you smell on the bottom of your shoe. It always happened that way.

"Hey, hey, hey! What's going on? I just asked you a question, Mrs MacCulloch. No need to start shooting at me. I thought we were just trying to have a friendly drink." She stopped in mid-sentence, took a breath and seemed to subside, letting her shoulders relax. Now she resembled a woman you could lend a shoulder to cry on. She had lost the tigress in her eyes. She looked more hunted than hunting.

"Look, Benny...May I call you that? My friends call me Mary...I know I've been foolish, silly, unstable at times, but I'd never leave Peter. He knows that."

"He may know more than you think."

"You mean about Alex? Peter doesn't care about Alex as long as we're discreet. So far we have been." She smiled an introduction to a confidence I wasn't expecting. "But Nesta would nail my fine tawny hide to the barn door if she ever found out. She's my best friend, after all."

"You share Alex's interest in pictures?" I asked, trying to see how much I could squeeze out of this run of luck. Thank God for guilt, I thought, as she sipped her drink.

"We share many interests. As you no doubt know already."

"Does that run to holding on to pictures that were supposed to be on loan?"

"Pictures? So what? Tallon's dead. What's the difference? There aren't any orphans. And George, Tallon's brother, is a big shot at Consolidated Galvin. Why not have a real drink, Mr Cooperman? Benny?"

I don't know what went into that drink. I don't know if it was Mary that slipped it to me. Maybe it was just two belts of rye on an empty stomach. Anyway, in no time I was telling her things that I should have kept to myself. Mary seemed fascinated. On the second round she was leaning closer to me and I was noticing the clever way her eye make-up was put on and the little lines around her temples and the dark roots of her hair. I was getting high, and I wasn't minding it at all.

"These pictures you have," I said, "you should turn them over to the estate, Mary. Easy as pie. No questions asked."

"Benny, why all this interest in pictures? You keep changing the subject. Can't we come to some sort of agreement? Just the two of us?"

"Your husband might not like that."

"Because he's paying you to spy on me."

"Have it your way. I never said a thing."

New drinks had come and it was bottoms up all over again. I try to stay away from situations like this. "No" is not hard to pronounce, but when I get a combination of somebody I want to know better and the possibility of shortcutting a long investigation with a bit of news that slips out between rounds, I bend an unaccustomed elbow or two. It's all in the way of business, as my Irish friend Frank Bushmill always says. And he should know; he's into more drink in a day than I see in a month. Still, today he was probably dead sober, working on somebody's corns in his surgery next to my office, and here was I, a poor sight of a man, with my cheek trying to get cool from the glass in my hand. Mary MacCulloch was still talking. Why had I stopped listening? I guiltily tuned in again.

"...can you expect from a girl from South Porcupine? You have to agree I've improved myself. I'm only five three, but I look taller. You want to know why?"

"Uh?"

"Peter Rowe said to me that I should get into the air force reserve. 'That'll make a woman of you,' he said. And he was right, I look taller because I have what's left of a military carriage. I was Sergeant Mary Boyce in those days. That was before we moved to Sudbury. Did you know I went in for law at the University of Toronto? Can you imagine me a lawyer?" She seemed to find that pretty funny. When she stopped laughing I tried to quiz her about Favell. That stopped the conversation dead. She sat back in her chair like I'd tried to get personal.

"I'd stay clear of Alex, if I were you," she said. "It's just a piece of free advice I'm giving you. It comes with the drink, like the salted peanuts. Alex can be as gentle as anything one minute, the next... Well, you just wouldn't want to be around. He can be quite ruthless. I wouldn't try to cross him."

"I see." I gave her a clear look in the eye to show that I'd taken in her warning.

"Are you sure you will be able to drive?" she asked.

"Like a fish," I said. "Where are you going?"

"I'm only going to the powder room. I'll be right back."

I waited a minute, then felt the urge to confess my rye and ginger. Drink takes me that way.

Chapter Four

"A *shicker*, Benny! That's what you are!"

"It was all in the line of duty, Ma. It's when I do it for fun that you got to get worried about."

"Fun?" my mother said from her end of the telephone wire. "Who ever heard of such a thing? My son, the drunk! Your father had a cousin who drank. It was a Harold or a Howard I think."

"He married money, Ma. There's a happy ending. Are you going to be home later?"

"Home? Where would I be going? I go out to have my hair done and to see my gynaecologist. I'm not due for either one this week."

"I thought I'd just drop by to say hello."

"Hello? You said it already. You want me to get the full effect? The unsteady legs, the powerful breath, the unfocused eyes? Benny, I've had a hard enough life without that."

"I thought maybe we could just... I could tell you about my move. I should give you the new telephone number."

"Benny, it'll keep until Friday. Let me hear all about it then. Your father wants to know why you need to take an apartment when you've got a perfectly good room right here. But I know you, you want to be independent. Benny, I'm your mother. I understand about being on your own. Your father just sees things in terms of the boys' room upstairs, which we had painted only a year ago, and that place over the chip shop."

"Tacos," I said.

"I don't care what kind of *chazerai* it is. What are tacos, Benny?"

"I'm not sure, but I've heard them described as omelettes with hardening of the arteries." Ma was putting all the anxiety about my move on my father, but I knew she was still struggling to deal with the fact that I was never going to live at home again.

"I think I can live without them," she said. "And as for you, Benny, give me a call when you sober up. Goodbye."

"Wait a minute! Wait a minute! Have you ever heard of Alex Favell?"

There was a pause at Ma's end of the line. Then she repeated the name a couple of times, tasting it on her tongue and moving it from cheek to cheek. "Alex Favell. I think I heard your father tell me about someone at the Mallet Club. This would be, oh, three or four years ago, Benny..."

"Sure."

"Well, all your father said was that he was a man with a bad temper. He wanted to know what Manny was doing there. Of course he was a guest. Either Lloyd or Alan took him, but he, this Alex Favell, made a big fuss about it. Why do you want to know?"

"Oh, I'm just fishing, Ma. Trying to get a line on a whole bunch of new people I never heard of."

"Your father thinks it's a shame about the boys' room, Benny."

"Ma, we went through that when I moved out nearly ten years ago!"

"I know. Nobody's ever slept in the boys' room since you left."

"What about Aunt Rose when she came to stay?"

"Except for your Aunt Rose."

"And didn't Linda Levine stay that time when she..."

"Benny, I'm talking about principle here! In the main, your father and I have kept the boys' room empty so that if ever you or Sam decide..."

"Ma, Sam has a wife and two kids. How are they...?"

"Benny, I can't talk to you when you've been drinking. We'll talk again when I see you."

"I could come over for dinner tonight."

"Your father's got a meeting. I'll see you Friday night as usual, unless you've got a date or something."

"Ma, I just..."

"Tacos, you call them? Have a good meal. Goodbye."

"Ma!"

I ducked out of the phone booth, but I couldn't see Mary MacCulloch sitting at the table. I decided to try to place another quick call before rejoining my rye and ginger ale.

"Hello?" That was a human touch. I'd been expecting something more formal like "Kesagami-Copeland, good afternoon. May I help you?" But I had to settle for what I got and that amounted to the information that, yes, Mr Favell was in, but, no, he wasn't seeing anybody this afternoon, thank you. Drink made me mutter something about "He'll see me," or "We'll see about that." I heard myself say the words, but I don't think I got the menace into my voice that I'd tried to imitate from television. I think that in the abstract, I'm an excellent actor. But, put to a practical test I often fail. I finally left my name with the secretary and hung up not knowing what I had accomplished.

When I got back to the table, I discovered that Mary MacCulloch had come and gone. Her cigarette had gone, the check had been paid and the drinks cleared. There was a note written on the back of a credit card slip, where I usually add the names of clients when

I have to buy drinks to drum up business. It said:

> Benny,
>
> *Sorry I have to run off, but I'm due to meet friends for tea in ten minutes. Remember what I said about AF. I'm not threatening, just passing on some good advice. See you around. Thanks for the lift.*
>
> M

She could have treated the drink as duty entertainment. I guess in her tax bracket it doesn't matter. Anyway, she had the idea I was working for her husband and not for a third party. Funny how guilty secrets come out when you least expect them.

I left the golf club and made it to the car without falling down more than once, slurring my speech, or failing to give a reasonable account of myself. Two and a half drinks did take its toll somewhere. How else did I get to Papertown in half the usual time?

There was a time when pyramids of pulpwood were the skyscrapers of Papertown. They grew along the banks of the old canal like mottled boils on a pockmarked skin. Yellow piles of sulphur tried to brighten the landscape, but it needed an enthusiastic sun to bring out their best side. They reminded me of a bad cold and a hacking cough. Most of the mills had been built during the heyday of the first Welland Canal and its successor. The canal brought pulp and chemicals to Papertown and took away ten-ton rolls of newsprint by the cheapest transportation in the country. Today, there were fewer mills. The landscape all the way up the escarpment was marked by silhouettes of abandoned walls and turrets of mills from the last century and the beginnings of this one. In some cases, an old dark structure had been saved and turned into a warehouse for used tires or scrap metal, but the transformations were cosmetic only and sometimes they didn't take.

The offices of the Kesagami-Copeland Paper Mills were located in a new, red brick, two-storey structure that tried to mask a dark, fieldstone main building that contained most of its outdated machinery. The company was originally set up by an American newspaper baron to make paper for his Chicago presses. Timber leases in the north had removed spruce and other marginal woods from the James Bay area for well over one hundred years. The local operation of K-C was a Canadian branch plant of its American parent. The Canadian flag hung limply from a mast in front of the main entrance. I knew before I opened the door that I would see a picture of the sovereign in the foyer. American outfits try to be good corporate citizens of Canada, but they do it with an American accent. An all-Canadian mill might have a picture of its founder in the lobby, but usually nothing more patriotic than an honour roll of those employees who served in the major wars.

I parked the car in front of a sign marked "Reserved" in the parking lot closest to the office block. The watchman gave me a dirty look as I walked towards the main door. He didn't challenge me because I was wearing a jacket and not a windbreaker. People who wear windbreakers have a hard time with parking-lot attendants.

The stairs to the second floor reminded me that I'd drunk my lunch at the golf club. I brushed my pants off with dirty palms and made an attempt at general repairs. My shin hurt where I'd barked it against the top step. When I had my breath under control, I walked through the big buff door into Alex Favell's outer office.

On one wall a huge blow-up of a photograph made during the twenties or thirties showed off the past of the paper mill. It was grainy and fuzzy in its details. The line-up of bosses in front of the mill looked out confidently at me while their dark business suits kept a note of panic at bay. Out the big window to my right, I could see almost the same view. But where was the bustle, where were the pyramids of pulpwood, where was the industry the beaver over the front door symbolized? Things were slow in the paper business? I made a note of it.

The drink gave me confidence I wasn't used to possessing. It felt like I was wearing a six-shooter or that I was six foot five instead of five foot seven. I was breathing courage when I went up to the woman behind the reception desk.

"Yes?" she said sweetly, like I was delivering rose petals. I went around her desk and tried to focus on the white letters on the door across the broadloom reading "ALEX FAVELL." "You can't go in there!" she said. "Who are you, anyway?"

"I've found a painting he's been trying to get. He'll see me," I said. I hoped she'd heard that line before. She fell back in her chair like I'd blasted her out of my way with a shot in one of her fleshy shoulders. Once in the inner office, I closed the door behind me and flopped into a leather and chrome seat in front of a vast black desk that looked like it had escaped from a sci-fi movie. On the far side I saw a tall, balding man with a moustache that would go well with his tennis whites. His eyes were wide with surprise, but held off judgment until I announced my business. After I'd given him my spiel about looking up Tallon's unrecovered inventory, he allowed an angry look to settle all over his face. What I got was a "My dear Mr Cooperman, we are not at all pleased by this visit" look. He allowed displeasure to make him look like he had touched a copper cent to one of his fillings.

"Well?" I asked. "What can you tell me?"

"You can go to blazes, Cooperman! I'm not obliged

to tell you a thing." I tried to see from his face whether I had a guilty creature sitting across from me, one whose fingers I was slamming in the cash drawer. On the face of it, it seemed unlikely. The suit he was standing up in was equal to the stress of being stretched as he gripped the edges of his desk and glared at me. It probably cost more than I'd put on my back for the last five years. Maybe ten. "Tallon was an imbecile when it came to keeping books and records. If his affairs are in disorder, he has only himself to blame. I warned him often enough."

"Have you got an aspirin?" I was suddenly becoming absorbed by my own problems. I should never drink on the job. I tried to remember where I'd got the drinks, and then I remembered the charming Mrs Mac-Culloch. Favell must have seen something on my face; he interrupted his telling me off and stopped himself.

"What?"

"I need something for my head. Have you got any aspirin?"

"Oh, er, yes. I'll get them." He began to move in the direction of what I took to be an executive washroom, when, for some reason, I continued asking questions. When will I learn not to provoke my benefactors until after the benefits have begun to take effect?

"Then you're not going to surrender any of the pictures belonging to the Tallon collection without a fight?"

"I've said all I intend to say. I've just got off the phone talking to somebody else you've been bothering. You can go straight to hell for all I care. Is that clear? I'm nobody's fool, Cooperman." He opened his mouth to continue the tirade and I was bracing myself for more of the same, when he stopped abruptly. He saw that I wasn't arguing with him. In fact, I was sitting in the chrome and black leather chair with my head in my hands. I couldn't see Favell, but I felt him near me trying to think.

"Aspirin," he said at last. "Yes, I'll be right back." I heard the door to his bathroom open. The pain in my head was getting worse. If I didn't know that I didn't suffer from migraines, I'd swear that this was a migraine. The light slipping between my fingers was blinding. Footsteps from a new direction came into the office.

"Mr Miles is here to see you, Mr Favell." It was the secretary. I straightened up and screwed on a smile. "Oh," she said. "What have you done with Mr Favell?" she asked suspiciously.

"He's in the toilet getting an aspirin."

She rolled her eyes. "It's those two-hour lunches," she said. "Honestly!"

A man stood in the doorway. "Alex? Where are you?"

"I'm afraid he's nursing a headache in the bathroom," the secretary said, trying to make eye contact with the visitor. She moved off after pausing near the door to the bathroom. She decided not to knock and left me and Paddy Miles staring at one another.

Miles was a long thin drink of water with thick dark hair, a high forehead and smiling eyes. The suit he was wearing looked older than mine, but its provenance was better. What is there to making a suit that they know on Savile Row in London that they can't learn on Spadina Avenue in Toronto?

"He'll be out in a minute," I said, offering him the remaining half of the room. "You're Paddy Miles, aren't you?"

"Yes," he said drawing out the "s" until it broke. "And you?"

"Benny Cooperman."

Miles's face cracked into a thousand lines. He suddenly looked very friendly and about ten years older than he had a second before. "Oh, you're the fellow doing some private investigating for Pambos Kiriakis.

Somebody should give Pambos a big gold medal. Once we have that list of his we can start winding up this estate." Favell came out of the bathroom. He looked at me and then at Miles, who had assumed a knowing, sympathetic look on his lean face.

"What the devil are you looking at?" he said, rather loudly and without disguising his anger.

"I just wanted to show sympathy, Alex. Thought you might be interested in a hair of the dog."

"Hair of the dog?" he asked, not understanding any of this. He shouted for his secretary through the closed door of his sanctum sanctorum. "Miss Bertolli! Get me MacLeod in Detroit on my private line. Mr Cooperman, I looked everywhere. I'm out of aspirin, I'm afraid. 'Hair of the dog,' Paddy, what are you raving about?"

"Sorry, Alex. I'm afraid I was confused by Mr Cooperman, here." The "here" sounded a little condescending. I felt a little like a specimen in a bottle. Favell glared at me. It was a crowded office, and I was being blamed.

"Look, Mr Cooperman," he said, "if you were sent to spy on me by that little creep, Kiriakis, you can tell him from me he's finished as far as I'm concerned. That goddamned Turk's not fit to wait on tables in a greasy spoon." I reared up in protest, but it didn't stop him.

"And what are you fit for, Mr Favell?"

"Me? We're talking about that snooping bastard, that *other* snooping bastard!"

"Hey, hold on, Alex! Mr Cooperman's only trying to help." Miles tried, but it didn't begin to dampen Favell's anger, which I was very happy to see demonstrated in such an obvious way. Where did it come from, I wondered. Who had been ruffling Favell's fine feathers before I came on the scene?

"Look, Mr. Favell," I said, trying to see if I could bother him some more, "maybe Pambos Kiriakis isn't the sort of fellow who rubs shoulders with you at the

Mallet Club or gets his name in the social register, but he doesn't steal pictures from a dead man, which puts him higher in my personal 'Blue Book' than a few others I could name."

"Going to bat for the little Turk, are you? I guess you guys stick together." I expected that the next salvo would have a fleeting reference to *Our Crowd*, but Paddy Miles cut him off.

"Alex, for God's sake! He's only doing his job!"

"Well, let him do it someplace else. There's no law that says I have to talk to him. He's not even sober. He just walked in here demanding aspirin!"

"Mr Cooperman, if that's true, perhaps you should abandon this meeting and try to reschedule one later on." Miles was trying to help, but Favell was not in the mood for it.

"In a pig's eye! Drunk or sober, I don't have to say a word to any investigator, public or private, unless he serves me with papers."

"Alex!"

"Just get rid of him. Show the little shit out the door and off the property!"

"Alex!" The secretary came in.

"I've got Mr MacLeod's secretary in Detroit, Mr Favell." Funny how her voice sounded like it was recorded on a balmy day without any ruckus going on in her boss's office. She sounded as calm and as matter of fact as an usher saying "Side aisles, please." I couldn't make out Favell, unless he really had come back from a liquid lunch ten minutes ahead of me. I only came to ask a few questions, not foreclose on his mortgage.

"Right, Miss Bertolli. I'll be right there." He sounded confused. He meant to say that he would take the phone. He went around to the side of his desk, which put the world in order for him. From there, with the flow charts on the wall and the view down into the yard on the familiar side, he grew a little calmer. His eyes even began to sparkle as an idea came to him. When he spoke, I got a good look at the gold inlays on the right side of his mouth. What well-insured villain gave Favell a left hook, I wondered.

"You think your friend Mr Kiriakis is blameless, don't you? Well, you'll find out that things are a little more complicated than that. His hands aren't so spotless. You should do a little more digging, a little honest research, before you come in here with your accusations. Before you start shooting your mouth off about something you're totally ignorant about."

"Hold your horses," I protested. "I never made any accusations. I'm looking for information. I didn't come to start the Third World War. But I see the welcome I get, Mr Favell. Maybe that tells me more than the red carpet treatment. As for being drunk, it's just not true. I had a drink with Mary MacCulloch half an hour ago at the golf club. Now tell me why Kiriakis's motives are so dishonest. He blew the whistle on you, didn't he? That sounds honest from here."

I liked the effect I'd made when I dropped Mary Mac-Culloch's name into the conversation. Favell and Miles looked at one another like I'd been giving her the third degree with a rubber hose and she'd broken, naming Favell and Miles as her partners in crime. It only lasted a second, but there was no missing it. I was surprised that Favell shared the moment with Miles. I thought, up to then, that Paddy Miles was on the side of the angels. He was one of the people representing the injured party, wasn't he? Arthur Tallon was the owner of the strayed or stolen paintings. At least his estate was. And Paddy Miles was as involved in trying to get the pictures back as I was. Wasn't he? I thought I'd better ask a question.

"Mr Miles, do you have any reason to distrust Pambos Kiriakis's attempt to round up the missing pictures belonging to your late employer? Do you know who would have taken the list of names that he asked me to try to recover?" Paddy Miles wet his lips with a nervous tongue.

"Tell him, Paddy, tell him. Educate the man!"

"Well," he began, trying to dissociate himself from Favell's hectoring. "While we were very happy to hear about Mr Kiriakis's list, which he says was given to him by Arthur Tallon, it is possible that he never had such a list at all. Arthur was erratic, God knows. I tried to keep books, but it was next to impossible. He may have made such a list, but again, he may not. It wasn't like him to keep records of any kind. I found no other lists of items on loan among his papers. And, to tell the truth, I wasn't surprised."

"So, if Tallon's list didn't exist, why did Pambos get me involved? Why did he manufacture a cock-and-bull story about a list that didn't ever get written? You knew Tallon. Can you guess at Kiriakis's motives?"

"Bloody Turk's as crooked as a bentwood chair!"

"Quiet, Alex. You're not making this any easier!"

"Detroit's waiting, Mr Favell."

"To hell with Detroit! Tell him I'll call in ten minutes!"

Miles thought a moment or two before trying to answer. He looked at me in a way that tried to break through the flak that Favell was sending up at us. He looked grave but careful, measuring his words in a metric scale. "We only know about this list from Pambos Kiriakis, Mr Cooperman. He is the only one who has seen it. If it was a fabrication, one obvious way to support it and give it life is to get an investigator involved. Since he's paying you to find it, it must be missing. It must exist. You're a sort of alibi. You stiffen his story. You give it starch." He paused a moment, then added,

"But we must always remember that he could be telling the truth. If he is, then what he has done in getting you involved would appear to be completely straightforward and logical."

"Bullshit! You can't tell me you believe that, Paddy! That creep is out to feather his nest, or out to become the spoil-sport of the year."

"There's something in what he says, Mr Cooperman. He may be hoping that we will give him the pick of any paintings he recovers. I'm sure that George would want to reward him if he uncovers items belonging to the estate. And I would agree to it as both fair and just. But that's not quite the same thing as saying that Kiriakis is without a profit motive in all this."

"That's the wee Turk all over!'

"And as I said, Mr Cooperman," Miles said, ignoring Favell, "we only have Kiriakis's word for it that his marvellous list ever existed at all."

"Well, Cooperman, well?" Favell was grinning at me with the golden side of his mouth catching the light. "You're looking a little greener now than when you walked in here. I don't think it's the drink. You better sit down." I sat and looked at both of them. I tried to see whether I had a feeling that I was being used. I didn't like it. It could have come from Favell's smug look on that business-as-usual face of his, or from the sour pinch in my stomach. Paddy Miles stood by, letting me see that he was a sympathetic soul and that he was sorry that the facts were so unsettling. My head was beginning to spin again. I needed that aspirin.

Although they didn't look like Stan Laurel and Oliver Hardy, I got a picture of the two of them looking at me. It stayed with me and I can see it now. Favell and Paddy Miles, Ollie waving the short end of his tie at me and Stan on the edge of tears.

Chapter Five

On my way back to the car, I started wondering whether the time had not come for another word with my client. His list was looking less substantial than it had when I first heard about it while unpacking my goods above Tacos Heaven. I intended to drive back to the new apartment, but found myself parked in the old parking place behind the City House, my home of many years. It wasn't the drink, and the headache had mostly gone. I was woolgathering, trying to find a solid place to put my feet in this business of Pambos's list. I backed out and headed for Court Street. In time the car would learn the new way home. There was a corner parking space with my name on it against the schoolyard fence. You could still read the names of departed tenants on the wooden panel with the word "reserved" in block capitals.

In the cupboard above the sink, I found some cans of soup left behind by A. Morris or P. Parretta or one of the other vanished former tenants. I read the instructions and looked for a can opener. I'd seen my mother doing this since I was just a youngster. She was very good at making soup. We often had green pea soup one day and mushroom the next. Of course, her chicken soup was her own. She would never serve canned soup with meat in it, although we did grow up on vegetable soup from Campbell's quite innocently for many years. It was only brought into question when Campbell's began to market something called

"Vegetarian Vegetable." I missed Ma's cooking and was looking forward to recreating some of her dishes now that I was on my own for the first time in an apartment of my own with a stove. I poured the soup into a saucepan and added a can of tap-water. I turned the heat under the saucepan to high and gave the mixture a stir, not enough to break up the tiny cubes of carrots and potatoes, but just enough to combine the water with the contents of the can. I was doing this when the phone rang.

"Hello?"

"Who's that? Is Phil there?" The woman had an English accent, from the north somewhere, but I couldn't be sure.

"This is a new line," I said. "It was only put in today. This is the first call I've had, actually." Her north of England accent prompted my "actually." Just like in the movies. She said she was sorry for bothering me and hung up. I put down my end and went back to the stove, where a cloudy bunch of small bubbles was beginning to turn the soup from orangish-brown to beige. I let it boil for five minutes, then served myself on my new coffee-table, which, when you pulled at it, lifted up to dining-room table height. I don't claim that the soup was as good as my mother makes, but it was familiar and on the right track.

It was nearly seven when I came out on the street again. The sun had set about half an hour ago and fingers of frost were in the air. Nowhere could I see any sign of the relatively balmy afternoon. Did I see golfers this afternoon or had I imagined them? This was always a tricky part of the year. The car started and I backed out of my space, the headlights illuminated the wire of the fence and cut off any view into the empty schoolyard.

I drove down King Street to Ontario and turned left.

Ahead of me a battery of highway signs prompted me in several directions. I knew them all, but I was always bothered for newcomers whenever I faced this choice. I could feel the pressure of cars behind me, urging me to make up my mind already. I wondered whether within a city there might not be some calmer system of signalling choices to drivers than these screaming capital letters. I made my choice before the car behind me began honking me to action. I turned right, went past the park with its huge cenotaph commemorating the dead of two world wars and turned right again at the television station. Wally Skeat would be finishing up his half-hour with the evening news, weather and sports. I was tempted to stop, but I headed down Yates Street and turned into Stephenson Road, which wound down the bank of the much-dredged canal and came towards the bright—but bright within reason and with taste—lights of the Stephenson House.

When I started out, when I put the key in the ignition of the car, I don't think all of me knew where the hell I was going. There were questions that I wanted Pambos to answer, things that came out of my meetings with MacCulloch, Favell and Paddy Miles. It's funny how a case begins to lose its abstract appearance after you've met a few of the characters involved. In their eyes you can see how real it is, and the abstraction disappears like the exhaust of a Mack truck into the night air.

I parked the car not in the lot in front of the colonial façade of the main building but around the back where the headlights interrupted an alley-cats' crap game. A couple of pairs of green eyes stared at me in defiance, but most of the dark shapes scattered in all directions. Other eyes looked out at me from the shelter of a row of garbage cans. There was a moon, a few days past the first quarter. It glinted on the metal bars on the windows and the frame around the back door. There was no light coming from this side of the hotel, although I could hear a rumble of exhaust from the kitchen stoves and even a little dinner music from the front of the house. I tried the door; it was open. I invited myself in.

It was a wide hallway leading to the kitchen of the hotel. I could hear voices raised in banter behind the closed double doors. The passage was lit by what came through the twin panels of wire-reinforced glass in the doors. A cart with empty garbage cans stood outside the kitchen. The hall smelt of the constant traffic of garbage-out and fresh produce-in. It was a heavy-duty location. On the floor I couldn't even find a cigarette butt to hold up to Pambos as a sign that his boys were letting him down.

I continued down the hall, turning left at the kitchen, and noticed that from here on the floor was covered in industrial carpet and the walls with wooden panelling. The hall ended at a single closed door with a window in it, like in a speakeasy in the movies. The window was closed. On the door, under the window, I read a discreet sign: C. Kiriakis, Private. "C"? What does the "C" stand for? I knocked and waited for the window to slide open. I expected to get the once over lightly from some beefy bodyguard, followed inside by a fast thorough search that made me feel like I was being measured for a pair of pants. Then I remembered that this was Pambos's office, not some movie casino run by some Raymond Chandler kingpin of gambling and related vices. This was Grantham, Ontario, and I was looking for the guy I'd had coffee with a few hours earlier. It made me feel better. Thinking of Pambos added a few watts of light to this blind-alley corridor. I tried the door. It was open like the other one.

In my head I could hear my mother yelling at me,

as though I was telling her all about my adventures behind the Stephenson House. "Benny! What are you trying to do to me! Scare me to death? Just tell the story,
leave out the scary parts." I could see her looking at
me in her tangerine living-room. "Benny, Ellery Queen
you're not. Just tell me the facts, like the fellow said
on... What was it? With Sergeant Friday? You know the
one. Bum-bah-bum-bump!" Why was I dragging my
mother into this place? It was scary enough without
her, what with the noise the hinges made as the door
opened inward. I stepped in and closed the door behind me, not quite cutting off my mother's voice inside me. In my perspiring imagination she was saying,
"You think I don't know what an open door means!
I wasn't born yesterday." For a second I wondered if
I'd see her familiar face appear at the window, if I slid
the panel open. I ignored the temptation.

"Pambos!" I called in a subdued yell that stepped on
its own intentions. "It's me, Benny!" The sound of my
voice vanished into the curtains, which hung down to
the floor. I could feel that old horror creeping up my
back as I heard the inner voice say, back away, get out
while there's still time.

A noise on my right. A section of the bookcases, filled
not with books but with antique toys and lead soldiers,
pivoted. Pambos came out into the room, followed by
an older man whose name I didn't know, although I'd
seen him around town for years.

"Benny! What a surprise! Glad to see you, sit down.
I'll get Renos to send in some coffee. Hey, do you two
know each other?" I looked at the man behind Pambos, and he looked at me. We stood in mutual embar-
rassment, waiting to be introduced. "Benny's a private
detective around town, Bill." Bill nodded.

"Investigator," I corrected. Pambos shrugged. "There
are a couple of things, Pambos..."

"Bill here's working for the *Beacon*. He's a reporter. Sit down," he repeated. We both did, while Pambos went around to the business side of his desk and demanded coffee through the telephone.

This wasn't the first time I'd spent an evening with Pambos, as I've said, but the evening had been relocated to its most glamorous setting to date. His collections were no longer kept in a box and brought out to be admired, but they were all around us. He pointed out the paintings and identified them: a Lawren Harris, an A.Y. Jackson, a small Pollock and a Wallace Lamb. The toys were mostly Victorian and early twentieth century. There were cars and buggies, trains, fire-engines, banks, jugglers, trick dogs and other animals and masses and masses of lead soldiers. "This fellow here," Pambos was saying, "is a member of Napoleon's Imperial Guard. They were his élite force and under his personal command. There weren't many of them left when he got back from Moscow after the winter of 1812-13." The figure, which stood less than three inches high, had been hand painted from his leather boots to his ginger-coloured whiskers. He carried one of those backpacks that French soldiers carried through the Napoleonic wars.

"Napoleon was a general by the time he was twenty-seven," Bill said. Pambos answered with a date. Seventeen-ninety-something. I had interrupted a meeting of the Tin-soldier League. I didn't have much to contribute. I was going to volunteer Napoleon's famous dying words, "Kiss me, Hardy!" but I thought that they both knew them as well as they knew the year of the Offensive of 1812.

"Do you think he was poisoned?" Bill asked me. I didn't know what to say. I thought he'd been beheaded like all the others. Pambos came to my rescue just as coffee arrived on a big tray. I sometimes thought that

Pambos lived on coffee; wherever he was, a cup was growing cold at his elbow.

"You've been reading that stuff by that Norwegian dentist, Bill. Come on!" Bill's smile lit up his craggy face as he leaned forward.

"Sten Forshufvud was Swedish and a respected biologist. Why are you underrating him? You can still argue fairly, can't you?" Pambos turned to me and tried to explain the history.

"The traditional story is that Napoleon died of cancer of the stomach on St Helena in 1821. But there are those," he said, pinning Bill down with a look that would have been withering if Pambos had been any taller, "who believe that he was poisoned by one of the Frenchmen attached to the Emperor's household."

"Montholon, the nasty Count of Montholon!" Bill added.

"So you say!" said Pambos. "You can't prove a thing!" Pambos said it so passionately, I thought he was taking the question of the count's guilt or innocence personally.

"Hey! Slow down. Let me be the jury. What I don't know about Napoleon could fill volumes. I'm as impartial a witness as you're likely to get." I picked up my coffee and began to sip. In a moment Pambos began to make a case for the fact that the Emperor had died of natural causes. He invoked books from his shelves as he went and soon the air was thick with names I'd never heard before: Montholon, Bertrand, Marchand, Hudson Lowe, Dr O'Meara, Dr Arnott, Dr Antommarchi and dozens of others. Every once in a while Bill would interrupt.

"I object!" he'd say. "There's no proof that there was a cancer found in the post-mortem." Or, "Hudson Lowe was only interested in his liver, he didn't care a damn about his stomach!" When I say that most of this went

over my head, I exaggerate. It *all* went over my head.
When Pambos finally began to wind down he brought
out a letter from the top drawer of his desk.

"I showed this post-mortem report to Agatha
Christie," Pambos said. I began to wake up. I'd heard
of her. In fact there were only half a dozen of her books
I haven't read.

"When did you hob-nob with Dame Agatha," said
Bill, not disguising his disbelief.

"A cat can look at a crime queen," Pambos answered.
"It was back in the 1970s. I was wondering about the
same thing you are, so I sent her a copy of the post-
mortem report, holding back the Emperor's name. I
didn't fool her." He looked down at the letter and read:

*Yes, I rather guessed it was Napoleon. It certainly argues
a cautionary tale in the use of emetics, doesn't it?*

Pambos waited for the effect of the letter to sink in.

"No word about poison. Not a word about arsenic
intoxication. Not a murmur about foul play."

"Well, she may have said that in the 1970s, but if she'd
heard from you twenty years earlier, she would have
had more to say. That's my bet," Bill said. Pambos put
the letter, which was handwritten, back into the neatly addressed envelope. I thought that they'd let the matter drop there, but they didn't. There wasn't a moment
for me to catch Pambos's attention for a few questions.

Bill took out a pocket flask and added a nip to his
coffee. Then he went on to describe the evidence for
the other side. I heard the same names tossed around
again, but now there were others: Ben Weider, Hamilton Smith and David Chandler. Like the earlier batch,
I wasn't able to place any of them, but I will say this
for Bill, he laid down the evidence like a good crown
attorney. We heard about antimony as well as arsenic,

about the contacts between Montholon and the Comte d'Artois, who became Charles X. It was a tempting theory, but the chemistry about making a poisonous almond drink from peach pits left me behind again.

I was about to ask Pambos if I could borrow his ear for a private moment, when the telephone rang. I looked at my watch. It was getting late. Nowhere in town did time disappear as fast as at Pambos Kiriakis's. I was surprised at the hour, but reassured that he continued to be the good host I remembered.

His sheet wasn't completely clean, however. There was the notorious Russian incident that, to hear some talk, nearly killed a Canadian-Soviet wheat deal. Pambos was giving a visiting Russian cultural attaché a medium-well-done steak at the old steakhouse, when a cartoonist from the *Beacon* walked in. When Pambos introduced the attaché to the cartoonist, Hugo Macduff, Hugo thought Pambos was having him on. To demonstrate his disbelief, Hugo treated them both to a trick he was working on. He thumped the table, then briskly whipped the tablecloth out from under the knives, forks, spoons and plates. He almost had the trick down pat, but, unfortunately, the board with the Russian's steak on it went sailing across the room and became lost among the rubbers and galoshes near the door. The Russian was not amused, nor was Pambos.

"By the way," Bill said, leaning in my direction, while Pambos was talking in an animated way to somebody on long distance, "my name is Palmer. Bill Palmer. I've heard Pambos mention you. He gets a kick out of knowing a private eye." He grinned. It was a beat-up, lined face, with drink written in every quarter. He wasn't even tipsy, but I was getting good at reading the signs. I thought of that Ben Hecht play they put on at the Collegiate a year or so ago, *The Front Page*. He looked like he could have stepped right out of a newsroom. There was a hunch to his shoulders and a lack of precision with his razor that reinforced my picture of the crusading reporter with his cry of "Stop the press! Hello, sweetheart, get me rewrite and make it snappy!"

"Have you known Pambos long?" I asked.

"I met him in Skylloura. It's a village north-west of Nicosia."

"That's in Cyprus, right?"

"Yeah. I was with a paper over there and I met him when his brother was killed." He automatically lowered his voice and cast a glance at Pambos, who was laughing into the phone and leaning back in his chair at a dangerous angle.

"They had a lot of trouble over there once, didn't they?" I guess it was a dumb question, but Palmer was generous.

"Yeah, they've been having a bad time since the days of the Argonauts and I don't mean the Toronto football club. I was over there when the Greeks and the British were fighting about independence. During the 1950s. The Turks came into it, too, near the end. Pambos's brother, Michael, was killed outside a Turkish village called Guenyeli in 1957. He was one of nine in what I called a massacre at the time. And since I still wake up at night when I have bad dreams about it, I guess I'd still call it that." This time Palmer didn't put his drink into his coffee; he took his snort direct, then offered me a pull at the flask after wiping the top with his hand. I shook my head.

"How did a Canadian reporter get to be covering a Greek war?" I asked.

"I was working on one of Beaverbrook's papers, the *Express*, when I was recruited by a guy named Charles Foley, who was starting up an English language newspaper in Nicosia. That was *The Times of Cyprus*." Palmer shrugged, not wanting to be taken for a hero.

"The fighting hadn't started yet and it looked like a warm place to spend the winter."

From the telephone, Pambos shot us all a helpless look. "All I can tell you," he said, "is that he sometimes drops by here in the evenings, but I never can be sure when. I'll give him your message if I see him. That's the best I can do." When he had hung up Pambos explained that the caller was a book collector from Boulder, Colorado, who was trying to find Martin Lyster, a book-tracer and dealer in rare books, whose name I'd heard around town before. Pambos described Martin as a slippery customer, always turning up like a bad penny when you least expected him. Bill suggested that the sound of a cork popping near an open window would attract his attention if he was within a hundred miles of it.

"Martin's a decent fellow," Pambos said, "but he's impossible to keep up with. He never tells you where he's staying. That's why I haven't been able to pay him for the last job he did for me." Here Pambos held up a calf-bound volume with gilt edging. Bill allowed that Martin was a living legend and took another swig from his flask, which was quickly nearing the empty mark. Bill took the book from Pambos and held it up to the light, examined the binding, sniffed at the open pages and nodded deeply like it was a rare wine in his hands and not a dusty tome with liver spots. Palmer handed it to me and I frowned at it and bobbed my head sagely.

"Mr Something Lambert in Boulder wants him to call," Pambos said as he took the book back into his possession and smiled slightly, no doubt because during my examination I hadn't cracked the spine. "So, if you see him," he said, looking at each of us in turn, "tell him it's important."

I was beginning to look at Pambos in a new light. For years I'd known about the brother who'd been

executed by the mob south of town and left headless
in a ditch. Pambos never tried to hide the fact. He was
as up-front about such personal information as I was
about my Uncle Morris's gold stocks. But he'd never
mentioned this second brother, the first of two to die
violently. I tried to imagine a brace of brothers standing beside the man lovingly replacing the calf-bound
book on its shelf. It was hard to add the necessary vio-
lence to the picture. But Michael had been active in the
movement to free Cyprus from the British and the other
brother had been an unsuccessful hoodlum. Brother
Costas had a record of minor violations long enough
at the time of his death to alert the cops to what the
younger brother, Pambos, was trying to do legally and
by the sweat of his brow.

"When did you come out to Canada, Pambos?" Pambos didn't look at me, he looked over at Bill.

"You were talking Cyprus politics while I was trying
to get Mr Lambert to cool off?" Then to me:

"Yeah, I came out here with my parents and brother
in 1960. As soon as Cyprus was an okay place to come
from again. Just after your paper went out of business,
Bill." He said that with a leer, as though Bill Palmer had
personally put *The Times of Cyprus* out of business.

"Now, wait a minute! When the Brits pulled back into
those sovereign base areas, the whole island suffered
a recession. All sorts of businesses went under. And
where were we going to get headlines once *Murder Mile*
dwindled into good old Ledra Street again?"

There was a brief lull in the conversation, and then
they went back to Napoleon again. I excused myself.
The bathroom had a print of the Mona Lisa hanging
above the tub. Nice touch. When I got back, fresh coffee
had arrived, and Bill Palmer had started filling a pipe
from a yellow oilskin pouch.

"He couldn't have invaded the coast of Kent,"

Pambos was saying. I had a good idea who "he" might be. "You forget the Goodwin Sands. Sandwich and Dover are the only close harbours. And you have the other Cinque Ports. There's pebble beaches around Deal and Walmer. Then you get the famous white cliffs." I wondered if I could retreat to the bathroom again until conversation came around to famous criminal cases or the movies of the sixties. I decided against it and tried to follow what was going on. I can now name the Cinque Ports, but I can't explain how there came to be seven of them.

About a quarter of an hour later, Pambos got up and told me to follow him. He took me into his "secret room" behind the bookcase. It was a crowded room that reminded me of the stacks behind the check-out counter at the public library. Who would have thought that the thing to hide behind a bookcase was more books? He had walls of them, some in mint condition, some in torn or faded jackets or without jackets at all. He told me about this being his treasure-trove of rare editions between parries and thrusts at Bill's theories about the last years of the late emperor of the French. I had just started to quiz him about some of the missing pieces in the puzzle he'd handed me when the man wanted in Boulder, Colorado made his appearance. Pambos and Bill warmly greeted Martin Lyster and introduced him to me. His face rivalled Bill Palmer's for the wear and tear of good times. "He's a decent old skin," said Palmer in a broad theatrical brogue, while Pambos found him a cup of hot coffee. Before he could tuck his long legs under his chair or get half a dozen sips of coffee into him, Lyster was arguing the case for the journal of the Irish Dr O'Meara, who attended Napoleon on St Helena. When I finally left, I'd had my fill of history all the way from the battle of Marengo to the massacre at Guenyeli. I took my weary bones home and put them into my new bath. How had I managed with only a shower all these years, I wondered, as I climbed into the bed we'd set up in the morning. I was asleep before I even noticed the clock ticking.

Chapter Six

I'd forgotten to set the clock-radio. The telephone let me know that when it started ringing. The useless time on the dial of the clock told a tale of being unplugged at the City House and then slipped into a box full of dirty shirts and paperbacks. It was a clear accusation of negligence. The phone rang again.

"Hello?"

"Is Phil there?"

"No. This is a brand new number as of yesterday." There was a pause as the woman at the other end took in the news. Did she know the woman with the north of England accent, I wondered. I added "I'm sorry" and waited for a "thank you," but all I got was a click as the connection was broken.

It was hard to orient myself in the new place. The light hit the walls differently. The morning noises were different. Gone were the sounds of heavy traffic moving steadily west along King Street. I could scarcely hear any traffic at all, but from the schoolyard, a din arose that would have rattled a VU meter at the TV station. It was all high notes, treble, no bass. I looked at my watch. It must be recess. I'd slept in on my first morning in the new apartment. A good sign, I thought, as I hoisted myself in the direction of my toothbrush.

An hour later I was sitting at the marble counter of the United Cigar Store. I hadn't tried making coffee in my place because it needed more thinking about than I had thinking time. Besides, I liked the company of the regulars. I looked through the Toronto paper and ate most of a piece of toast before walking past the magazine rack to the street. I could feel the heat the moment I stepped out the door. St Andrew Street was warming its old stones and bricks, flushing the winter out of its joints under a sun that was almost visibly teasing and encouraging the weeds to grow up around the telephone poles and between the cracks in the sidewalk. I headed to the library.

The Grantham Library is a nerve-racking place. I find it difficult to read for a long time at a stretch with the sound of running water in my ears. Somehow, architects find libraries call out for fountains and waterfalls. Maybe it's an over-compensation for all of the faceless commercial blocks they put up, without a statue, or a column or a classical detail of any kind. They have to save up these frustrations and get rid of them on public buildings. Now, I don't mind the fountain at the new court house. On my way to get a writ or a copy of a judgment, the sound of water goes very well, but when I'm just sitting and reading, the water soaks into my brain and sends me off to the "Men's" before I really need to go. The sound of water and the mysteries of the Dewey decimal system are equally distracting. Maybe that's why I have for many years gone directly to Ella Beames in her office in the Special Collections Department with my problems.From her second-floor room, the world looks different, more organized, with past and present coming together in one of Ella's hundreds of files.

I told her what I wanted and she went away sighing. Was our relationship beginning to show signs of stress? Was it time I learned how to do my own research? I was over-reacting. I guess she doesn't get asked to bring out files on the troubles in Cyprus and the local art scene by the same customer all that often.

"Here they are, Benny." Ella said as she plunked down a load of books and files of clippings in two separate places on the heavy table in front of me. "There'll be things on microfilm too, of course. But this is a start. You can read yourself silly trying to follow a war in the papers. Best to find out the dates you need and then go to the *Globe* or the *Star*. On a big international story like Cyprus, the *Beacon* got everything through the wire services. But they'll be your best bet on running down the stuff on the Contemporary Gallery and Arthur Tallon." Ella tried to catch her breath and brushed a loose strand of hair out of her eyes. I think it was greyer than when I saw it last. I liked to look at her velvety cheeks and her small, perfect nose. Her face wasn't beautiful—in fact you might say she'd been plain as a girl—but there was the beauty of tidiness about it. There was wit and humour in the way her features related to one another. And she still liked helping me! What was I going to do?

My sudden interest in Cyprus was pure indulgence and curiosity. I guess I was sharpening my research instincts for the real work that lay ahead in the art clippings. The curiosity was genuine enough; I resented being left behind last night, being unable to contribute anything. Cyprus, I thought, I could bone up on so I wouldn't look a dummy. Napoleon would take longer, a summer holiday or a long cold winter. Even I could see that.

As I opened the books and began to get a measure of the troubles in Cyprus, Ella disappeared only to return with more information. The first book was *Island in Revolt* by Charles Foley. I guess he couldn't very well call it *Revolting Island*. Foley. I remembered hearing the name last night. It was good to feel I was this close to the inside track so soon in my research. I read on. In the 1950s, after the loss of India and Palestine,

at the time of Suez, the Domino Theory of foreign poli-
cy was very big. The Brits couldn't see how they could
keep their military bases in Cyprus without running
the whole island. Cyprus wasn't exactly the jewel in
the crown of the British Empire, but it was the only
thing giving off a fading semi-precious glitter. From the
Foley book it appeared that most of the leaders of the
movement to get the British out of the island were
British-trained and -educated Greeks, who loved British institutions and traditions. They were shocked that
the Brits thought that as far as more self-government
was concerned, it was just "not on." There were other
books and key clippings to go through. I could see myself becoming an overnight expert on the subject. I
checked Guenyeli in the index of Foley's book. Yes, the
massacre had occurred. A group of about fifty Greeks,
hearing of trouble in Skylloura, a village north-west of
Nicosia, started out to help. I checked where I was on
the map. They were intercepted by a patrol of Security
Police and taken first to the police station in Skylloura
and then to one in Nicosia. When Security couldn't find
any grounds for holding them, they were driven by
truck and let go near the Turkish village of Guenyeli,
on the way to the resort town of Kyrenia on the north
coast. Somehow the Turks were expecting them. As the
Greeks crossed the fields on their way back towards
Skylloura, a gang of Turks armed with clubs and axes
came to meet them. Some were riding motorcycles.
They attacked and nine Greeks were killed, one was
beheaded, others were injured. There was no mention
by name of any of the victims, including Pambos Kiriakis's brother Michael. When the story of the massacre
began to spread, it was at first denied and then different official versions were circulated. The Greeks, in one
version, were the aggressors. In another, only two bodies had been found.

Reading on, both in Foley and in other books, I found that there were other *incidents*, as the Government Security Police called events like the massacre at Guenyeli, between the various island communities. In fact I seemed to remember that things were still tense over there. Hadn't the Greeks—or was it the Turks—invaded? Wasn't the island split between the two factions, with the English staying safe in their sovereign base areas, as Palmer called them. I read on, but I didn't learn much more. I mean, there was lots to learn, but it didn't help me with Pambos or his late brother. The nagging question this Guenyeli thing left with me was "Who let the Turks know that the Greeks would be let out near their village?"

The next pile of books and clippings were less impressive for a start. There was no book about Arthur Tallon and his Contemporary Gallery. There were obituaries and clippings, reviews of shows and an interview given to a *Beacon* reporter ten years ago. In the handsome collection of art books, Tallon was a footnote or a brief citation preceded by "And of course this chapter would not be complete without..." His name turned up often among the acknowledgements, and reproduced pictures in several of the books about the Canadian art scene were credited to his own personal collection. After a pretty fast shuffle through these things I began to get the idea that Tallon had contributed a great deal to the development and encouragement of Canadian art, but for all his efforts the critics in Toronto were not passing around the glory. The obit in *The Globe and Mail* was brief and factual. The one in *The Toronto Star* ran two inches shorter than the obit for a former *Star* bookkeeper who died of lung cancer at 72. The *Beacon*, as I would have expected, went on and on about our local loss. There was a photograph in the file, not a clipping but an eight by ten glossy. It showed

Tallon standing with his head thrust through the opening in a marionette theatre. Beside his face stood five or six variously designed puppets. It looked like the cast of *Jack and the Beanstalk*, judging by the hoary old ogre, the cow and the beanstalk running up the back. Tallon's head was impressively framed in the proscenium arch. Great eyebrows, like the wings of a startled bird of prey about to take off, dominated a wide forehead. His eyes behind thick, steel-rimmed lenses looked back at me so strongly I felt obliged to look up from the page. Tallon had alert, knobbly, Lincolnesque features. With a beard and shawl, he could have passed for the assassinated president. He would have had to drop the cigarette butt that protruded from a corner of his mouth. There were other pictures of him among the clippings: Tallon with Wallace Lamb in 1944, Tallon in a canoe in Muskoka, Tallon with the Director of the National Gallery, Tallon with someone named Kahnweiler in what looked like Paris before the fall of France in 1940. Tallon looked about twenty-five.

"Having fun?" Ella Beames picked up one of the clippings. "Half the time I thought he was certifiable," she said, "the rest of the time he was like a lanky bear. You wanted to hug him."

"I didn't know you knew him, Ella. What was he like?"

"I just told you. There's a picture in the file he gave me. There it is. He made those puppets. He worked as an apprentice to some marionette-maker in the States. New England somewhere. I should be more precise than that. No wonder they're talking about retiring me."

"Retiring *you*? You're pulling my leg. They'd as soon put horns on the bust of Andrew Carnegie."

"Just check around here a year from now. You'll see."

"Ella, the world's falling apart. They're talking of shutting down the United, after nearly ten years I abandon the quiet of the City House, and now this. What am I going to do without you?"

"Benny, it isn't as bad as that. I'm not going to Victoria to live with my sister after all; I'll be right here in town. If you get really stuck, you can always call me. Don't look so glum. The world's not coming to an end." I managed to change my expression, but my heart wasn't in it. Ella had been my right hand for so long I always felt guilty whenever I cashed a cheque from a client. Wonderful Ella came free with the public library. What Ella didn't know about the present and past of Grantham and vicinity wasn't worth knowing.

Ella asked me about my mother and how she was getting on with her television-watching. I told her that she still doesn't miss much, but the TV doesn't cut into her reading time. She still devours about four novels a week. The last time I looked it was Julian Symons and Ruth Rendell. "She told me, Ella, that she had a hankering to go through Dickens once again."

"I think she's got most of him in paperbacks. I've got *Hard Times*. She lent it to me.

"I'll tell her." I took a breath. "Ella, how does the art scene work here in town? Most of the stuff in those books is about New York, Montreal, Vancouver and Toronto. Where does a place like Grantham fit in?"

"Well, I'll tell you what I know, but that's not much, Benny." She settled into a wooden Windsor chair on the other side of the table. "Let me see," she said. "Tallon was a sport, a square peg in a round hole. He belonged in a bigger place than this. He should have gone to a gallery like the Equinox in Vancouver or set up in Toronto. Toronto was always trying to get him to set up a branch there, but Arthur liked to do things his own way and in his own time. He was downright eccentric about most things. I could never guess what he was going to do from one week to another. He held on to his Contemporary Gallery, but he didn't look after things. It was a filthy mess most of the time, if you ask me. But, then, he had all of those paintings he bought when he was young. He came back from Paris with a lot of things that were by total unknowns then, but which would fetch unbelievable prices at an auction today. But Arthur stuck by Canadian painters mostly. He collected Emily Carr and the Group of Seven. Landscape painters, most of them. You probably saw silkscreen versions of some of their stuff in school when you were a kid. You know, they did Georgian Bay and Algonquin Park and Carr did totem poles..."

"I know that bunch. They were in banks too and on calendars. So that's the Group of Seven. Was Lamb one of them?"

"Heavens no! He came along later. But he's just as good. Better, I think! He was a wild man, yet Tallon became his dealer. They were a very unlikely pair, I'll tell you that for nothing."

"Was Tallon the only show in town?"

"Oh, no, Benny. There's the public gallery at Rodman Hall, with Mrs North in charge, and there's Hump Slaughter's auction room. He's the biggest dealer in antiques and fine arts in the Niagara District."

"Hump?" I asked.

"Humphrey, really. But everybody calls him Hump. I know a lot of people who avoid calling him by his first name. For a long time people didn't think it was quite proper. But nowadays nobody seems to mind. What's happening to the power of words, Benny? Time was I used to blush at the words scrawled on fences, and now I hear them—everywhere. How are writers going to write books if language is going bland on them?" I shrugged. I was still working my way through the Russians. It was taking quite a while. *Crime and Punishment* became easier when I saw that it was really television's *Columbo* backdated. As far as language and its shocking power goes, I guess you can get sated with four-letter words as well as you can with popcorn and strawberry shortcake. In the old days in England when they used to hang people in wholesale lots, the horror may have bothered the bumpkins visiting London for a rare visit, but for the locals the slaughter only provided opportunities for pimps and pickpockets.

I spent another half-hour at the library flipping through the material on the buying and selling of pictures and the art of collecting. When I got tired of that, I went back to Cyprus. The troubles apart, it sounded like a great island. It sat with its tail pointing up into the armpit of the Mediterranean where Syria and Turkey came together. I tried to imagine the weather. In the book called *Romantic Cyprus*, a travel guide by Kevork K. Keshishian, I didn't see any pictures of parkas or windbreakers. Life without winter. Now *that* I wouldn't mind at all.

Out on the street, the weather wasn't at all Mediterranean, but it would pass for late March in southern Ontario. I walked up James Street past the old Court House and the Oille fountain with the empty geranium pot at the top. Traffic along St Andrew Street was moving along steadily. The parking spaces by the meters were all full. Everybody was making a buck. It was time I joined them.

Chapter Seven

"Windermere," the voice said. "Good morning."

"Good morning. I would like to speak with Jonah Abraham, please."

"Just a moment. I'll connect you to his secretary." It seemed a reasonable approach, so I waited on the line, trying not to whistle through my teeth the tune I had stuck in my head. It was a hymn we used to sing in public school. Old Miss McDougall used to spend more time on singing hymns than on the rest of the curriculum. I tried to identify the present tune, but it escaped me. Something with "...where only man is vile..." in it. I looked around the office from my usual place behind my desk and tried to appraise it with a stranger's eye. I must get around to spending a day just getting rid of the things I never use: the broken electric fan, the trio of wigless manikins, the coat rack still marked "Size 10 & 12." I should replace the rug with the worn patch in the middle. The file drawers too needed cleaning out. The bottom one contained galoshes I hadn't worn in three years. They were mossy with dust, and I started wondering what kind of character it is that keeps useless junk underfoot year after year without ever once throwing up his hands and saying "Enough is enough!"

"Mr Abraham's secretary. Good morning."

"Good morning. Is Mr Abraham in this morning?"

"This was in regard to...?"

"Private business," I said, rather more bluntly than I'd intended. I could hear an intake of air at the other end. Could her job run that smoothly, I wondered, that my answer filled her with dismay? I felt immediate sympathy for the woman. Why can't I be as tactful as I would like to be?

"I am Mr Abraham's private secretary. Could I have your name, please?"

"Ben Cooperman."

"Of?"

"Just Ben Cooperman. I'm a private investigator, if you want to tell him that."

"Oh! Just a minute." There was another delay. This time I mentally cleaned out the second of my file drawers. I knew it was full of plastic bags that had held lunches and other goodies. I don't know why I started that collection, but once begun, it seemed wasteful to begin throwing them out. What I needed was to extend my trade routes. Figure out ways of taking things out of the office in plastic bags. If I ate more lunches at my desk, there would be more garbage. That was a thought, but it would also speed up my accumulation of more plastic bags.

"Yes? Mr Cooperman? This is Jonah Abraham. You wanted to discuss a private matter?" Good. I liked the way he came to the point. Already I liked Abraham.

"I've been trying to trace some paintings that have strayed from the Tallon collection, Mr Abraham. Apparently at the time of Mr Tallon's death, there were quite a few pictures out on loan. In order to complete an accurate inventory for the estate, we would like to identify as many of these as we can. With your help, we should be able to clear this up in a short time."

"You're doing this for Patrick Miles, is that correct, Mr Cooperman?" He'd kicked me in the knee and he didn't even know it.

"It isn't usual to give out the names of clients, Mr Abraham. But we do know that your name appears on a list of people who have works from the collection."

"That's very interesting. Perhaps you could have Mr Miles call me. Without meaning to give offence, Mr Cooperman, I hardly think we need to involve a private investigator at this point. Get Paddy to call me. Naturally, I would be very glad to cooperate with Paddy and Arthur's brother in clearing up the estate as quickly as possible. Good…"

"Just a moment, Mr Abraham. What if my client doesn't represent the Tallon interests?" He thought a moment before answering.

"I can't see how there can be collateral interests. You intrigue me, Mr Cooperman, but, if you are not representing the estate, I can't see how I can help you without authorization from the estate. Goodbye." It took me longer to think of an answer to that than it took Abraham to hang up the phone. I sat there looking at my dusty venetian blinds, with the phone in my hand, listening to the echo of the broken connection.

I'd now talked to all of the men Pambos Kiriakis had told me had access to where he kept the list. Where was that exactly? In his secret cubbyhole behind the bookshelf? How secret was that anyway: it was the first thing I saw in his office. It didn't appear to be something he kept secret from his close friends or even casual acquaintances. Maybe it was less a secret room than it was a kind of folly, a childish dream realized. Maybe he saw some of the same Saturday matinées at the Granada Theatre that I did.There were enough sliding panels and secret doors in those movies to fire a few imaginations even here in Grantham. I must ask Pambos about that: where was the list, what did it look like physically, was it typed or handwritten, and on what kind of paper. I made a mental note to call Kiriakis and clear up a few loose ends.

I made a few calls to some people who owed me a couple of favours. The harvest wasn't a big one, but there were a few interesting things that turned up. Peter MacCulloch was in his seventh year as vice-president of Secord University. He was well respected in academic circles, but spent most of his time hob-nobbing with people who could build a new stadium or kick in with the cost of football uniforms when the call to the building fund was answered. He went to Toronto at least once a week, sometimes more often. He had been a chemical engineer early in his career and made a name for himself as the man who built up Godden and Garber into one of the biggest names in the Canadian petrochemical industry. He lived in Calgary and Edmonton for many years before a dramatic break with G & G eight years ago. After a year as head of a community college in Vancouver, he returned to take up the post at Secord, which had become vacant suddenly on the death of Dr Clendennan. One thing I found that stirred my heart a trifle was the fact that MacCulloch and the late Arthur Tallon were second cousins. Did that mean that he might have legitimate claim to some of the paintings he had forgotten to confess to holding? Not certainly until the will is probated, I guessed. It raised a question of a family feud. Since I stopped doing divorce work, I'd done my best to stay away from quarrelling families. My best was not always good enough.

I thought for a moment about the inside information I'd been handed on a platter about the affair going on between Favell and MacCulloch's wife, Mary. Shakespeare probably said something about what you can learn from guilty parties when you ask about whether it is going to rain or not.

But I was straying from my subject. Mary MacCulloch

was not my client, in spite of the high heels that had
followed me down the corridors and out into the Secord
University parking lot. She was an unfaithful wife in
mid-affair, and afraid of being found out both by her
husband and by Nesta, probably Alex Favell's wife and
Mary's best friend. What did that have to do with the
missing pictures? Probably nothing, but it was free information, I thought, and it might come in handy before the week was out.

What did I know about Alex Favell? My telephone
contacts told me he was another local product. His
father was a member of the Grantham hunt when there
was a Grantham hunt. He also operated the paper mill
for its American owners. Alex grew up in the firm. After doing an MBA he went trouble-shooting for the
owners in places like Baie-Comeau, Chicoutimi and the
company's home base, Chicago. Like his father, he was
a horseman. He collected pictures, and married the
former Nesta Holland, who belongs to another of the
oldest families in town. I think they are still taking
musket balls dating from the War of 1812 out of the Holland barn near St. Davids. What else did I learn? Oh,
yes, he played golf and tennis and kept a boat at Port
Richmond. I thought I recognized that competitive edge
in our conversation at his office. His secretary, I remembered, suspected that his long lunches were not totally in the firm's best interests. He was a big giver to
charities, as was MacCulloch, and both served on many
boards of directors and were listed on the stationery
of charitable groups across the province. There was no
shaking the respectability of either MacCulloch or
Favell.

On the suggestion of Ella Beames, I borrowed a copy
of the recent paperback edition of *Distiller of Our Times*
by Paul Coldham, the former magazine editor and more
recently chronicler of the doings of the rich and

powerful. I flipped through this five-hundred-page opus about the Abraham dynasty and found that Jonah was not the most dynamic member of the third generation of the family. Between bites of my chopped egg salad sandwich at the Di, I studied up on the growth of this remarkable clan, whose North American career began when an immigration officer decided to stop writing after Jonah Abraham's grandfather had given him his first two given names. The family name was never put on his landed immigrant papers. In fact it took Coldham some time-consuming research to discover that the family name was Yakobowsky.

After trying its collective hands at everything from selling button hooks and needles to making ornamental glass beads from old bottles, the family discovered booze and the money that could be made from the manufacture and sale of it. When Ontario went dry in the 1920s, part of the operation went underground. Coldham had difficulty getting his facts about Prohibition. Survivors are still reluctant to talk into a tape recorder even at this late date. By 1976, the date of Coldham's book, Jonah Abraham at forty-eight was about to become chairman of the board of one of the most sure-footed and diversified international conglomerates in the world. Outside business, his main interests were his investments and his remarkable art collection.

Reading between the lines, it looked like Jonah partook of the family money, but did little to earn any of it. Becoming the grand old man at forty-eight is young. And living in Grantham kept him away from everything but the occasional board meeting in Toronto. The Grantham operation merely dealt with local wineries: big bucks locally, but to Windermere, small potatoes. Jonah, true to his name, was beginning to look like he was unlucky in his own family business. He was overshadowed by his more flamboyant siblings who made headlines in Toronto, Montreal, London and Paris with their marriages, divorces and separations, remarriages and one suspected murder. For some reason, Jonah had avoided all this and retired to the relatively peaceful Mies van der Rohe-designed house on the escarpment overlooking greater Grantham.

"You want coffee or milk with the sandwich, Benny?" the waitress asked. She looked like a young Myrna Loy in her starched uniform. She carried her tray with a difference.

"Milk, I think," I said after deliberating for a few seconds. For a few more I watched her uniform swing away from me towards the front of the store, where she disappeared behind the counter. I watched traffic run eastward past the glass front door and windows. I admired the stained cherrywood booths and walls. The Di was one of the treasures of Grantham. It should have a brass plaque on the front wall protecting it from the whims of change.

I eat out a lot, I was thinking. Maybe now that I have my own place, I'll try cooking for myself a little. My spirit is as adventurous as the next guy's. Besides, I've been learning a lot about food over the last couple of years. Being trapped in my room at the City House had cramped my style. I was even getting the itch to make my own instant in the morning, instead of having to get dressed and head out to the United. There were a few things I'd like to try cooking, a few of my mother's specialities that with practice I might be able to copy.

I knew I was going to be glad I left the City House. Ten years in a hotel room is plenty. Settling-in problems were only temporary. In the long run, I'd be glad I made the move.

I was drinking my milk when I saw Bill Palmer come into the restaurant. He was with a reporter from the *Beacon* that I knew, Barney Reynolds. I picked up my check and walked by their table. "Hi, Barney! You keeping ahead of the rewrite boys? Hello, Mr Palmer."

"Bastards!" said Barney, who was always telling me about how his pieces were cut to ribbons by the editors. Bill Palmer looked like he was trying to place me. After I let him sweat for a minute, I helped him out.

"Of course! Now I remember. We were talking about the death of Napoleon."

"They killed all the great strips," Barney added. "Remember *Bringing Up Father*? Hell, I go back almost to the *Yellow Kid*. Remember *Abbie an' Slats*? Raeburn van Buren drew it and Al Capp, the guy who drew *Li'l Abner*, wrote it. Now *Napoleon and Uncle Elby* was a damned well drawn strip."

"You got the wrong Napoleon, Barney," Bill interrupted. "We're talking about the late emperor of the French, the man of Elba and St Helena."

"Able was I ere I saw Elba," Barney said.

"What?" I said.

"That old chestnut. The best-known palindrome on record, isn't it?" Palmer smiled across the table.

"What's a palindrome? A Persian airport?" I asked.

"In a palindrome you can read the line from either end and it reads the same," Bill said.

" 'Live not on evil, madam, live not on evil.' "

"What are you guys talking about?" The world was going mad.

"Sit down, Benny. 'Was it a rat I saw?' "

"Huh?"

"That's another. 'Red rum, sir, is murder.' That's another. There are millions of them." I sat down next to Barney, facing Bill Palmer. On the whole, I wished they would go back to the comics. I could hold my own there. When the waitress came, I ordered coffee, since the boys looked like they weren't in a hurry to leave or in the middle of a private conversation.

"You said last night," I said to Bill, "that you met Pambos Kiriakis in Cyprus?"

"Oh, God, here we go again!" moaned Barney.

"That's right. Not Barney's favourite topic. He thinks the Turks were sold down the river."

"That's right. The Greeks controlled the press."

"Horse---!"

"I knew I'd get a rise out of you! Works every time. Bill's devoted to all lost causes. Enosis is only one of them. He'll also sign you up in the Flat Earth Society. Show Benny your membership card."

"Ah, Barney's sore because this was one war he missed."

"The paper said that they didn't need the old touch. Used wire copy! Pablum!"

I could tell that although this conversation might be a lot of fun for people who'd been exposed to long hours of radiation from a green word processor, it wasn't helping me pay my rent. After another ten minutes of Barney ribbing Bill and Bill trying to explain it all to me, I picked up my two checks, paid my bill and walked east on St Andrew Street.

Chapter Eight

That night I tried making Campbell's split-pea soup. I used the same saucepan that I'd used the night before. While it was boiling—I thought I should boil it for ten minutes anyway—I called Pambos at the hotel.

"Charalambous Kiriakis."

"Is that you, Pambos? It's me, Benny. Is this a good time?"

"Benny! I'm glad to hear from you. Have you got good news?"

"What I've got won't take long to report, but I do have a few more questions I'd like—"

"Benny, why don't you come on over. I'll put on some top sirloins and we can talk. Since I got so good at delegating authority around here, I got nothing to do at the dinner hour."

"Well, actually, Pambos, I got something on the stove as a matter of fact."

"Using that little kitchenette already. Good for you. Something complicated?"

"No, just simple down-to-earth cooking like my mother makes for me when I go home. I'm working on her style."

"I didn't know you had this interest in cooking, Benny. It's a whole new side of you. Have you read Brillat-Savarin?"

"Hey, Pambos, I just moved in, eh? Give me a break."

"Okay, why not come over when you get finished.

No dirty pots in the sink. Nothing left drying on the counter. Don't get hooked by bad kitchen habits, Benny. They're the hardest to break. Believe me, I know what I'm talkin' about."

"I'll come over when the pot is gleaming. Around seven-thirty or eight o'clock?"

"Sure. See you." He hung up, and I turned down the heat under the soup. It looked like thick yellow lava bubbling in the saucepan. A dry crust had formed above the waterline. I stirred it back into the mix with a wooden spoon. When it looked ready, I served myself and dined at the table I'd set. I tried to find a record, but I remembered that I still had to rewire the record-player. It wouldn't take long after I found the diagram I'd made before I pulled it apart. The soup was delicious.

Once again, the headlights broke up a convention of cats behind the hotel. I parked the Olds and climbed out into the alley.

This time there was the welcome of familiarity about the dark entrance to the back of the hotel. A busboy with a dirty apron was putting out the trolley with full garbage cans. It was good not to hear my mother's voice in my head, adding footnotes as I went down the hall to the office door. I think I even smiled at the plastic plate with "C. Kiriakis" on it. I now knew his real name. What was it, Charalambous? Something like that. I tapped a tattoo on the door and waited for the panel to slide open. It stayed closed. I repeated the knock and tried the door at the same time. The door was open, but I waited a few moments before barging in. I tried calling.

"Pambos!" I called. My voice, I think, sounded strong. When I came yesterday, I could hear a strangled quality in it. "Pambos! It's me, Benny!" No answer.

The office looked unchanged. The glasses had been cleaned away and replaced by brand new dirty cups.

One stood on the blotter in front of Pambos's place at his desk. The secret panel was closed. The ancient toys and banks smiled a greeting. I thought of Napoleon on St Helena as I surveyed the leaden troops. They were comfortable things to live with, I decided. Like the brass lamp with the green glass shade: easy on the eyes, easy to live with. The wonderful thing about Pambos was that every object had been picked with love and kept close to where he could look at it every day. I looked at the oils on the wall: the Harris, the Jackson, the Lamb and the Pollock. For the first time I really saw them. With all the knowledge that my morning in the library brought to the fore, I examined the brushwork and the composition critically.

Then I sat down hard in one of the deep-breathing leather chairs. It let out a noise like a sigh that mingled with a similar sound that came from me. "Oh, God!" I said, or something like that. I don't remember exactly what I said. I just remember the letter-opener with the words St Louis World's Fair written on the handle. Another of Pambos's antiques. It was something I'd seen him playing with last night as we sat and talked about Napoleon and the town of Guenyeli in Cyprus. Now, nobody was playing with it. It was stuck up to the hilt in Pambos Kiriakis's shirt. He lay palms up on the broadloom under his desk.

He was wearing the same pants as he'd worn while helping me with my unpacking. The shirt was different; a blood-stain beginning at the wound had followed a crease down to the belt-line. Here it had pooled, sending the overflow down the side of his shirt, soaking his back as far as I could see it and the carpet. I kept my eyes on the details. I didn't look at the slack jaw or the surprised, protruding eyes. I was glad he was behind the desk, where he all but disappeared from sight when I stood up. In my brain I could hear my mother's stern voice telling me not to touch anything.

"All right!" I said. It came out like the cry of a half-strangled peacock in the zoo. It startled me. My mother bumps into all of her bodies between the covers of paperbacks. Me, I wasn't that lucky. Just when I thought I was handling myself with professional calm and detachment, I knocked over the cup of cold coffee on Pambos's desk. I watched the stain darken the green blotter. I cursed my clumsiness, but cut myself off abruptly. There was something in the cup. I fished it out with my trusty ballpoint pen. It was a silver bracelet made of large flat links and an oval disc inscribed "Arthur Tallon." On the other side: "The wearer is allergic to penicillin."

Why had Kiriakis dropped it into his coffee? Was it Pambos who did it? Or was it his murderer? I was trying to figure out the answer to those and a few other questions, when I heard that we were about to have company. I pocketed the bracelet. I didn't hear the outer door open, but I heard it click back into place after it had been opened. There was somebody between the way to my car and where I was standing above Pambos's body. No place to be caught with my feet this close to the blood-stained carpet. Another glimpse of Pambos and I had the familiar tugging at the top of my stomach. I tried to shelve that for the moment by concentrating on something neutral. Vanilla ice cream was a bad idea, but I was having trouble replacing the images that had recently taken root in my head. Panic was coiled in the back of my throat. I moved the curtains behind the desk to see how much room there was between them and the window. Footsteps were getting louder. I slipped behind the curtains and waited. My breath was coming quickly and noisily. I tried to make my diaphragm do what Mr MacDonald, the high-school dramatic coach, said I should do with it, make it control my breath. I forced myself to breathe easier, but the dusty closeness of the curtains made the noise about the same. I tried to listen for the intruder. Hell, if he was an intruder, what was I, the Flying Dutchman?

The door to the study opened. I could feel rather than hear someone making his way to the desk. Papers were shuffled, a drawer was opened. Had he missed the body? I didn't think so. Still, I heard no gasp, no sudden intake of air. The search continued: a rattle of paper, then quiet, while he was looking through the papers. Through the curtains I could make out only the pinpoints of light at the desk lamp and the overhead light. Occasionally a shape obscured the desk light. I only got an impression of size. I couldn't even sex the intruder, although there was something large and bulky about the shape blocking the light that made me use male pronouns as I was trying to sort out to myself what "he" was going to do next. I heard a drawer close and then a slight "ah" sound. Had he seen it, or was it something else. I hoped it wasn't something else.

"Your shoes need shining," the voice said. "You needn't stay behind the curtains on my account."

I pulled aside the curtains and stepped back into the light of the room. "Thanks for the tip," I said. "It was stuffy in there."

The man on the other side of the desk was bald, with eyes that were slightly oriental. He was a little taller than me, and wearing an expensive tan. The eyes looked to have a suppressed smile behind them, like he enjoyed seeing the world in its ironic underwear. Right now, he was focused on me and asking himself the same questions about me as I was about him. He hitched up the corner of his mouth on the right side; it wasn't a smile, but it stood for an acknowledgement that we were the living in the presence of death behind the desk. I liked the face, and it now began to dawn on me that it wasn't the face of a complete stranger. I'd seen those flat ears, the slightly uptipped eyebrows and that generous nose before.

"I don't believe I've had the pleasure," I said, trying to come up with a name to fit the place before he gave me the answer.

"My name doesn't matter," he said, changing the subject. "But I think you should explain what you were doing hiding in the draperies.

I'd seen his face in the *Beacon*, not so long ago. He had something to do with business. Then it came to me:

"I was just testing your powers of observation, Mr Abraham. I think I've seen your picture in the business section of the Toronto papers and also the local one. I'll be glad to explain what I was doing, if you can explain why you were going through the papers on Kiriakis's desk. Especially since Pambos can no longer tell you to push off. By the way, did you misplace your letter-opener?"

Abraham smiled. There was some pain behind it, but it must have seemed the right gesture at the time. "The one in our friend behind the desk, you mean? No, I didn't mislay it." He moved a few steps back away from the desk. This permitted me to clear the area. I felt more comfortable with the desk to my right, and Pambos's body concealed by the angle and the top of the desk itself.

Hadn't I told Pambos that I couldn't imagine Jonah Abraham going through the papers on his desk? Now I'd seen it and I couldn't share the joke with the little guy. I started feeling sick again.

Abraham wore a silk tie with a lot of green medallions floating against a ground of yellow. It was tied too tightly for my taste, made him look uncomfortable. "The letter-opener is part of Pambos's collection of American turn-of-the-century memorabilia. He kept it on his desk." He tried that smile again. He was trying to be ingratiating. I knew a little about that game too. "I hope you don't imagine it has my fingerprints on it. I assure you it doesn't."

"You didn't act very surprised to run into a corpse."

"I must compliment you on the quality of your vision. Those curtains are thick brocade." I ignored his observation.

"You just dug into those drawers like a little beaver. You must run into a lot of bodies to take them so coolly."

Jonah Abraham, if it was Jonah Abraham—and he had neither affirmed nor denied my guess—sat down in one of Pambos's leather chairs. Again the leather heaved a great sigh. He crossed his hands in his lap, like a little old lady, and gave me a taste of that near-smile with the pain behind it again. I nearly leaned back on the desk, but I decided that I would try to keep the Cooperman fingerprints on the Cooperman knobs and glass surfaces and not spread them around indiscriminately. Abraham looked like he had a confession to make. I sat down opposite him, and when the cushion stopped protesting my weight, he began:

"When I was here ten minutes ago, I was very shocked to discover ... what I discovered. I would decribe it as more than 'very surprised.' I was surprised enough for the two of us. I left the room to telephone the police. I didn't want to touch the phone on his desk. They should be here in a few minutes. If I had had anything to do with Pambos's death, I wouldn't have raised the alarm, would I?"

"So you thought you'd kill time going through his mail."

"Nothing of the kind, my friend. I was nervous, that's all. And I didn't feel like looking at that large Wallace Lamb over there. Death and Lambs don't mix very well." I glanced over at the painting he referred to. It looked like a Dutch still-life reflected in a broken mirror.

"So that's what a Lamb looks like. It looks like a Dutch still-life reflected in a broken mirror."

"Really?" He didn't sound interested in my opinion. He looked back at the picture and something happened to his face, like it had softened and then tightened again fast, before the eye could register it.

"That's 'Breakfast in Ayton,' one of his best. I'd give a pound of flesh to own it."

"Whose?" Jonah Abraham ignored my question. He didn't like people near him sounding off. I guess I came on like a TV cop show. Silence flowed and filled the gap. Then he looked down at the figure on the floor. From where I was sitting, I could see the top of his head and the arms thrown back. He looked like he'd been shot after being told to put his hands up. But, of course, I knew this wasn't so, even though the wound and the letter-opener were out of sight. I thought for a moment about how Sam, my brother, and I used to practise being shot standing at the top of a small rise in Coleman's lawn. Once hit, we would corkscrew down to the ground or fling ourselves backwards, imitating the best deaths on celluloid as seen the previous Saturday at the matinée at the Granada Theatre on James Street. I wondered where Jonah Abraham practised his dying. Then I was looking at Pambos's pale palms again.

"Pambos," Abraham said. I didn't know whether he was answering my question about the pound of flesh, or whether it was an involuntary response to the fact of death in general and that of an acquaintance in particular. "What's that he's holding in his palm?" I got down on my knees and leaned closer.

"It's a button. Looks like it comes from a woman's coat or jacket."

"Let me see!" Abraham moved closer.

"Better let the police pick it up first. There might be prints. Looks like there are threads attached to the underside."

"So, that lets both of us out, my friend. He was killed by a woman."

"Or that's what the killer wanted us to believe."

"You're making a television melodrama out of it. Simple solutions are best." I could just make out the beginning of the sound of a far-off police siren. Or maybe it was a fire somewhere. I couldn't tell the difference. But my own involvement with this murder made me select the police as the most likely source of the sound. As it grew closer, my guess was confirmed. Both Abraham and I got up off our knees and sank back into the responsive leather chairs and waited.

Chapter Nine

I thought about Jonah Abraham, my fellow suspect in the murder. It provided a more interesting way of spending the time than counting the change in my pocket without looking, or culling out-of-date membership cards from my worn wallet. I tried my hand at mentally redecorating the corridor in the downtown offices of Niagara Regional Police, discarding the furniture and putting down a thick rug to deaden the footsteps of innocent and guilty alike. But I couldn't concentrate on anything for long. Abraham held my attention. He was real. I should have an unread paperback sewn into the lining of my coat for unexpected long waits like this. I always get stuck this way and I never have a thing to read.

I knew I had to stay away from Pambos. He was too good a friend and his dead face was much too recently dead for me to think about him in a personal way. For the moment, he was the body in the Stephenson House, the reason I was being questioned. There would be time to mourn him, but not that night.

I had already been through the usual mill at the scene of the crime. I had told all, or nearly all, to the first officers at the scene and then to the detectives that came with the clean-up boys and the medical people. At least the medical people didn't want to know what I was doing there. They concentrated on Pambos. Like a team of make-up men on a movie set they worked him over, bagging his hands like they intended to run him through a beehive. The fingerprint boys left me alone too, except for the fellow who had seen me on the scene of at least two other crimes I could think of. In a big city, it would all be more anonymous. Imagine getting asked in London or in New York about whether you were the same Benny Cooperman who left fingerprints on the sink in Dr Zekerman's office five years ago, and found the hanging body of a movie star in a Niagara Falls hotel room three years ago. He greeted me like we were lodge brothers who'd strayed from the convention floor and found ourselves holding up the same bar at three in the morning.

I looked at my watch. It was nearly ten o'clock. The cops had arrived at the Stephenson House just after eight-thirty. We had danced around Pambos's study and then transferred the action to a small meeting room in the new part of the hotel. In the background we could hear the staff having hysterics about their fallen leader or the possibility of changes in the next regime. By the time we were told we were needed downtown, it was nine o'clock. They had Abraham wait in a separate room. I'd noticed that from the moment the cops took out their day books, they were treating Mr Abraham with kid gloves.

Jonah Abraham, I thought. He was rifling the desk. That meant he was looking for the list. That meant it must be either Favell or MacCulloch who took it. It sounded right, but I wasn't sure I bought it. Abraham could have seen my shoes under the curtains when he came into the room and saw that by going through Pambos's papers he would appear to be innocent of stealing the list. I tried to let that drip through the filter. It came out looking thin and unappetizing. This was a murder investigation not a treasure-hunt for some list of paintings and who has them. Pambos was murdered, sure, but who could tell me that it was because of the things he had talked to me about. Maybe he had an argument with his chef about wages. Maybe it was some waiter or housekeeper he'd fired. It could be a dozen different things and none of them close to the fine arts.

That seemed the sensible thing: Pambos's death was not an event that had a single answer. Not yet, anyway. But Abraham being there. The connection with the list was clearer. Pambos said that Abraham was known to have been on the list and that he was one of the three people who had an opportunity to have taken it. I needed to learn more about that. Maybe Jonah Abraham was an old family friend. Maybe the Stephenson House was his favourite watering hole. Maybe he and Pambos were cronies who used to talk about fine art long into the night. I could picture some of that.

Abraham said that he called the cops. The cops came, so likely he was telling the truth about that. Step one. He tells the truth about small things. What about big things? Time will tell, time will tell. He took the death of an old friend coolly enough. No shouts or tears, no prostration or obvious grief. Now wait a minute. We don't know he and Pambos were pals, do we? He recognized the murder weapon. He was familiar with the office. And when it comes to showing signs of grief, neither of us carried on. We didn't rend our garments or don sackcloth. Not made for showing instant grief. What are the cops making of that? They like neat packages. Okay, so maybe Abraham's no sentimentalist. He takes death as he takes life, as he finds it. How inconvenient of him to find it in Pambos's private study, under his desk.

There was a floor-model coffee machine in the corridor of this part of NRP Headquarters. When you put the right number of coins into the right slots, the machine poured a brown liquid into a styrofoam cup, then lightened it with a chalky shot from another opening. The sweetener, as I'm sure the manufacturer calls it, was already in the mixture that in the end was not hot or recognizably coffee. It tasted like death but it killed the time. When I finished with the beverage, which I doubted had ever seen a coffee plantation, I began methodically destroying the cup it came in. First I scored the top around the rim with my fingernails, than began tearing off strips of the foam and putting them in the ashtray beside me along with the butts of my last three cigarettes. I wondered if the law would allow them to install a machine that would, for good money, sell cigarettes that bore as remote a relationship to real tobacco as the product of the machine I'd just been swindled by. I continued tearing up the cup, wondering whether Mr Abraham was sitting in a similar corridor on the other side of the building, or whether the well-known distiller was already on his way back to his little place on the escarpment. I was working on this when my old friend and fellow defender of the law, Staff Sergeant Chris Savas, came out of his office and glared at me.

"Hello, Benny." I was expecting something with more energy, more of Savas's brand of sarcasm directed towards private investigators. He sounded a little hoarse, the way he did when we batted evidence back and forth in the small hours. I swallowed my opening line, deciding to save it for another time. I'd been savouring the information that Pambos had let slip when we'd been talking at the United: Chris's first name was Christophoros and not Christopher as I had always supposed. I guess in Greek it amounts to the same thing, but I'd planned to spring the name on him. But with Pambos dead, the joke went flat.

"Hi, Chris. I'm sorry about this. Pambos was a nice guy. I liked the little bugger. I'm sorry he had to go out that way."

Savas gave a sort of a nod, then tossed the crown

of his head in the direction of his door. I followed him inside. "C'mon," he said. "I'll getcha some real coffee."

The office hadn't changed from the last time Chris and I had reason to talk professionally. The rust-stains on the linoleum still showed where the furniture used to stand before it was moved to the present set-up: the stack of files by the door, a cabinet of official manuals, a desk made of grey metal, bumped and chipped by heavy traffic. A serious-faced Chris looked down from his Aylmer Police College graduation picture along with two dozen other equally serious young officers. Elsewhere he was grinning in a shot taken on the firing range. Large earmuffs protected his ears. The sober look returned in a framed photograph of him getting some honour or other from a former lieutenant-governor. He never told me about that picture. Chris was a good cop, and that included all the shy vices beginning with modesty.

I took the usual chair reserved for guests and left enough leg-room for Chris to get past me when he came back with two mugs of real coffee. Both of us spend long hours drinking the worst coffee ever to stain a pot; that's why we both appreciate the good stuff whenever we're lucky enough to get a sample. Outside the door which Savas closed behind him with a swing of his hip and a kick, I could hear the normal sounds of the NRP on duty at a late hour. Two-finger typing was going on next door, a badly distorted PA system blared indecipherably, and occasionally I heard the sound of a male voice raised above the normal drone. Savas sat. He opened a file in front of him.

"Okay, we come to bury Pambos not to praise him," Savas said, throwing down a few scanty handwritten reports that came from the investigating officers. "We'll have a wake for the guy some other time, Benny. Right now this is just another routine investigation. What do you know about it that isn't down here in black and white?"

"It's all there, Chris. Just like I told Vic Vittorini and his partner. It's a new guy; I don't know him."

"He's not so new. Name's Jack Harasti. He'll go far if he can get his mind off crossword puzzles. That's your vice too, isn't it, Benny?"

"It's not a vice when you know how lousy you are. I'm strictly an amateur."

"I'm glad to hear that, Benny. Now let's get down to cases, as they say." I nodded that that was fine with me, and Savas stared at me for a long time. "You know," he said, "in all the years I've known you, you've always been straight with me." I started to get worried. Savas didn't need to flatter me. This time he was winding up well back of the mound and I knew it was going to be a fast ball. His face was putting on that phoney avuncular look that he used on lost kids when he was walking a beat. It cut no ice with me, and usually, when our mutual friend Pete Staziak was standing with us, he'd give me a look that said Savas was at it again.

Chris and I went back to the winter of 1980 or around about there. I was getting my butt kicked by a colleague of his in a way that bothered Savas's set of scruples. So we put our heads together and concentrated on the art of the possible. Since then, I'd seen that big head of his in and out of several investigations. Sometimes I knew he'd like to nail me for a B and E or a felony of some sort just so he'd be one up on me, but I've always been too dumb to make an illegal buck and Chris knows it as well as I do. He has a big face with a big helping of nose in the middle. When he takes off the "Mr Nice Guy" sign, he looks friendly enough, but as soon as he gets serious or worried, his eyes get hard and stony.

He started in on me, taking me through my earlier

statement. I told him about meeting Pambos at the United Cigar Store and about how he helped me unpack in my new apartment. I even told him about the list he wanted me to find. I could tell that Savas didn't want to know about all those pictures that hadn't been returned to their rightful owners after the death of Arthur Tallon. I asked him if he knew anything about Tallon's death and he didn't. But I'd planted a seed. Tallon was a long way from Pambos Kiriakis on the first night of an investigation, so we tried to keep to the body on the carpet. He took my being at the scene of the crime seriously, as he was supposed to. He also didn't like the fact that his other key witness had mentioned that he first came across me in the draperies of Pambos's office.

"For the love of Mike, Benny, open up or I'm going to let you fall off the roof! And don't go saying you were pushed."

"I told you three times what I know! You want me to start making things up?"

"I want the whole story, not fragments. What were you doing in Kiriakis's office? Why did you hide behind the curtains? What are you really working on beside this picture business? What women are involved?"

"Button, button, who's got the button?"

"I've got it, Cooperman, and I want to know where it came from." He let the button fall on the file folder. There, on the top of his desk, it didn't look like our best clue to who'd killed Pambos Kiriakis.

"I don't suppose there were any prints you could get off that?"

"Smeared. The way you're going to be if I don't start getting some answers." He was looking at me like I was a bottle full of answers to all the questions he could think up. I tried again to think of something I'd forgotten to say, but my conscience was clear; I'd been as up-front with Savas as he'd ever been with me. He had dropped a hint about the direction his investigation was leading. I thought I'd see how serious he was.

"Chris, do you honestly think Kiriakis pulled that button off some woman's coat? A death struggle and all that?"

"Well, it's not off a seaman's greatcoat or off the fly of a fireman, is it?"

"You're barking up the wrong spruce." I picked up the button and turned it around in my hand. "All you're going to get from this is bud-worm."

"How come?"

"Chris, I saw the button when it was still lying in Pambos's palm, before the forces of law and order had had a chance to pass it around and bag and label it."

"I hear you. Keep talking."

"When I saw it first it was lying front side up."

"So?" Chris was beginning to look testy. It was one of the professional looks he did best. "Cooperman, don't ration it."

"If I pulled a button off your coat while in a death struggle, trying to get out of here to catch up on the early night I promised myself yesterday when I finished moving and unpacking umpteen boxes in my new place, the front of the button would be touching my palm and the ripped off, dangling threads would point up. This thing was lying the other way round. So, I suggest that it was planted. It didn't get there by normal or natural means. That's all. It didn't grow there."

Savas thought about that, unless the process of scratching his late-night beard absently meant the opposite. He seemed to be turning it over in his mind, but what do I know about what goes on in Chris Savas's head. "Okay, he didn't pull the button off a female murderer's coat. Who did it then?

"It has to be the same character who filed the letter-opener between Kiriakis's ribs. That's my best shot. Not too many innocent people carry around a button belonging to their hated enemy in hopes of finding some cold palm to leave it in."

Savas sipped his coffee and I took a long drink from the mug in front of me. It was nearly cold. How long had we been sitting and talking here? Hadn't Chris just brought in the cups a moment ago? What was going on with time in Niagara Regional? It was often said that they could fix anything but a parking ticket. Now I believe it. "The question to ask, Chris, is who had it in for one of Kiriakis's lady friends."

"Okay, spill. Who are they?" I tried to watch myself; I didn't want to tell Chris for the fifth or sixth time that I had already told him all I knew about Pambos's private life.

"You haven't been listening, Chris. There is only one fact I haven't passed on to you that Pambos told me. And it's irrelevant and you already know it."

"Christ. Cooperman, will you let me be the judge of that? That's my goddamn job not yours!"

"Okay, he let it leak that my old friend Chris Savas's first name is Christophoros not Christopher. You want me to add that to my statement?" Chris shifted a bubble of air behind his upper teeth and sucked on it. His big face went through the motions of returning to a calm and placid appearance, but muscles under the flesh of his cheeks pulsed with irritation. I tried to make it better. "Chris, I was just doing a job for Pambos. I don't know any more about him than you do. In fact you probably know a hell of a lot more. I don't know about his love life. I don't know his friends or enemies, male or female." I stopped, maybe a little more abruptly than was expected. I added:

"Come on, Chris. He wasn't my best friend. I liked him and I'm going to miss him, but I'm a limited resource if you want to know what he did apart from what I just told you. I knew him best in the old days when he was working in the steakhouse. We used to sit up till all hours in those days talking everything from art to politics and back again. There was a gang of us: Wally Skeat from the TV station, Harold from the *Beacon* and sometimes Ned Evans from the Workshop Players, when he was sober enough."

Chris slapped both thighs with his large hands and stood up. "Okay," he said. "Let's leave it there for now, Benny." I got to my feet and started for the door. When I was part of the way through it, I turned back to face Chris Savas.

"Was there a lot more to Pambos than met the eye, Chris?" Savas winced. At first I thought that was all I was going to get, then he volunteered:

"There's this whole Cyprus thing." I waited for him to elaborate, but he had told me all he intended to. We shook hands and in a minute I was walking down the broad front steps of Niagara Regional to the friendly trees of Church Street.

Chapter Ten

"Hello, is Phil there?" This time it was a man. I explained that this number had been recently reissued and suggested that he should check with the directory or the operator about the whereabouts of his friend. I envied Phil his devoted friends and was inclined to be a little hard on him for not keeping them abreast of his moves from place to place. I wondered if I would get calls forwarded to me from the City House. I made a mental note to phone Gus at the bar and give him my new number. For some reason, known best to my marrow, I didn't get around to it for several weeks.

I tried to get Pambos out of my head. He was dead. There'd be no more viewing of his treasures, no more discussions about the poisoning of Napoleon. Pambos was dead. It seemed strange, hard to accept. The image of him moving his coffee cup closer to me at the counter at the United was still at least as clear as the one with the letter-opener. As I looked around the room, I could see him disposing of the contents of my cardboard boxes and then flattening out the cartons and tying them with string. I thought I'd better give myself time, and began with a big bath in my new tub.

Climbing out and drying myself with one of the new towels I'd bought to mark my progress from King Street to Court Street, I began to feel better. I guess it comes to those who discover themselves to be, in spite of a narrow miss, still among the living. I'd just settled down to a book with a title that began *The Man Who...*, when the phone rang. I thought that I would be angry if it was Phil calling to pick up his messages.

"Hello?"

"Mr Cooperman?" It wasn't a voice I knew, and I was slightly alarmed that my new number had been traced so quickly. I began to regret the unkind thoughts I'd entertained for Phil's pals.

"That's right." He didn't speak up immediately. I added: "Who is this?"

"Sorry to bother you so late..." he continued, ignoring my question.

"Nobody else worries. Who are you and what's on your mind?" Again, the silence between the question and the answer was alarming, not enough for me to grab my clothes and retreat back to King Street, but just enough to make my throat feel dry.

"Mr Abraham would like to see you."

"Mr *Jonah* Abraham?"

"That's right. He said he'd make it worth your while." So, my friend from the other side of the curtains wanted to compare notes or get me to back up what he told the cops about his being in Pambos's office before I got there. He must be a worried man, judging by the hour.

"Not a social call, then?" I gave him a few seconds to respond. He didn't. "Tell him I'll see him tomorrow. He can find out where my office is. I'm in the yellow pages."

"He'd like to have a drink with you tonight," the voice said, stepping up the insistence.

"It's past my bedtime. I'll see him tomorrow." I didn't want Jonah Abraham to think he could get me for a drink, like a stale pretzel. "Look," I said, "I'm tired and ready to turn in. Your boss will understand that this hasn't been an easy day for me." The voice at the other end, even silent, had the sound of not listening.

"Mr Cooperman," he said at length, "if you look out your window, you'll see that Mr Abraham has sent a car to pick you up. He naturally doesn't want to inconvenience you."

"He shouldn't have bothered. It's after office hours."

A hand or handkerchief went over the mouthpiece of the distant telephone. I thought I heard, but I might be inventing, the other voice say:

"He says he won't come. How do you like that? A guy like that!" Still more distant, another voice came through. It sounded familiar:

"Give me the phone, Vince." The hand came away from the phone and I could hear clearly again. "Hello, Mr Cooperman?" It was the real thing. It was like being called on the phone by the best rye that money can buy. He went on: "I hear we are not going to have the pleasure of your company tonight. I was looking forward to our second meeting."

"Look, Mr Abraham, I'm tired and it's late. Why not call it a day? As for the pleasure of my company, I'm sure you'll get used to it. Think of all those days that preceded tonight. Or, if you want to confess to something, you can do it right now on the phone. It'll save gas and the line hasn't been mine long enough to have a bug on it."

"I like to do important business face to face, Mr Cooperman. It's a rule of mine. Call it an eccentricity."

"As far as I know, we don't have any business to discuss."

"I want to make you an offer."

"What kind of offer won't keep until morning?" I'd said that without thinking. I wasn't purposely playing hard to get, I just wasn't thinking fast enough. I mean, with Pambos in the cold room at Niagara Regional, I wasn't working for anybody. With Pambos dead, I could go back to tracing a line of credit card receipts that would lead me to Matt Kirwin, who had picked up his daughter after school one day three months ago and vanished with her and her homework. The credit cards told me Kirwin was careless about details and I would be able to put that file away just behind the Kiriakis file. "I'm a reasonable man, Mr Abraham, but I just got out of a hot bath and am looking forward to half an hour with the classics and then sleep. There's an unpleasant sight I want to get out of my head. I think you know the one."

"I do, indeed. When we first met," he said, his voice trying to sound casual and even friendly, "we could both see that your business with Mr Kiriakis had come to an end."

"I ought to take up a solider line of work."

"What I would like to suggest is this. I would like you to stay on the case. That's my proposition. Same terms you had with Kiriakis. I want you to find that list."

The place Jonah Abraham called home had been designed by Mies van der Rohe in 1938, when the German architect came to North America. It was said that he never saw the house either while it was under construction or later after it had been completed. He was kept informed of the project through detailed photographs and long-distance telephone. The builder was Jonah's father. He'd started with the idea of having a simple house designed around an atrium. The spot he picked commanded a view of Lake Ontario and the plain rising from it to the Niagara Escarpment, immediately below the proposed windows. Somewhere between the initial sketch and the final installation of a doormat, the plans got out of hand. The simplicity of line was still there, as you drove up the curved approach, but the lines were longer higher and deeper than those first clear intentions. The place was a mansion. Jonah told me that his father and mother could never leave well enough alone. Everything got embellished and exaggerated, even the plans of Mies van der Rohe. On weekends you could visit parts of the house for two dollars a head, but I never got past the velvet ropes before.

I'd relented on my stand. A position taken on the tel-ephone requires face-to-face negotiation. Besides, I thought that the night air might do me good, help me sleep, after the pressures of the day. I wrote out a note about where I was going and left it under my pillow. It was a silly tactic, but it made me feel better as I closed the door to the apartment and headed down the stairs.

Two of Abraham's boys were sitting in the front seat of the car. They didn't look particularly happy to see me; they kept eyes front, while the driver put the car in gear and moved smoothly on a fine German engine out of the downtown area.

When the car came to a stop, I didn't wait for the royal treatment, I opened the door and walked towards the big front door. The car moved away soundlessly with the boys still maintaining radio silence. I rang. The ser-vant who answered the door moved on oiled ball-bearings. We walked through a succession of screens and frames to an open space that appeared to be the reception area. I could tell that because there didn't ap-pear to be anything else going on there, and it was here that I first saw Jonah Abraham coming towards me, with his pal Vince, a respectable three steps behind his master. "Ah, Mr Cooperman! I'm so glad you changed your mind." He was wearing a green turtleneck sweater, which surprised me. I guess I was expecting a smok-ing jacket with an ascot tie. Vince was wearing both a tie and a dark suit. Informality is for those who can afford it. "I don't think you've met Vince, here. Vince Davey. Vince is something of a right-hand man around here."

Abraham kept on talking. It was the sort of banter that fills up the empty spaces: "I was in the market for company tonight. My daughter has abandoned me for the dubious charms of the younger generation." Abraham held out his hand and I took it. His clasp was firm but not extravagant. He didn't need to prove anything, least of all to me. The sweater looked new up close, but his eyes, in spite of the smile they offered, looked old and tired. He smelled of talcum like he'd come from a late-night swim or rub-down. "Come," he said, taking my arm, "we'll talk."

The servant who'd let me in had vanished. Vince began backing away from us, and disappeared when Abraham asked him to look after the boys from the car. To be honest, I didn't see where he went. The geography of the house eluded me; I couldn't find any doors or windows. It was all screens and pictures in large tidy frames with a lot of white matte showing. There were chairs too, but not the kind you can slip your jacket around the back of. It was a private house, but it had the chill of a dentist's office or maybe, to give it credit, a retailer in high-quality business furniture.

We walked through halls and places that were almost rooms, except that one bled into the next in a confusing way. The house might have gone up in the thirties, but it was doing that modern thing with more gusto than the new police headquarters or Secord University, and they were hardly five years old. Abraham was leading me, with some purpose, through the screens. Here and there I saw a familiar velvet rope pushed out of the way on its two brass stands. Suddenly, Jonah stopped. "But you must forgive me," he said, giving me his most charming smile, "I've forgotten my manners. May I get you something to drink, Mr Cooperman?"

I thought we'd come to talk, but maybe Abraham was given to walking around his target. "Thanks, but no thanks," I said. "I'm not much of a drinker."

"Ah, but you must have one of my Bloody Marys. My father got the recipe from Hemingway in 1947 in Cuba." We resumed walking, but in another direction. When he stopped he was standing before a professional-looking bar. "You need to make a whole pitcher of these," he said, pulling out a long cylinder of ice, and letting it slide back into the pitcher again. "Ernest taught Dad to use tennis-ball tubes to get the right amount of ice. If you use cubes, the drink gets diluted with the melt-waters. A big chunk of ice like this is what you need..." He went on and on about how Hem added the Tabasco and the Russian vodka. I didn't pay attention. I was wondering why he was buttering me up. He knew I had accepted his offer to continue the investigation when I agreed to come up here, so why was I getting this spiel about how the great Hemingway made his Bloody Marys?

When he finished talking, he handed me a frosted glass and took another himself. I tried it. I recognized the Tabasco and a trace of lime juice. People say you can't taste vodka; was there ever a sillier statement made about strong drink? It was rough on the way down, but it was sneakier than rye or Scotch. Abraham leaned in for my opinion. I held the glass at the end of my arm, like I could taste it two feet away. I nodded with enthusiam, and Abraham grew quite rosy with appreciation.

We sat, and finished our drinks while Jonah kept on talking about the mixing of drinks. He let me in on his version of the perfect dry martini. I don't know whether it came from Hemingway, his father or from his own artistic imagination. He kept the olives in the freezer and used just enough vermouth to cover the bottom

of the glass. He used the same tennis-ball tubes full
of ice to chill the mixture. It sounded like Hemingway
to me, but he didn't admit it. Maybe he wasn't a complete snob.

When he had finished his drink and saw that I was
not going to get any further into mine, he pinched the
creases in his trousers and got up. "I'm glad you decided to come and work for me," he said as he moved his
right hand in the direction he wanted us to walk. He
managed to balance the business of being my host and
employer very deftly; I could feel the tug of ownership
and the salve of hospitality rolled up together in his
gestures. We walked by a huge Japanese screen about
half the size of Albania, without a word. "You may find
it awkward working for one of your suspects."

"You may be a police suspect, Mr Abraham. Remember I'm not looking for the person who killed Pambos
Kiriakis. That's a Niagara Regional matter. I'm looking
for some missing pictures, that's all. But now I'm working for you. I guess if you have some of them, I'm still
going to try to find out about it. I'm not a specialist in
this art stuff. I tell you that straight out. Still, maybe
finding pictures isn't a lot different from finding other
lost or strayed property."

"Through here," Abraham said. He held open the left-
hand side of a large double door that didn't appear to
be part of the original design. "I feel like showing off
my collection." We entered a large gallery full of pictures and glassed-in cabinets. "Here we are. What do
you think?"

It was impressive. The walls were lined with paintings, with a few slim sculptures thrown in to break up
the monotony. I recognized many of the pictures; I'd
seen them reproduced in books and magazines, I guess.
I looked deeply and tried to give back to Abraham's
proprietary grin, the response required. "Nice," I said,

"nice. Very nice. It must have set you back." He walked towards one of the pictures.

"This Thomson is the only known portrait painted in his maturity. The National Gallery still badgers me about it."

"Nothing like practice, eh?"

"This Lamb, now. What do you think? I'd part with the Pissarro next to it or the Miro over there by the Klee before I'd give this up. Look at the underpainting! What a marvel!" I tried to look at the underpainting, at the same time wondering what weather conditions would ever make underpainting necessary. I wondered if paintings ever leaked after a Canadian winter. I couldn't see it, but I was still learning.

"Did you get it from Tallon?" I asked, trying to keep a foot in the conversation.

"I got most of my Canadian pictures from Arthur at one time. My father is responsible for most of the European things like this Giacometti figure. That's a Laurens over there. He missed on Lipchitz, Maillol and Brancusi," he added with a flattering smile. It worked too; I was quite proud of myself for being taken for somebody who can recognize the holes a few missing Lipchitz and Brancusis can make in your sculpture collection. "Father was one of Kahnweiler's only Canadian customers." I nodded and tried to remember where I'd heard that name tossed around before.

"With all this European stuff, Mr Abraham, why all the panic about the Canadian things like the pictures on Pambos Kiriakis's list? The Canadians must represent only a tiny part of the value of, say, a collection like this one."

"A good question, Mr Cooperman." He rubbed his hands together like he was going to enjoy answering it. While he talked, we continued to walk around looking at the pictures. "The European pictures were bought

by my father years ago. He bought them in France mostly as I've said from dealers like Kahnweiler. Others he
bought here from people who deal in European canvases and sculptures. They represent the largest part
of this collection, which my father left me in a sort of
Gertrude Stein-Alice B. Toklas arrangement. I mean I
have a life interest in it. I couldn't begin to estimate the
value of this part of the collection should it ever come
to light at a public auction. The smaller part of the collection is something I've built up myself. These are the
Canadian things like those Cullens over there and these
Colvilles and Pratts. In monetary terms, you can't compare them with the European part of the collection,
although I should think I could get six figures for every major Canadian work in this room.

"The reason for the panic about Mr Kiriakis's list is
that it represents free gold. Tallon, as I'm sure you know
by now, was notoriously bad about keeping track of the
paintings he dealt with. Some, no doubt, were left with
him on consignment, but he had a regular dealer relationship with most of the painters. He was always buying things from them in order to keep them in paint
and tobacco. I've heard stories that he bought many
canvases at prices that would now be considered
ridiculously low. But in those days there was no market for these works. You see, many of these painters
had no reputation when Tallon took them on. When
their reputations grew, they went on to other dealers
in many cases. Tallon's operation was always under-
financed. The collection he built up was built with love
on a shoestring. The irregularities that you are investigating involve trifling amounts of money when compared to the total value of Tallon's collection as a whole.
You will be cleaning up loose ends, enabling those
settling the estate to get on with the job."

"Then why was Pambos Kiriakis killed?"

"Mr Cooperman, I'm sorry to puncture your balloon. I am only guessing, of course, but I think when the police uncover Mr Kiriakis's murderer, it will be, like most murders, a rather sordid domestic incident: perhaps a vindictive room clerk or waiter that he fired who carried a grudge. The money involved in the pictures represented on Kiriakis's list would never be worth a human life."

"Maybe you put a higher price on it than other people?"

"Yes," he said with a sigh, "you are right. To some a life has no value at all."

"Your Canadian pictures came from Tallon?"

"I got most of them from him at one time. I do have connections in Toronto and Montreal, but he was the only local dealer I'd give the time of day to. Years ago, Arthur took me under his long, lean wing and taught me how to look at pictures. That was one of the things my mother and father took for granted. It probably accounted for the turmoil it took six psychiatrists years to sort out. Tallon taught me what my parents thought I'd learned with breathing and walking. Tallon showed me what to look for, and later, what to buy. He had a remarkable eye. Uncanny."

"So, you believe in the list?"

"Oh, yes; I believe in it," he said, his eyes developing a network of smile lines as he looked at me. "And I have a better reason for putting you to work on it than poor Mr Kiriakis had. He was just trying to put the cat among the pigeons. I need to find this list, because without it there is a shadow cast on the whole Canadian part of my collection. Without the list..." Here he broke off. He was looking over my shoulder. I turned to see a young woman standing at the far end of the gallery. I hadn't heard a sound. She was wearing jeans and a denim jacket over a white shirt. She crossed the room with a glide that didn't seem like walking at all. Jonah held out his arm and reeled her into an affectionate embrace.

"I came back," she said simply. "I got sick of it, so I came back." She turned to me, and looked up at me with salamandrine eyes.That moved her father to make the necessary introductions. This was Anna, Jonah Abraham's youngest. I felt my throat going dry as I made with a minimum of small talk. If her father had continued about his grafting of rhododendrons, I wouldn't have noticed. I didn't know where I was and I didn't care. Suddenly all of my interests had been absorbed by the five-foot-seven figure standing beside her millionaire father.

Chapter Eleven

When I came to my senses again, Anna had gone and Jonah was maundering on about paintings again. He was worried about the appearances of things. If some of Tallon's paintings were unaccounted for, and Abraham had the largest private collection of Canadian art in this part of the country, then naturally, he felt, suspicion would attach itself to him no matter how many bills of sale he waved in people's faces.

"Without that list of our dead friend, I'll never enjoy title to all this in a clear and uninterrupted way." He waved his arms at particular paintings, looking at them as he spoke, a special look for each of his treasures, like they were his children, each with its special talents and associations.

"But, you'd have papers..."

"I'm not worried about legal ownership. I do have a few battered receipts from Arthur for most of this, but people will talk, and I hate talk. A man in my position. I have to be twice as honest as the next fellow because my money was made in the family liquor business. In the twenties my father and uncles were bootleggers running booze over the border. Today, nobody says that to my face. Nobody." From the expression on his face I wouldn't want to challenge him. Jonah Abraham was his own man. He knew his worth and the extent of his power. I felt like I should make some gesture to show that I had no intention of rubbing his nose in his past. And to me, growing up on the edge of the Niagara River practically, the rum-running days were part of our colourful history, like the battle of Queenston Heights in the War of 1812. I knew vaguely of elderly people around town who were known to have played a part trafficking in Canadian liquor moving across the river to New York State. A high-school friend's father had run a boat above the falls on the Niagara River, hoping that the US Coast Guard wouldn't come as close to the upper rapids as he did. Savas had a friend near Queenston, an old rum-runner who now ran a prohibition-style after-hours roadhouse and restaurant. Here they served drinks openly, not even in teapots. To me, the whole era was colourful and full of the excitement of death-defying feats of bravery. Of course, there was a lot about it I didn't know. Al Capone in Chicago and the Purple Gang in Detroit seemed to belong to another legend entirely. Abraham continued talking and I tuned in:

"But," he said, "I'm a realist. I don't lie to myself. It doesn't matter that I've never had a parking ticket in my entire life. It doesn't matter that I have next to nothing to do with the business end any more. I still have to be twice as public-spirited as the next man." He smiled and went on. "You know that pool for kids in Emerson Coalsworth Park? That was me. You think I wanted that plaque stuck on it with my name two inches high? Look around you and tell me if that's the sort of man I am." He seemed to be speaking rhetorically, so I kept my eyes on his. "But people have to be reminded. You can't give them a minute to forget." I nodded slowly and Abraham's eyes relaxed their grip on mine. He took my arm again and led me through to the room we'd started in half an hour ago.

"Will you have another drink, Mr Cooperman?" he asked, reaching down for his lethal concoction of

Bloody Marys. He poured one for himself while waiting for me to make up my mind.

"Sure. You make a good drink, Mr Abraham." He poured me a refill, but in a fresh glass. I guess he wasn't doing the washing up. Our exchange of "misters" had formalized things again. He was in the act of hiring me and I'd just been put through an interview. I wasn't sure how I'd come out. He could have noticed that my attention drifted away from time to time, but maybe he was one of those ear-breathers who talk a lot but don't pay too much attention to whether much listening is going on. I didn't know. I still felt the sting in my eyes from his intense brown eyes. I sipped the drink, feeling the chill against my cheek of the glass in my hand.

"Your health, sir."

"Thanks. Happy days." A herd of angels flew by while we worked on our private thoughts. Finally, I heard myself speaking my doubts out loud. "Mr Abraham, why me?"

"I beg your pardon?" He set down his glass on a glass-topped table.

"Why me? You can afford the best private investigators in this country and in our neighbouring republic. Why do you want me looking into this? Because of our chance meeting earlier?"

"You know that's not true," he said. "I told the police exactly what happened. I might like you to protect me, but not from anything that happened tonight at the Stephenson House."

"How do I know what you told them?" I said.

"You don't know any more than I know what you said. There's no advantage to either of us, either way. In fact, it was you in the curtains, remember. You need me more than I need you if it comes to that. What if I said you were covered in blood, or that you had a desperate look in your eyes. No, Mr Cooperman, I'm not trying to buy from you anything more than Kiriakis was. I want the same information."

"A Toronto outfit could have six men on this by morning."

"I know something of your reputation, you know. I do have connections in Grantham and I have done my homework." I shrugged. What could I say. And he'd got me for the same money I was getting working for Pambos. Only Jonah Abraham hadn't helped me unpack all my earthly possessions and set my new home in order. I gave Pambos a bargain. Abraham was Mister Big Bucks. I kept my mouth shut. I'd wanted to leave Pambos out of it. I felt bad about him getting killed. Giving Abraham a cut rate made me feel better about that, I guess.

"You know, Mr Cooperman, I could have dozens of Lambs and Milnes and Roberts in my cellar and no one would be the wiser."

"So, you hire me to take the heat off. That makes sense."

"What heat?" His voice broke a little around the edges. I was hoping he was going to do a retake, but he went on instead. "Paddy Miles? Tallon's brother? Believe me, there is no heat."

"You're forgetting tonight."

"Yes." He rolled the glass between his palms and thought about that new element in the equation. He went on after a moment. "Whatever idiot it was who killed Kiriakis has definitely raised the temperature. But, I think I'm out of scorching distance. His death was very likely unconnected with this picture list. That only happens in books and moving pictures. But it means that the police will be paying attention to you and your movements from now on. I caution you to be careful."

"Did Kiriakis approach you about the list directly?"

"He telephoned. Said he was making inquiries. Very much in the manner you telephoned me."

"Kiriakis said that you were in the hotel the night the list went missing. Did you ever see it?"

"No. But I believe Kiriakis. He had the little man's pathetic desire to be liked. He was trying to be useful. If he had been able to unearth any, all, or some of the missing paintings, George, Arthur Tallon's brother, would have given him the pick of the recovered canvases. Arthur specialized in Lambs. That's what Kiriakis was out for. A free Lamb for his tiny collection. What a pity."

"The Lambs aren't wagging their tails behind them."

"No, indeed. At least not as far as we know."

"Are you suggesting that the lost Lambs have returned to the fold and we have been allowed to think they're still missing?"

"It's a possibility, isn't it? As long as everybody's under suspicion, we might as well make sure we mean *everybody.*"

"Paddy Miles, George Tallon and all the heirs. Did you know that Peter MacCulloch was a cousin? He might have reason to think he'll get something from the estate. He certainly has pictures belonging to Tallon's estate that he won't return unless forced to. The same may be said of Alex Favell."

"Alex Favell is one of those people I was born never to understand. He has a way of bringing out the primitive instincts. I don't trust him and I dislike him. I don't know which came first."

"Speaking of the estate, as we were, how well do you know George Tallon?"

"George is in charge of the Niagara region for Windermere's largest competitor, Consolidated Galvin. We know one another. I suppose our rivalry has led to a friendship of a kind. Why do you ask?"

"Could you get him to give me permission to look through his brother's medical records at the General? You need permission of the next of kin."

"May I ask why?" Jonah was looking at me with a peculiar expression on his face. Maybe he was thinking that he should have brought in a Toronto firm after all. And I wasn't even sure why I was asking. I only knew that the medical alert bracelet I took from the spilled coffee on Pambos's desk was a problem. I didn't know what kind of problem, but it existed and it wouldn't let me sleep at night until I knew more about Tallon's illness and death.

"I don't think I can answer you, but I think it might be important. Can you get it?"

"I think so. I'll let you know."

Jonah Abraham's way of winding up a conversation, I discovered, was to walk his guest around to the hall and face him towards the front door. It was subtly handled. There was no hint that the conversation was ending, not a silence that passed between us or a strained expression. But suddenly, he was opening the door for me and instructing me to keep in touch with him directly. He'd left instructions for me to be put through to him night and day. But I was cautioned by his tone that it had better be important when I called. I said goodnight and stood sniffing in the paper mill on the night air. In less than three or four seconds, Vince's pals were back with the car. Vince got out of the front seat and handed me an envelope. "Mr Abraham wants you to have this," he said. I looked long enough to see my name written correctly in ink on the front, before putting it into my inside breast pocket.

I enjoyed the silent running of the big car's motor all the way down the escarpment and through town. When it stopped in front of my place, the door was opened for me; I sat still until it was. I was just testing.

Tacos Heaven had closed its doors for the night. The street was quiet. I couldn't even hear the big car sliding off into the night as I rattled my keys to open the outside door.

Chapter Twelve

"Mr Cooperman? Hello?" It wasn't a dream, although it was a voice from my dream. I steadied the instrument under my chin and propped it with my pillow. I had been wind-surfing through the Amazon, I think it was, with Anna Abraham watching from the shore. Her father, mounted on an unlikely piranha, came in hot pursuit. And now he'd caught up to me by telephone.

"Yes? Cooperman here. Mr Abraham?"

"Good-morning," he said in a voice that smelled of aftershave and a good breakfast. "I hope you were able to catch up on the sleep our discussion deprived you of. It's nearly ten o'clock." I checked my watch and he was right. The ruby digits told the truth: nine-fifty-seven.

"I did all right. What's the trouble?" I thought there had to be trouble. Part of it was my dream, the rest was simple deduction: what would he be telephoning me for, if it wasn't because something had fallen apart since our midnight conversation.

"My daughter Anna, the one you met, she went out again last night and didn't come home. Is she with you by any chance?"

"Look, Mr Abraham, that's very flattering, but it's highly unlikely that your daughter would end up in my place above Tacos Heaven. I hope you have other guesses." I pulled my legs out from under the blankets and placed the sole of each foot into the deep pile of my new carpet. I can't describe the luxury of that sensation after all those years of cold City House linoleum.

I felt tension on the other end of the line and the frustration it produced began to point at me. "I consider that it goes without saying, Mr Cooperman, that you'll always be straight with me?"

"As a flagpole, Mr Abraham. But as to the whereabouts of your girl, I haven't a fingerprint to go by. I'm looking for a list, anyway. Remember? Does she often take off like that without leaving word?"

"I had the idea you were on her mind when I went up to bed. She asked me as many questions as you did. Only hers were about you."

"Sorry I can't help. I'll keep an eye peeled."

"Keep both of them peeled and call me if you see anything."

"Yahzir, I'll do that." Abraham hung up, I did the same.

I got up and brewed some instant coffee. I began a list of things to buy for future breakfasts, things like butter and jam and orange juice. Under orange juice I wrote "Anna." I don't know why I did that. She wasn't something I was shopping for. But I guess she was on my mind. I thought about her in the shower. What did she want to know about me for? Is she a little simple? Must be if her old man's worried where she is. She didn't end up here, so she was laying a false trail. So, she's not so dumb after all. But why pick on me, I wondered, while I did my armpits for a second time.

Once out of the shower and into my clothes, I put the list with jam and Anna on it into my pocket. I wondered as I let myself out of the apartment whether I was stuck with showers for the rest of my life because of my years at the City House. Here I was on the second morning in the new apartment abandoning the bath and taking the quick, easy way out. I sometimes thought that my character should be sent out, like my father's old fedora, and reblocked.

Once out in the street I felt a little bewildered. I'd had my morning coffee, so why was I heading towards the United? Breakfast done, I should be on my way to work. Only it didn't feel right. I did it anyway. The right way to start the day was with a coffee at the United; especially when all around me were rumours that the place had been sold and was going to be pulled down. I had to let my vote of protest be counted. I'd have a second cup of coffee at the United for as long as it was possible.

Last night's *Beacon*, of course, had nothing of the murder in it, but I went through a discarded copy on the counter for the news I'd missed waiting to be questioned by Chris Savas. In the box marked *City and Vicinity* I saw that Humphrey Slaughter was having a show of contemporary paintings beginning on Friday. This was still Wednesday. Friday was the first of April, which still seemed more than a month away.

"Hello, Benny? How's everything?" It was Pambos Kiriakis's friend Martin Lyster, the book-tracer. He was well over six feet tall but so thin that he couldn't have weighed more than one hundred and fifty pounds.

"Morning, Martin." Seeing a ghost from that last evening with Pambos made me nervous. Idiotically I asked him: "Found any good books lately?"

"Never mind the books, did you hear about Pambos? What's this bloody planet coming to?" Martin adjusted his long legs around the pedestal of the stool he was sitting on as he leaned in my direction. His long, lined face was dark with worry. "They'll be murdering us all in our beds next!"

"When did you hear about it?" I asked, moving the paper to give him elbow room.

"I was having a jar with Wally Skeat around closing time last night and he told me. Shot through the heart.

Bang! Bang! and good luck to you! Terrible!"

"Wally gets some things right too," I muttered to myself.

"And Pambos Kiriakis of all people! What did the likes of him ever do to anybody?"

"Might have been a fired dishwasher or an old girl-friend. I don't know much about his private life."

"I still can't believe it. The night I saw you, Bill and I were with him until nearly three in the morning. He was an old dear friend."

"Tell me about his wife? I only met her a few times."

"Linda? She's not been near him for two years at least. You know they were separated? She's living in Mon-treal. She was, I mean, last time I heard. But, Benny, you don't think she would have done it? Pambos was generous with her, to a fault, I hear. He was sentimen-tal about the girls."

"That's something for the police to run down. Was there anyone local on the scene?"

"Now, Benny, I don't like speaking ill of the dead," Martin said. "I'm depending on your discretion, Ben-ny." I nodded and made the required noises. "There's a German girl he was seeing. He called her *Schätzchen*, which I gather is nothing very flattering. Her name's Mathilde Lent. She lives in a room or apartment some-where on lower Queen Street. Place is run by Dutch people." I made a mental note then tore it up. I didn't want to get mixed up in the police side of this investi-gation. I'd crowded Chris Savas before, and I didn't like the sensation.

"Where are you staying, Martin? Pambos never told me and I see you're not in the book."

"Well, now, Benny, I'm always on the move. Best thing is for me to get in touch with you. Never know where I'm going to be. Right now I'd like to be down in Flori-da to watch spring training."

"I didn't know you were a baseball fan."

"I nearly swapped a mint copy of the *Criterion*, October 1921, for a single for one World Series game. If it was a pair, I would have done it. Well, almost. I take books seriously too."

"What's the *Criterion*, October 1921?" I asked.

"*The Waste Land*. You know, T.S. Eliot and all that. That's where it first saw the light of day. Now, Benny, are you into this Napoleon business?"

"I wasn't there, I don't know anything about it. Why?"

"I've got a copy in fair condition of Dr O'Meara's journal of his time in St Helena. Pambos was going to buy it. I'll try Bill Palmer at the *Beacon*; he's interested, but a poor risk."

"You cleared up the angry man in Boulder, Colorado?"

"Where'd you hear about that, now?" He looked down into the depths of the green marble counter-top. "That night, I guess. Well, Benny, you see that fellow's a terribly wealthy man, and he's bloody impatient with people like you and me. He'll have called everyone I know trying to reach me. Oh, I talked to him. Settled him right down. I told Pambos it was all fixed. Storm in a teacup."

"So you can't be contacted directly, Martin?"

"Well, I'm staying not far from here, but the lady in question has a reputation I wouldn't like to tarnish. But, I'll drop by here again, and catch you at your eleven o'clock break like today."

I didn't tell him it was breakfast, or the second half of it. A man should have minor secrets to practise on. Days of large deceits may not be far away. I paid the check, bought a pack of cigarettes and helped myself to the penny matches with United Cigar Store written on the front. For all I knew, this branch might be closed down the next time I need matches. I thought of all the places I knew whose only monuments were the books of paper matches in my winter coat or bottom drawer or overnight bag.

The office looked like neutral ground. It always looked that way after I'd spent a night waltzing with Niagara Regional. My name on the door and window gave me assurance that I really existed. I took out Abraham's envelope and opened it; the cheque gave me further assurances of existence. Quickly I signed the back and wrote the account number underneath. I tried to plan out the rest of my day so that I'd pass my bank before 3:00 P.M.

After moving a few library books, some apricot pits and my old electric fan, I got out the city directory. I flipped through it and stopped at Queen Street. I found the block I wanted, then carefully checked the east and west sides of the street. Near the south-west corner of Duke and Queen, I discovered:

> Dirk and Gertrude Bouts
> 35 Queen St., freeholder
> Mathilde Lent, tenant

Good, I thought, then remembered that I'd declared Pambos's murder out of bounds for this private investigator. For years I'd been telling clients that the cops are a hard act to follow when it comes to investigating serious crimes. So, what was I doing even thinking in this direction? It wouldn't hurt to pass by the house and have a look, I thought. I have to get to the bank don't I? It wouldn't hurt to look. I tried to imagine what kind of girl Pambos would call *Schätzchen*. There was so much about the little guy I wanted to know and now it was too late to ask. I wasn't being fair. Until I met him on moving day, he was a casual acquaintance. Okay, a friend, but nothing close. Then he became a client. He told me all about the list of pictures. That's all. I'm no authority on his private life, his business, his taste in women, books or booze. We were never close. That's it; we were casual pals and then we were doing our first stroke of business together. Why should I even care who killed him? What's it got to do with me? Jonah Abraham's picking up the tab, so I can see Pambos right. I can finish the job he hired me for. But that's it. The cops can nail the killer. Let Savas go dig up Mathilde Lent. Let him see where she was last night. All I want to do is do what I'm being paid to do and get paid for what I'm doing.

I think there was room in my head for this argument to run a few more laps and I was inclined to let it rip just to see if any nuances occurred to me that I missed on the earlier circuits, but I was suddenly uncomfortably aware that I was sharing the space with somebody. I could tell without looking up. I didn't hear anything, but I knew I was right. When my head moved in the direction of the door, I could see. I wasn't alone. Anna Abraham was standing in my doorway. I hadn't even heard the door open.

"Is this where you do it?" she asked, walking in and peeking through my venetian blinds. She was still wearing the jeans of the night before, but had put on a man's pink shirt, the kind that buttons down at the collar. There was nothing mannish about the effect.

"Do what?"

"You know, detect things." She was winding the cord from the blinds around one of her fingers.

"It serves its purpose. It'll do. What brings you slumming?" The dust from the blinds began to get to her. Silvery motes glistened in the bands of light coming around her head. She walked over to the filing cabinet and tugged one of the drawers open. I may have fallen in love with her for a moment the night before, but just then she was giving me a pain. "What do you want, Anna?" She looked at me like I've never been looked at.

"You don't seem very busy."

"Interesting opinion. What do you want?" She continued giving my place the once over, as though I was out of town and she had all day to kill.

"I suppose you have cameras for taking pictures through keyholes?"

"Six or seven of them. Thirty-five millimetres down to eight. If you want smaller, it can be arranged. Anna, what the hell do you want?" I felt the anger that had been simmering in my stomach begin to boil over. "Just because I'm doing a job for your old man, it doesn't mean I have to entertain his kids during working hours!"

"What about after working hours?"

"We never sleep." Anna smiled at the quotation and I liked that. I suddenly didn't feel as chair-bound as I'd felt with her wandering around the office, looking at my certificates and licences hanging on the wall. "Tell me, Anna, does your old man keep office hours?"

"He has an office at the Windermere Building downtown, if that's what you mean."

"But does he spend any time there? Does he keep office hours?"

"Daddy!" She enjoyed the joke by herself. Then she started wandering the space again. "His secretary keeps office hours for him. If something important comes up, she can get him wherever he happens to be. Daddy's always hated business."

"But he enjoys the fruits of it well enough."

"Don't be cynical. It's easy to be cynical. What kind of hours do *you* keep?" The boiling started again. Again I was trapped in my chair, barricaded behind my desk. "Anna," I said, "get lost."

She didn't move. She looked like I'd slapped her, but she held her ground. I wrote Mathilde Lent's name and address on a piece of paper to look busy. Anna came closer and leaned over the yellow block of foolscap, with her arms supporting her as she gripped the edge of the desk. "You're not very friendly, Mr Cooperman." I debated about looking up and decided against it. I tore the top sheet off the pad and put it in my pocket. "Just tell me what the hell you want, Anna." She picked up the plastic top of an inkwell in the penstand I'd inherited from my father and stared into its dry bottom. She replaced the lid and began examining a jam jar full of pencils. "Stop rearranging my desk!"

"Want me to leave you alone with those three bald ladies?" She'd seen my trio of graces under their unbleached cotton covers — left-overs from the days when my father ran his one-store retail empire from this room.

"So, okay, I'm kinky for group sex. Go home and tell your father. You wouldn't understand, Anna, I'm trying to earn a living. Now scram!"

"How old are you?"

I got up, took her by her left wrist and spun her around so that she faced the door.

"Hey!" I didn't hurt her, but without changing my grip, I was able to propel her through the open door, I closed it and slipped the spring lock with Anna Abraham on the other side. My collar was burning. I had to loosen my tie. The nerve of that kid...! I thought. I went back to my chair, far more angry than I should have been. I could hear her clomping down the stairs slowly. If it's possible to clomp in a sullen manner, she was doing it. What the hell had she wanted?

I waited ten minutes, during which I cleaned up the place for the next visitor, and walked down my twenty-eight steps to St Andrew Street. I couldn't see any sign of her. I closed the door behind me.

St Andrew Street on a spring morning was on the move: a truck was unloading cartons of books and greeting cards across the street at Graham's; shoppers were coming out of Bevitt's Fine China with packages; two farmers, father and son maybe, stood peakcap to peakcap in worn, heavy cloth jackets, arguing on the curb. The familiar panhandlers were plying their trade, unsuccessfully, when I passed them on my way to the Upper Canadian Bank at the top of Queen Street. I waited in line behind the ropes, which divided the customers who were unable to cope with the machines from the others, until a cashier accepted Jonah Abraham's cheque. While I was waiting, I read the latest notice that began, "In order to serve you better..." My heart fell whenever I saw one of those. It meant that some valued service had been discontinued. I lived in dread of the day when they would no longer allow me to deduct cash from a cheque that was going into one of my accounts. They'd tried to wean me a few years ago from this practice on the grounds that it led to messy bookkeeping. I suggested that the slide into fiscal confusion had begun when they did away with the stubs in my chequebook. It was a spirited counter-attack, enough to get me a reprieve, if not a pardon. I didn't look forward to another argument with Mr Alistair Openshaw, the manager of this branch. I'd had discussions with him before and had formed some biased and badly based generalizations about bank managers from the encounter.

Back out on the street, I wondered if it would hurt to see whether Chris Savas's investigation had extended to the other end of Queen Steet. It was a short walk past the *Beacon* on the left and the bookstore on the right down to the address I'd memorized. Thirty-five Queen Street was a square three-storey brick building that looked like it had once been a private house. There were two tall windows on either side of a curved entrance with pilasters, and six similar windows on the floor above. The top floor was a handsome mansard roof with dormers on at least three sides and a diseased-looking rail running around the flat centre of the roof. There were signs of a lopped porch on one side, and the hooks which used to restrain shutters still protruded from the smoky red brick.

"Yes?" It was a woman's head that came through the front door when I rang the bottom bell. I'd got no reaction to the bell above that. The woman was short and blonde with a smile but a certain distrust of strangers written on her face. From inside, I could hear the sounds of morning television and of an infant crying.

"Mrs Bouts?" She nodded, continuing to wipe her hands on the dishtowel she'd brought to the door for protection. "My name is Cooperman, and I'm trying to reach your tenant, Mathilde Lent."

"Oh, Mattie's not here. She's out."

"Do you know when she's coming back? It's important."

"I see, well, you could give me your name and I'll have her telephone you when she gets back." Gertrude Bouts had a trace of an accent that was probably Dutch. "Will you come in? I have to see to the baby." I followed her down the hall and into a large front room full of comfortable contemporary furniture with a large TV set supplying the focus of all the arrangements. Only the baby's playpen was set on a different axis. Mrs Bouts picked up the child, who looked to be under a year old, and began to address him as Willum. I sat down into the deep comfort of a piece of sectional armchair-sofa, and waited. At last she put Willum back into the playpen and smiled again in my direction.

"Sorry about that," she said. She had the idiom

exactly, but there was an accent under it which escaped her ear. "My husband's in Hamilton this morning. He works as a dot-etcher for a photo-engraver. You said it was important that you see Mattie?"

"Yes," I said. "A friend of hers has been killed."

"Oh, no!" she said, holding tightly to the arm of her chair. "How awful!" I told her what had happened, the whole schmeer. She didn't seem to recognize Pambos's name when I got that far.

"When do you expect her back, Mrs Bouts?" Here she looked awkward and failed to meet my eyes.

"To tell you the truth, Mr Cooperman, Mattie's not here. I mean, she's gone away. She left nearly a week ago."

"Do you know where she went or where she's staying?"

Gertrude Bouts shook her head. She didn't know anything. I began to feel a tightening at the bottom of my stomach. I took a breath before asking any more questions.

"Are you from the police, Mr Cooperman?" She tilted her head like she was asking if I liked the temperature of the room. I explained that too.

"As a friend of the dead man, they will try to get in touch with her before too long. They'll want to know where she went."

"I see," she said. "I see." She stared at the carpet.

"What can you tell me about Mattie, Mrs. Bouts? I never met her."

"Well, she was a very pretty, fun-loving thing, you know." She put her hand to her mouth suddenly. "Why did I say *was*? Oh my God, you don't think...?" There wasn't a particle of evidence to suggest that any harm had come to Mattie Lent, but I found myself sharing the same fear that Gertie Bouts had voiced. We were both fearing the worst for that pretty, fun-loving thing.

Chapter Thirteen

"Oh, no, Mattie is Austrian, not German. She comes from Schruns, the skiing centre up in the Montafon Valley in the Vorarlberg. Her father had an inn on the Kirchplatz, or as you would say 'Church Street.' " Gertie handed me a black-and-white photograph of a pert blonde, smiling through snow-glare at the camera. In the snapshot, Mattie was standing in an up-to-date ski outfit in front of an inn. Snow-laden firs flanked the end of the inn, and late-model cars that owed nothing to Detroit were jammed together along the street.

"So this is Mattie." I waved the photograph, turning my statement into a question. Gertie nodded. "When was she back there last?"

"That was taken in the early winter of 1986. She went back to see her parents. Her mother's been sick. They're both over seventy."

"Looks like a nice place."

"Oh, yes, beautiful. It has green and white plastered houses and the church has a green dome like an onion."

"What's she like?"

"Oh, like in the picture. She likes to go skiing and dancing. She likes a good time."

"Does she have a job?"

"That I wouldn't know. She pays the rent on time. She wears nice clothes."

"Did you ever hear her talking about Mr Kiriakis from the Stephenson House?"

"No, she didn't go for little coffee-klatch confessions. She didn't pull her hair down with me, although she lived with us for nearly five years."

"I see. And you've no idea where she went?"

"Oh, no. She just left. She didn't take more than an overnight bag."

"May I see her room?" Gertie didn't answer right away. She was trying to remember when she'd changed the bed last, maybe. Her lips were very pale when at last she nodded.

"If you like," she said.

She got up a moment after I did and led the way up a staircase that was a little grand for a rooming house. She paused outside a door on the second floor and knocked, for form's sake, then we went in. It was an ordinary bedroom without anything that struck me as odd or unusual. It was clean, tidy, with clothes in the closet and more in the bureau. In a drawer of the bed-side table I found a few letters with Austrian stamps. The writing looked German to me and authentic enough to convince a non-German-speaking person. I examined some black-and-white photographs and postcards from Schruns. It looked like a nice place to visit. After slipping the letters back into their envelopes and tucking the collection back into the drawer, I turned back to Gertrude, who was trying to stay out of my way. "Are you at all worried about her disappearance, Mrs. Bouts?"

"'Disappearance'? Why, Mr—I'm sorry, I've forgotten your name..."

"Cooperman."

"Mr Cooperman, yes. Mr Cooperman, until you came I didn't think it was anything like that. She's a young girl, but I thought, you know, that she's a modern wom-an. 'Disappearance' is strong language for staying out all night. I mean, without knowing what you just told me about her friend, Mr Kiriakis. She still may come home all together, you know, in one piece. This isn't the first time she's been away without leaving word. Oh, no. At Christmas we didn't hear from her for nearly two weeks. But that was Christmas, and we were busy and the time passed more quickly. Now, this time, I don't know."

"Well, maybe 'disappearance' is a big word for what's happened. But coming just at the time of Pambos Kiriakis's death... It does pose a question. I think you would be wise to inform the police of what's happened."

"Yes. I will speak with Dirk about it."

"Has she had any visitors, any family coming to look for her?"

"I told you that they are in Austria, ah, but I was forgetting. Her sister Greta came last October. She stayed for three or four days and then went back to New York. She's a translator at the United Nations."

"Do you think that Mattie went to see her sister?"

"I don't think so," she said with the beginnings of a testy look coming to her face. "I don't think they get along. Greta is very old fashioned, very serious, very religious."

"I see. What about other friends?"

"I'm sorry. I already told you. And now, I must get back to Willum. I'm sorry that I can't be of more help. Dirk and I want to do the right thing, Mr Cooperman. Do you think that the police will come to see us?" We moved out of Mattie's room and down the staircase with the wine-coloured walls that told of grander times, when the living was easy and supported by an army of servants. In the front room again, before moving to the door, I tried another tack.

"Did Mattie have any interest in art? You know, paintings, oils, watercolours?"

"Oh yes, she talked about it. She went to Buffalo and Toronto to see the galleries there. Dirk said he'd show her the Hamilton gallery one day. But she wasn't a painter herself. She liked to see the pictures."

"I see. Thank you for your help, Mrs Bouts. I'm sorry to have troubled you." I made my way back through the hall to the tall front door. We shook hands formally and a moment later I was looking back over my shoulder at the house, trying to think whether I was imagining the feeling that Gertie Bouts wasn't telling me everything she might about this business. The house, tidy in its nineteenth-century reserve, wasn't helping either.

Further up Queen Street, I passed the familiar office of the *Beacon*. Through the window on the ground floor I could see customers placing ads or picking out words for obituaries and wedding announcements. News of last night's dirty deed at the Stephenson House had not yet reached the street. The *Beacon* was an evening paper; it rarely hit the pavement before three-thirty in the afternoon. Next to the *Beacon*, an old house, formerly used as a real-estate company's head office, had sprouted a "For Sale" sign. I knew it wouldn't be long before demolition crews would start pulling down the last of the surviving houses on this part of Queen Street. I could almost imagine the original owner of the property stepping out of a carriage and complaining to the contractor that there must be some mistake.

I walked past the window of the Upper Canadian Bank. As I expected, there were no customers standing in line behind the velvet ropes. Four tellers stood idly at their posts waiting for their eleven o'clock break. I felt a warm surge when I recalled that Jonah Abraham's cheque was, even as I walked along the main street of Grantham, turning me into a man of wealth and property, comparatively speaking. At least it wouldn't sink into my overdraft without leaving a trace. That thought led directly to a rut in my recent thinking. I was obsessed with the idea that I had given Abraham a good deal when I'd agreed to continue the investigation I started for Pambos. I wondered when was the last time Jonah Abraham had got a bargain.

A tune came to my lips, a spring to my stride and I almost felt my girth increasing through its association with affluence. A couple of people said hello to me as I came east along the south side of St Andrew Street. I almost felt like an established merchant on the street, a bit like my father nodding at his competitors as he passed them standing between the large display windows of their stores.

My sunny daydream died. Jonah Abraham's daughter was leaning against the street door leading to my office. She looked like she was trying to hold up a falling building.

"Hello, Mr Cooperman."

"Goodbye, Miss Abraham." She blocked my way to the door handle. "Excuse me," I said, and I tried to say it politely. I pushed past her.

"Why are you so mean to me?" she asked. "I've never met anyone as rude as you are."

"That comes of a sheltered life. You don't know how lucky you are." I got the door open and headed up my twenty-eight steps. She was right behind me. I could hear sharp heels on the linoleum. I didn't even try to close my door. She wandered in and shut it with a flat white palm.

"You didn't answer my question. Why are you so mean?" She moved away from the door and walked behind the client's chair. "I could tell Daddy," she said with a smile.

"Right now I'm on better terms with your old man

than you are, so don't threaten me with an empty gun."
I flipped through the mail that I'd scooped up as I came
in. There was nothing of interest, except for a bill from
an oil company with an enclosure offering me a device
for inflating my punctured tires, with nothing to pay
on it for six months.

"Don't call him that. 'My old man,' I mean. You don't
know anything about him."

"I know he's worried as hell about you." I picked up
the telephone and moved it across the desk. "You want
me to dial the number?" She crossed her arms and held
onto her elbows for a second, then slumped into the
client's chair. She looked at me like I was the third
school principal in a row to tell her she was a candidate for expulsion.

"I can't talk to him now. Not with you here. I'll call
him later, I promise." She gave me a blast of those
salamandrine eyes again. I wondered if a private investigator is *in loco parentis* to his client's offspring. I
hoped not.

"Okay, I believe you will. Now, what can I do for you?"

"I just wanted to talk. I know you're working for Daddy. He told me."

"So, you're checking up. Is that it?"

"He's always getting short-changed. He can't buy a
stamp for the going price. Everybody nicks him. You
don't know what having money's like." I thought about
that, but said nothing.

"Do you know why he hired me?"

"Naturally. He wants you to find some kind of list
of paintings or other. He said that he is suspected of
taking the list from a man who has just been killed.
Now I can tell you right now that he didn't do that.
He was home with me all night last night."

"That's a big help." She slowly lost the pout on her
face and began to look quite proud of herself. "I hope

you'll keep this information to yourself. I wouldn't share it with the cops if I were you."

"Why should I do anything you say, Mr Cooperman?"

"If you want to keep your old man out of jail, you won't complicate things by inventing phoney alibis that are about as watertight as a broken coffee filter. You were out last night and didn't get back until after I got to your place. Besides that, the cops know he was at the scene of the crime. He called them. So, please go take a creative writing course somewhere and use your inspiration on paper."

She didn't like me again. She'd almost become friendly, but I put things back about a hundred years. She slouched and fidgeted in her chair. I decided to try another tack, just to see what would happen. "What do you know about Mary MacCulloch?"

"Mary Mac...? She owns a picture Daddy wants. A Lamb, I think. She's very beautiful, and Daddy says she's very spoiled. He sometimes calls her 'Bo Peep,' because of all the Lambs she owns."

"You share your father's interest in painting, I gather?"

"I love pictures. Yes. But neither one of us...!

"Hey! I'm on your side, remember? You don't have to protest your innocence with me. I just thought you might be able to help me out, that's all. What is this Lamb that Mary MacCulloch has that your father covets?" I switched from "old man" to "father" to illustrate the fact that I too could be reasonable when others were prepared to be so.

"It's a major painting, but on a small scale. It's only about that big." She indicated a rectangular shape about three feet by two. "He said he would trade shares in Windermere Distilleries to own it. And you have to understand that Windermere Distilleries is bread and butter to the family."

"He has a soft spot for Lamb too, hasn't he. He's

another Bo Peep. Do you think he's any good?" I expected the look she gave me; the question was a vague probe. I don't know what I was after.

"Wallace Lamb's pictures will still be hanging in galleries long after a lot of abstract expressionist garbage has been cleared from the walls of our major galleries," she said with a face like Joan of Arc or maybe an English suffragette.

"Hey, that's a little hard on the abstract expressionists. In what way is he so good?" She took a deep breath and began exploring her opinion while she talked.

"Well, Lamb has a way of dividing up the proportions in a painting between the subject and the background that … that tells you it's a Lamb. You don't have to look for his signature, you just know a Lamb when you see one. That's just one thing."

"What do you know about him?"

"He came from some place north of Toronto. A place called Varney. Have you ever heard of it?" I shook my head and she nodded, agreeing that Varney wasn't a familiar landmark in her life either. She went on:

"I only know what Arthur Tallon told me about him. About his drinking and womanizing. That sort of thing. His life story would make a great book."

"He was an important painter for Tallon, wasn't he?"

"Well, yes. Tallon kept Lamb alive. Gave him enough to go on painting at a time when there was no market for his work. Tallon created the market by selling a batch of his paintings to a well-known diplomat for a song. The diplomat announced that he was supporting Canadian art, and Tallon said 'The price was right.'"

"You liked Arthur Tallon, didn't you?" I deduced this from the smile that accompanied Tallon's *bon mot*. It was her first big smile, and it was worth waiting for.

"He was 'Uncle Arthur' to me when I was little. I can still remember the thrill of running up the stairs to that chilly, white-walled gallery on King Street. He taught me to open my eyes and really look at things. Oh, I loved that man. I told him I wanted to marry him when I was seven or eight and he said he'd wait for me. He never did marry, you know."

"Oh? What was that all about?"

"He just wasn't sexy at all. He was really the 'uncle' type. That's as close as he wanted to get to people. To women, anyway. The bigger I got, the farther apart we got, as though he was afraid of me. But we were always good friends. He was like Lewis Carroll. You know, the man who wrote *Alice in Wonderland*." I was familiar with the book, but the private life of the author was his own business, something unconnected with missing lists and paintings.

"Carroll was 'funny' about little girls and couldn't abide little boys at all." I nodded, trying to put an end to the digression, since neither little girls nor boys seemed to be involved in the present investigation. I made a stab at restoring order.

"Did you finish telling me all you know about Mary MacCulloch?"

"You're still on her, are you?" She made a gesture that I knew would mature and become useful in middle age, if she lived that long. I kept my eyes on my hands folded neatly on my desk.

"I just asked a question. No need to snap off at me like a sick cat. Why does she make your back hair stand up?" She gave her mouth a tug that showed me that she didn't like to be questioned about anything. She enjoyed having the conversation on her own terms.

"What do you want me to say? She's pretty, right? Okay, she's even better looking than pretty. She has a way about her. She's rich enough to do what she wants and has a husband who is prepared to look the other way. Daddy says she's no better than she should be."

"What does he say about MacCulloch?"

"Isn't that hearsay?"

"It would be in a court of law, but this is still 200A St Andrew Street and not the new court house. I withdraw the question. I'll ask him myself."

"It's just that..."

"Forget it, Anna. It's not important."

"That's the first time you've used my name."

"It's considered good technique in cross-examination. It disarms the witness. Why are you so suspicious of me?"

"People are always gouging Daddy. Always taking advantage."

"Oh, fine! I was in bed when he called me to come over last night. He sent a car to make sure I wouldn't disappoint him. I'm sick of rich people and their tender sensibilities."

"There's an exchange between Scott Fitzgerald and Hemingway about rich people being different from other people."

"Yeah, they have more money."

"Oh, you know it then? Why do you pretend that you never read anything more complicated than the comics? I saw you talking last night. You let Daddy do a lot more explaining than he had to do. You know a lot more than you pretend to know."

"That's an occupational hazard. A lot of the time I pretend to know a lot I don't. It works out." I kept on going without taking another breath. I asked, "Did Mary MacCulloch have a grudge against Pambos Kiriakis, the man who was killed?"

"I don't know. I heard she did. But who knows about things like that? I may have a grudge against you, but I'm not going to kill you."

"I hope not." I felt my collar getting tight again. "Now don't forget to call your father."

"Are you trying to get rid of me?"

"Look, Anna, your old man isn't paying me to shoot the breeze with his daughter. I've got work to do. What I've got to do, you can't be any part of."

"I've heard that before somewhere."

"Well, drop me a line when you figure it out. Meantime, look, I really have to show some work for the money. Okay?"

"Well…"

"Look, if you're around the Beaumont Hotel around ten tonight, I'll buy you a drink in the bar. The place they call The Snug."

"You can tell me about the progress you're making," she said, getting up. I breathed a sigh of relief. She was actually going.

"Yeah, that's right. Around ten, in The Snug." A moment later she was gone and this time I didn't even have to twist her arm.

Chapter Fourteen

F or twenty minutes I enjoyed the silence, played around with the names on a list I'd been making, names that included everybody I'd heard about recently except for Hemingway, Scott Fitzgerald and Lewis Carroll. Then the phone brought me back to the world of the convenience store and the six o'clock news.

"Hello?"

"Hello, there. I just looked you up in the yellow pages and there you were. Just where a real detective should be. This is Mary MacCulloch."

"I knew that. I'm pretty good on voices. Your ears must have been burning, I was just talking to someone about you."

"Look, Mr Cooperman, I'd appreciate it if you wouldn't bandy my name around like it was an old pingpong ball. I should think a reputable detective would know better."

"Detective's the wrong word, Mrs MacCulloch. I'm an investigator, just like it says in the yellow pages. You get to be a detective by wearing brass buttons and a badge first. And speaking of buttons, you've lost one from your jacket."

"Oh, damn! I'm glad I'm not sitting in my slip, Mr. Cooperman. How did you know that? I'll never match it. Double damn!"

I hadn't imagined that she'd still be wearing the same jacket, but I didn't mind having a reputation for X-ray vision over the telephone. Her response sounded innocent enough. I would have liked to have warned her about where the button was found, but I was sure that Chris would recognize true innocence but might get confused by her response if I warned her. So, I dropped the button. "What can I do for you, Mrs MacCulloch?"

"I thought we'd got to first names. It doesn't matter. I wanted to know if you intend to drop the investigation now that Pambos is dead. Poor Pambos."

"Are you offering me honest work, Mrs Mac-Culloch?"

"Why no! No, I was just asking. My husband and I have no secrets from one another, Mr Cooperman. He told me about your visit. I could shoot you for letting me ramble on in your car and at the club the other day. You should have told me about that absurd list."

"If I stopped every flow of free information, I might not make the rent, Mrs MacCulloch. You can't say I led you on."

"Well, let's shut up about that for now. Why would anyone want to kill poor Pambos?"

"Are you going to miss him?"

"Mr Cooperman, I'm more discriminating than that. Pambos made me wish there was a table with a white tablecloth between us at all times. He had that head-waiter manner."

"When did you start collecting paintings?"

"Finished with Pambos already? You must be able to think of more to ask me about him than that. Oh, well, I'm my own favourite subject, so let's talk about me. I don't mind. But, you have to understand that Peter's the real collector. I dabble the way poor Pambos did. I watch Peter at auctions, but I don't bid. I've just learned about pictures from watching people. I watch the prices and the look on people's faces."

"Faces like that of Jonah Abraham?"

"The very face I was thinking of. I must never talk to you fresh from the shower. You are an amazing man, even if you aren't a drinker."

"You have a picture he admires, I think."

"'Admires'? He practically begged me to put a price on it. I rather like the idea of a millionaire wanting something that I won't let him have. It's almost medieval. Like something in an opera."

"Did Arthur Tallon help you in your art education? He seems to have been running classes around town. Were you in on any of them?"

"Arthur was very sweet, yes." Here she paused while I could hear her lighting a fresh cigarette. She coughed and then went on. "He always let me know when some particularly nice pieces were coming up for auction in town or across the lake in Toronto. That's how I got the Lamb Jonah wants."

"Too bad Lamb didn't live to see the fancy prices people are paying for his pictures." I heard a laugh at the other end and quickly reviewed what I'd said for hidden witticisms. I didn't find any. The laugh was repeated.

"Lamb? Dead? What are you talking about? He's as alive as I am!"

"I thought all painters were dead. Where is he keeping himself these days?"

"Oh, he's not social. He keeps to himself. He drinks and recites Shakespeare from the balcony. The neighbours call the police. Happens all the time. He doesn't go to openings."

"That's how I've missed him. Where does he live?"

"The last I heard he was living with a woman on Facer Street in the North End. Wentworth Apartments, I think. But, Benny, if I may call you Benny once more, be careful! Watch him! He'll rob you blind if he's sober, and never turn your back on him if he's drunk!"

"Charming!" I said.

Instead of taking the car in to have the snow tires removed, which was item number one on my own personal list, I drove the Olds out Facer Street to the Wentworth Apartments. It gave me the opportunity to see my favourite street sign announcing "Elberta Street." For some reason a misprint in cast iron was funnier than one on paper. But, maybe the joke was on me. What do I know about given names? I know some people make a study of them, noticing which names are in and which are out of fashion. Information like that I have to get from women like Martha Tracy. Women make a study of names. There's an endless fascination there somewhere, but it escapes me.

Facer Street, on the northern side of the old canal, never had class. Not even when steamships were running up and down carrying the produce of the western provinces out to the St Lawrence and the Atlantic did Facer Street reap any joy from what was going on under its nose. And now that the canal has moved to another setting altogether, and even the scar left by the old canal cut is now more or less buried under suburban streets, Facer Street has lost even the promise of happier days. The street runs straight for the most part, making only one big curve before it gives up at a railway siding. There are a few warehouses along one side and a messy run of frame houses along the other. Aluminum doors with flamingos decorate the houses that have been cared for. The others stood peeling under a hot sun, as I parked the car a few houses down from the apartment building.

A three-storey structure of red brick, the apartment's appearance among a row of frame bungalows caused less sensation than you might imagine. The general state of dilapidation that began in the makeshift porches and rough fences was continued in brick that needed repointing and windows that needed reglazing. In one apartment a generous portion of aluminum foil applied to the picture windows blocked out the sun completely. Inside the front door, the lobby smelled of stale beer. To the right of the door, the metal frame of what was once a directory of tenants hung from one hinge. Little white letters in plastic clung to the corners like confetti. A pile of a former tenant's belongings was stacked against the front inside wall. Battered lampshades and a floor lamp leaned over a carton of magazines and newspapers. A piece of Danish modern furniture from the 1950s, minus one of its four legs, rested as well as it could against the cardboard carton. When I pressed the elevator button, I smelled urine by the emergency exit's stairs.

"Hey, Mister, lend me a buck!" It was the boldest of three kids ranging from nine to maybe thirteen. They looked at me not with expectation but already getting ready for the blow or the hard words that would follow their leader's request. It was the smallest who spoke in front of his taller friends. Before I could answer, a woman opened a door.

"Get out of here, you kids! Blast off! Beat it!"

"Aw, screw off!" said the youngest.

"You don't live here. I'll call the police like last time! I'll tell your mother, Alvin. I know who you are. Now go on home!" The woman lifted her ample arm to show that her threat had fire and vinegar in it. The kids didn't wait for an exit line, they left in a tight group laughing through the front door. "And what do *you* want?" It took me a moment to realize *you* meant me.

"I'm looking for Wallace Lamb's apartment." She looked like I'd cracked a joke. I didn't know how to top it.

"*Him?* You gotta be kidding. You from a collection agency?"

"Not exactly. Is he here or not?"

"Look, I could tell you he died, or went off with a registered nurse, but you'd find out anyway, so who're we kidding?" I wasn't sure what I was nodding to, but I nodded. "He don't have nothin' worth repossessing if you ask me. All they got is that colour TV and that's it." I tried my testy look and got the apartment number, just like in that old play: the third floor, back.

I could hear the sound of the television as I rang the bell to the right of the door-jamb. I tried to look pleasant at the beady lens in the middle of the door. It must have worked; the door was opened by another large, middle-aged woman in a housedress like the kind my father used to sell in his store.

"Yeah, well, what do you want?" she asked, blowing the ash from the end of her cigarette in my direction. I could see her trying to place me. I wasn't carrying a clipboard or any papers that might need signing. That was a mark in my favour. "You hear those kids? Running around up and down the stairs? I told Shirley (she's the super's wife) that our rent includes a little protection from stuff like that. I didn't mince words with her, I told her straight out." I found myself nodding again. I tried to concentrate on her eyes. They were her good features. They were bright blue, surrounded by forgotten mascara. The rest of her looked like it was about to ripple or shake. She might be the only woman in town who had never read a magazine article on *anorexia nervosa*. "Damned kids, breaking everything in sight. You from Welfare?" For a moment I weighed the advantages of letting her think I was, but it seemed a temporary gain easily disproved. I just grinned and let her make whatever she wanted to out of it. "If you are, it's about time. He's not getting any better, you know. Come on in and see for yourself."

She led the way into the apartment. I heard the noise

of a daytime television program. It was a game show and the host's voice rippled with the fun of the diabolical games he had in store, while the audience roared with delight. "Well, since you can't take the Cadillac home with you, what about putting your other five thousand on *twin* Triumph sportscars!" The audience clapped and cheered and the contestant lost her bankroll when she couldn't remember the world-famous American president with the initials "F.D.R."

"We got company, Wally! Wally? Can chew turn that rotten thing off?"

"Go drown yourself, woman. Do something useful for a change."

"Watch your mouth, Wally. We got company. You did say Welfare, didn't you?"

"No, you did," I said, looking at the back of an overstuffed chair facing the TV. The top of the head that had its back to me was a faded red, like weak tea. He reacted to my confession at once:

"Ha! She's tone deaf when it comes to money." The man in the chair got up and stared at me. "You don't look like money at all," he said. "Not city money or any other kind."

It's hard to assess someone who is giving me the same treatment at the same time, but I tried. What I saw standing in front of a large colour TV screen was a man in his late fifties or early sixties. He wore his dying red hair over his forehead in bangs, like he was an extra in *Henry V*. It was a wide brow with penetrating eyes below wild eyebrows. The face, which narrowed rapidly from the nose down, was unshaven. The pale red was deepest under his nose, where he may have recognized a moustache, but it all looked like meat for the razor to me. His glasses were framed with a plastic that echoed the rusty colour above and below it and were mended with adhesive tape where the right temple met the frame. He looked like he needed watching. If I had been carrying a bankroll, my right hand would have automatically checked to see that it was still on my hip. Lamb tilted his head to one side, to get me from a slightly different angle, then smiled a one-sided smile and indicated a chair. "Sit down. What's your pitch?"

I tried to picture Lamb standing in front of "Breakfast in Ayton" with a palette and brushes. It didn't work. He looked like he'd be more at home standing on the sawdust of a carnival pitch. There was something beat-up and used in his appearance, as though he'd spent time in jail or the prizefighting ring. I thought of the metal furniture in Chris Savas's office. He was wearing dirty corduroy trousers and a plaid shirt of flannel. I sat in the chair next to his. It too faced the television set, so I had to turn to keep Wallace Lamb in view. I hoped he'd turn off the television set; I'm very susceptible, especially to junk programs like the one now playing. I tried to think of where to begin.

"Pambos Kiriakis told me that Arthur Tallon gave him a list of your pictures that were out on loan. Kiriakis wanted to see a few before making up his mind to the one he wanted to buy. Then, Tallon died, the list disappeared and now Kiriakis has been murdered." Lamb moved his jaw, like he had a cud in his mouth that he kept moving from cheek to cheek.

" 'Murder's out of tune, and sweet revenge grows harsh!' You're not the police. Where do you come in? Is it money after all?"

"There's quite a bit tied up in those pictures. Tallon's estate can't be settled until a proper inventory can be made. Pictures belonging to the estate have to be located and identified."

"I charge big money for authenticating. I don't get a cent for the bloody canvases. They're all bought and paid for."

"I don't think that's the angle they're worried about. They know a genuine Lamb when they see one. It's more a question of proof of ownership." Lamb's cud changed sides. He was looking for another crevice he could get a foothold in.

"Kiriakis, eh? Murdered. 'To be too busy is some danger.' How do you come into this and who the hell are you, anyway?"

"My name's Cooperman. Benny Cooperman. I'm a private investigator. Kiriakis hired me to find that list."

Wallace Lamb snorted at my profession and turned to the large woman framed in the kitchen doorway. "Just as I thought, Ivy: he's a lousy sleuth! Money-grubbing, not bestowing. Whatever happened to Lady Bountiful?"

"Wally, turn the bloody sound down!"

"Ivy, shut up!" He turned back to me, as Ivy moved out of sight into the kitchen. "What are you paying for information?"

"That depends on what you have to sell." Ivy reappeared and turned down the TV a little herself. She used the opportunity to take another look at me. She blocked the whole of the screen.

"If you're out to find information, it's going to cost you," she said, putting a heavy arm to the back of her head as though she was looking for a stray or errant tress, but none had escaped the tight-fitting hairnet which imprisoned all her mouse-brown curls. "We didn't invite you here, so you better show us the colour of your money."

"Ivy, bugger off!" Ivy held her ground and her tongue. "That list that Tallon gave Kiriakis made a lot of people sore, eh? What's your name again?" I told him. This time it may have sunk in.

"I've talked to a few of the people on the list. Names Pambos thought important enough to remember. They had access to his office and possibly knew where he kept it. One thing I'll say for them, Mr Lamb: they're all great fans of yours."

"Fans? Oh, I've got plenty of fans. In 19...I can't remember the year, what's his name, the governor-general? He bought twenty paintings from me at ten dollars each. They say he's a great patron of the arts. I say he knew a bargain when he saw one. Tallon had sawdust where his brains should have been, but his heart was as sound as a good oak hull."

"You knew him a long time."

"I never knew where I stood with him, but I could always touch him for a few dollars even if I didn't have any canvases to peddle." Ivy moved from the television set, letting a blast of colour into the room, and came to rest behind Wallace Lamb's chair.

"He got them pictures dirt cheap, if you ask me," she offered.

"We didn't ask, Ivy. He wasn't as fair to me as a bank—he wasn't any damned computer for one thing—but he gave me a fair price if I worried away at him. He was a gentleman, you know, and had that way of letting money and talk of money embarrass him. He'd go beet-red if you tried to haggle. Like if I puked on his old school tie or unzipped in front of his lady friends. So, I'd have to settle or try it again later. He was a hard man to get around. Maybe it was because he was so damned honest."

"Breeding has its advantages."

"Ivy, why don't you get us a beer?" Lamb looked like he was trying to mine my face for the money he was sure was there somewhere. All it needed was to find the right words, the right angle. He had to try to guess what it was that he had that I wanted badly enough to pay for it. Ivy moved back into the kitchen where I heard a refrigerator door open and close.

"Wally?" she called.

"What do you know about the missing list?"

"Wally, we're all out of beer!"

"That woman's a great extravagance. An Ivy I can ill afford. 'As creeping ivy clings to wood and stone, and hides the ruin that it feeds upon.' For a moment he looked regretfully in the direction of the kitchen, then sighed. "You're paying, I hope?" he asked.

"If there's any money going, I'll see that you get some. Right now it looks like all people hope to get out of this are a few pictures with your name on them. That's not much for you to look forward to."

"Look, my friend, I'm finished with painting, washed up. I can't hold a brush any more, not even with both hands." He watched as I nodded sympathetically. "Can you let me have twenty bucks on account?" he asked. "I'll see you get it back." I temporized by feeling for my cigarettes. I found the package and offered it to Lamb, who shook his head. "Those guys who do it with their feet have it all over me now. And it hurts. You think I can sit in Hump Slaughter's auction room and listen to the bidding on my stuff? You see, when I was good, I was bloody great! I was right up there with the big ones. Trouble is, I didn't die young."

"Wally, is that guy still there?"

"Put a sock in it, precious! We're talking!" He leaned over and turned the sound down a notch lower. Now the neighbours had no reason to complain.

"How did you meet Pambos Kiriakis?" I asked, just trying to join together fragments of what I knew.

"I saw him at openings. I could tell from his clothes that he wasn't one of the well-heeled buying type, so I knew he was there to look. I liked that. I'd been in his shoes myself. Tallon introduced us and later told me he was a chef at a steakhouse and that he had a small perfect drawing by Lawren Harris. We started to talk and that was it. I had an interest in antiques at one time. That was another thing. He knew the Early Canadian stuff and he swotted up on information from the library so he could keep up with me. He was a funny guy for things like that. Tenacious. Once he got an idea in his head, he was driven. Hound of Heaven after him. Sorry he got himself killed."

"Yeah, it's not likely it had anything to do with that list of your pictures."

"You talked to Mary MacCulloch yet?"

"Uh-huh."

"She got away with some of my best. Her old man's supposed to be the collector, but she's the one with the eye. I bet Paddy Miles has let her steal him blind. He's a pushover for a pretty face."

"Wally." The voice came from the kitchen, plaintive and intimidating. I got up to go. It was that kind of moment and Wally Lamb didn't try to stop me. I slipped him the price of a case of beer minus the bottle deposit and got out of the apartment. Before I got to the elevator, I heard the TV set again. The sound followed me nearly out to my car. So, that was Wallace Lamb.

Chapter Fifteen

I drove back to my place and dropped into Tacos Heaven for a bite of lunch. I found myself confused by the menu; the print was so large I had to hold it at arm's length in order to get it all in focus. It was altogether a bad experience. I ordered badly and got up, after an unhappy adventure with refried beans, shaking a lapful of tacos fragments to the floor. It was my first attempt at Mexican food, so I didn't know whether to blame the negative reaction on me or on the lunch. I paid up with nine dollars and a cowardly smile. There was a sense of resentment as I pocketed the change. I thanked the man behind the cash through clenched teeth. *"Muchas gracias,"* I said.

"Szivesen," he replied.

It was just after three o'clock when I parked behind Hump Slaughter's auction house. The lot was posted like a game preserve, threatening everything short of summary execution to illegal parkers. There were only three cars in the lot. I was encouraged by them and the four other empty spaces. I found a back door beside a nearly full bulk-loader, which carried the stencilled name "Bolduc" in capital letters. The message on the door read "Private," just in case you'd missed the theme up to this point. I ignored this sign too and found the door was unlocked.

I was in a dim loading bay surrounded by packing cases. I'd stepped into one of those B movies with Lloyd Nolan playing the detective. He always found himself in a warehouse like this with the heavies lying in wait for him somewhere ahead in the dark. I was getting lost in the idea that I was Lloyd Nolan, when I began to remember that Slaughter's auction house was on the site of the former Skippy's Bowling Alley. I hadn't spent too many years bowling, but I still remembered the place where I'd learned to keep score and run balls down the gutters, saving wear and tear on the hardwood alleys. I was getting a pin-boy's eye view of the place. I began to remember where the rest of the space led.

Light entered this back part of the former bowling alley through three tiny square windows at the top of the back wall. Most of this was absorbed without a highlight by the thick velvet curtains that separated this behind-the-scenes area with its rubble of wooden packing cases from whatever lay beyond. I moved through a zigzag alley between half-opened crates with glimpses of gilt antique mirrors, furniture under plastic wrappers and stacks of paintings with cardboard guarding their vulnerable edges. In a corner stood a group of marble nymphs playing at archery in unlikely costumes. They reminded me of wet T-shirt night at Widdicombe's pub on Ontario Street. Maybe those Greeks had the same idea in mind that Terry Widdicombe had. I guess in those ancient days, before photography was perfected, a cold chisel and a lump of marble were the fastest way of putting down a permanent image.

These musings were interrupted by voices coming from the other side of the curtain. I tried walking in their direction. The old yellowed plaster that I remembered had been cleaned from the walls to my left. Now naked brick ran up to the honest rafters and beams of the ceiling. This brick was covered with paintings hanging from a track that ran along the wall and disappeared into the curtains. Catching some of the light, a couple of wood goddesses were cavorting with unicorns on a faded tapestry. The poor unicorns looked grey with age and not at all happy about the crowns around their necks or the attentions of the goddesses. Close up against the curtains, the voices were nearly human. One belonged to Mary MacCulloch. It had her superior teasing quality even at this distance. The other voice was new to me. I heard something about "keeping your mouth shut" and "sewing mailbags for a living." That was Mary.

"If I go over," the second voice retorted, "I'll take you with me!" There were English overtones here, although the words were our common Canadian stock. "There's nothing I did you weren't part of." I found the parting in the curtains and struggled with the heavy velvet until I could see light again.

The front end of Skippy's had been turned into a theatre. The floor was raked, supporting two hundred empty seats facing me. I stood on a raised platform. To my left stood a speaker's lectern, stolen from a church by the look of it, surmounted by a microphone standing on the end of a gooseneck curve. Mary and a dumpy, round-shouldered man in shirtsleeves were standing at the back. They hadn't noticed my entrance. It was just like that at the Collegiate when I came on as an actor. Even in my mother's green hat, I was still part of the scenery as far as the customers were concerned. The guy with the slouch didn't drop a stitch either:

"Why in five years, Mary, we could both be out on parole and writing this up for the magazines. They like tear-stains on the glossy pages…"

Slaughter, if it was Slaughter, had a leer on his face that I wouldn't want pointed at me. The two of them were at that stage in a quarrel when it becomes pleasurable to throw the worst things imaginable at the other. Neither one seemed to care about putting back the pieces and shaking hands afterwards. For me, at least, it meant that I was still invisible as I climbed down off the stage, taking shelter behind a large ormolu grandfather's clock and a crate of rolled oriental rugs in front of the first row of seats. The battle continued:

"You low life!" Mary shouted. "You won't get away with this. I'll see you take the drop by yourself. And now it isn't just stealing. It's murder. Somebody did in Kiriakis. Why not you?"

Slaughter, as I was now pretty sure it was, backed away from Mary. He lost the leer and replaced it with something almost desperate. His mouth hung open and his chin shook as he tried to find words for an answer. Meanwhile I worked my way down a side aisle to the front of the auditorium. But it wasn't because I couldn't hear; even poor Pambos might have caught some of the exchange from his file drawer at Niagara Regional's cold room. "The...the little guy wasn't hurting me," he said. "I don't have any of the pictures on that list. I never handled that stuff. That's more your department." I could see he liked the way it sounded. He had turned the ball back at Mary faster than she'd imagined. For a moment she looked confused.

"Paddy told me not to trust you," she shouted, a second before she saw me moving. She turned her head in my direction as I reached the mid-point of the aisle. "He...Oh! Benny!" Slaughter's head spun around, his jaw dropped. Mary looked stunned, but coped with it better than Slaughter, who glared back at Mary and then again at me. He must have seen a conspiracy in the fact that she recognized me. After giving me a fast once-over, he turned back to Mary.

"Who the hell is this guy? Mary, if you're..."

"It's an investigator. You know, Cooperman."

"We're closed!" he yelled. He said it like this was a nuclear warhead assembly plant and I was without the proper security clearance. "The place is closed! You ever hear of doors and knocking on them?" He started across the back of the hall to intercept me as I came to the end of my aisle. "We were talking private business. You have no right…"

"I'm just one of those little pitchers with big ears, Mr Slaughter," I said, continuing to move in his direction. "And Mary's right. It isn't just stealing. Not since Kiriakis joined the heavenly chorus. But there may be a way to come out of this without doing a long stretch in Kingston."

"Who the hell…?" Slaughter was closing in on me, blocking for a moment my view of Mary and the door to the street.

"Shut up, Hump! Listen to what he has to say. He may be right." Slaughter started to look back at Mary, but ditched the notion before he'd turned his head more than a couple of inches. I was his target, and he wasn't going to let me out of his sights. It was a big, meaty face, now blotched with angry red patches from agitation. His big sloping shoulders under the sweater looked strong and menacing. Mary glared at both of us, then tried to recapture the situation with a smile. It didn't match the caught-in-the-act look on her face. "You're always about doing good works, aren't you, Benny? Asking questions of all the right people?" Something in her voice slowed Slaughter in his tracks. He moved more cautiously.

Mary was wearing tight-fitting jeans, a white blouse and a denim jacket. She had the outfits all right. Always the right clothes for the occasion.

"Right now I'd trade all my questions for a couple of half-decent answers," I said. That didn't stop anybody, and Slaughter was getting close. "For instance," I went on as though I had all day, "of how much were you bilking Paddy Miles and the Tallon estate?"

I didn't see Slaughter's hand as it came in my direction. I felt his knuckles on my jaw as I fell backwards over the aisle seats. There was more shock than pain. Above me, Slaughter hung there, his expression somewhere between triumph and concern. Mary grabbed him by the arm. "Hump, let him alone! He can be big trouble. Benny, are you okay?" I went on stroking my jaw. It was still the surprise of the blow that bothered me. What pain there was was mostly in my back where I'd hit the armrest of the seat. Slaughter was breathing harder than I was. His Irish sweater was puffing in and out under a face that had grown sweaty from the exertion.

"I'm dandy. Just hang on to him while I get on my feet."

"You son of a bitch, coming in here...!"

"Hump, he's faking. He doesn't know a thing."

"You better just get the hell out of here. I'll have the cops run you in for trespassing!" I used the back of the seat nearest me to pull myself back into an upright position.

"You make that sound tempting enough to wait for," I said. "But I didn't come here to call that bluff or any of your other bluffs."

"Benny, you don't have any proof that there has been anything irregular going on. Whatever you think you know will take a lot of proving." I kept the back of an aisle seat between Hump Slaughter and me. It seemed prudent. I didn't examine its uses in a pinch, but it felt good just holding on to it.

"Mary, I'm not out to prove anything. I'm not even looking for Pambos's killer. That's police business. I got my hands full just trying to find out what happened to something belonging to Kiriakis that disappeared a few days before he died."

"The famous list! God, I'm so tired of hearing about that damn thing! You could buy everything on it for two or three hundred thousand!"

"Pin money to you, maybe, but that's meat and potatoes for lots of people for five years."

"Benny, please try to understand." She and Slaughter were standing in front of me. Both wore the same expression of anxiety. Both needed my belief in their accounts of themselves. In Slaughter, that competed with aggression. I watched the way he held one hand back with the other. Mary had stuck one thumb into the wide belt at her waist. Her other hand still checked Hump.

I started talking more quickly now, hoping to scare one or the other of them to guilty glances or stout denials. People put off guard say more than they mean to say. And I was listening with both ears. "Slaughter, I'm sure it would be interesting to compare your books with Tallon's. Paddy Miles kept books as well as he could. I'll bet those books would tell a fine story about selling original paintings to a middleman, Mrs MacCulloch, here, who then puts them up for auction and pockets a tidy profit, even after splitting it with you." Mary dropped Hump's arm. She had her shoulders back now. I could count buttons on her white blouse. Hump needed a shave and maybe a low cholesterol diet. They didn't speak. "Tallon's death pinched a lot of greedy fingers in the works. Yours," I said, looking at Mary and then at Slaughter, "and yours. Maybe Miles got his share too. And we're not talking about the pictures on that list any more." Mary gave a start and her lips parted like she was going to say something, but didn't have the breath to make up the words. "Oh, no, we're talking about paintings that were never on that list."

"You're talking through your hair, Cooperman! I run

a legitimate place. We get a fair price for all this stuff."

"Benny, if you'll only listen to our side."

"Everybody and his brother took advantage of Tallon. You, your husband, Alex; yes and maybe Paddy Miles and Abraham too. Tallon was a sitting milch cow, just asking to be milked. The only thing that caught everybody with his pants down was that old heart of his. He died, fast. No warning, no chance to put back the money. You can't hurt a dead man, but it looks like this dead man can hurt you plenty."

"That's all talk, Benny!" Mary said. "What of it? You can't produce a shred of evidence that would stand up in court. Paintings were bought and sold. Nothing was stolen. It's your word and half-baked theories against ours. My husband's name means something in Grantham. So does Hump's. Who'd believe a sleazy detective like you?" It was a good defence from Mary. I liked the part about being protected by her respectability. They all had that: Tallon, MacCulloch, Favell, Miles and Abraham. Pambos Kiriakis and I were on the other side of that line. It all depended on how dearly Grantham would defend her own favoured sons and daughters. And they couldn't all be guilty. Grantham would be right to show some suspicion. I needed proof that would stand up to a stiff blast blown through the long straight noses of Grantham's best people.

Mary MacCulloch came over to me and took me by the hand. Her hand was firm but gentle, very intimidating, very sure of its powers. "Now, Benny," she said in a voice that had banked the fire that had been there a moment before, "why don't you try to be reasonable? We're not *bad* people. Do we look like the people on 'Wanted' posters? Benny, why do you hate me?"

"Mrs MacCulloch, I may not like you very much, but I don't hate you. I'm not on a class vendetta either. I'm just trying to make sense out of what's been going on here. And speaking of hating you, there is somebody who hates you. Yes, Miss Mary, you have an enemy I wouldn't want standing under my window at night."

"What do you mean?"

"Somebody's trying to pin Kiriakis's murder on you. Was it your partner here?"

"Watch it!" Slaughter said, and then to Mary: "I don't know what he's talking about, Mary. Honest!" He looked back at me. "Why would I want her out of the way? What's the percentage? If she bought the pictures, like you were saying, then I needed her. Without Mary, there was no business in Tallon's pictures." I had to allow him that, but I didn't say anything.

"Why would Hump want to break things up?" Mary asked as though she was reading my mind. I tried to answer and I liked the way it came out:

"Because with Tallon dead it was game over, Mary. Time to make up new rules and settle old accounts." She chewed on that for a moment then got back to the question that had been gnawing longer.

"Benny," she said, "why would anyone want to implicate me in Kiriakis's death? Why would I want him dead anyway? He was such a harmless little man."

"Maybe he tumbled to your harmless scam here. He found out about the borrowed pictures. He'd had the list stolen. It wouldn't take much to guess that there was more involved than a few missing paintings. You and your partner here, or either one of you acting alone, could have wanted to keep Pambos from doing his guessing in public. And what better way to shut somebody up?"

"Stop suggesting that! We're not that sort of people."

"You're wasting your breath on him," Slaughter offered. "Look, Cooperman, this is a private showroom. I've got to be careful about who I let in here." He took an aggressive step in my direction. I'd been waiting for it. In a second I was backing down the aisle as I'd planned. I could already feel my hands parting the velvet curtains. I was at the point where I was hoping the car would start on the first try, when my backing away from trouble banged me right into it.

"Look out, Benny!"

"Oh, my God! Cooperman?"

"Wh...?" The lights went out and the stars came out to play, dancing a jig around my head like a nest of wasps. Then they disappeared too and it was quiet for some time.

Chapter Sixteen

I was running through Jonah Abraham's house chasing after something just up ahead. I can't remember what it was, but it was terribly important that I catch up to it. The rooms in the house kept melting into one another in a way that Mies van der Rohe might have approved. Then it became clear to me that not only was I chasing something, but that, in turn, I was being hunted as well. What the plot needed was faces. All I had to show was a sense of agitation running into panic. When I opened my eyes, the long galleries had vanished, but the sense of the hunt was still fresh in my nostrils. I was alone in the auction room. The head of an ancient Greek woman was in my lap. The rest of her and the column she'd been standing on were in fifty pieces all over the floor. Neither of my hosts had stuck around to collect breakage. The white pieces looked more like plaster than marble, so it figured. The head in my lap with the foolish hat on was probably a refugee from a school art class, a Minerva on the lookout for better things. I moved her gently towards the largest chunk of her torso and made good the second part of my escape.

I came out of the auction house and into the daylight, blinking from light reflected from the automotive showroom windows across the street. I brushed more plaster out of my hair and off my clothes. People passed me on the street without looking back. A woman with a child tugged the little girl closer as the tot tried to turn and stare at me. I was just beginning to collect my thoughts. They ran in two directions and I had difficulty getting a firm hold on either one of them. Mary and Hump had made off, but I couldn't see which way they went. They most likely took to the cars out back. That led me to the second thought. I was in front and my car was in back. When I think of it now, it doesn't throw me, but it did then. Suddenly the world was too much with me and I was headed for a crack-up sooner than later.

I tried to get back into the auction house by the door I'd just come through: it was locked from the inside by one of those pressure bars. I was going to have to walk around to the nearest alley to collect the Olds. I was in the midst of trying to remember the Grantham street plan well enough to catch the nearest way when a car pulled up in front of me. It was a Lincoln of dark aspect and impressively long. I heard a door slam on the driver's side. In a moment I was looking into the angry face of Alex Favell.

"Cooperman! What are you doing here?"

"I've just had a tussle with Minerva. Maybe it was Athena. I couldn't tell which. You wouldn't have an aspirin on you, would you, Mr Favell?"

"Goddamn you and your bloody aspirin! Get out of my way!"

"They're gone. If you're looking for Mary and Hump Slaughter."

"How many times do you have to be told to keep your nose out of my affairs? Just stay clear of me." He tried the door and found it as locked as I had a second or two earlier. He was taken short. His plans hadn't allowed for running into either a locked door or a private investigator with a sore head. He paused.

"I do my best to stay out of everybody's affairs, Mr Favell. Divorce work is a hard living. Nowadays it's not even a living. So, you can have your affair and welcome to it. Are you ever going to give back those pictures to Paddy Miles? You got them from Tallon, Tallon died, so, now they're wanted by the estate. But you know all that, don't you?"

Favell looked up the street and then down, just as I had done. His luck was no better than mine. "Look, Cooperman," he said, pulling me close to him by the scruff of my neck. "If I gave Paddy anything I'd be taken for a bloody fool. I've got Lambs and Milnes, three by Harris and a fine late Thomson. Why should I part with them?" He thrust me away from him. I think "thrust" is the word. His action was so dramatic, I couldn't get over it happening on Ontario Street in front of the old bowling alley. He went on talking, obviously very rattled too: "No power on earth will take them off my walls until it's time to settle *my* estate. Arthur should have listened to me. He should have paid attention to what all of his friends were telling him through the years. Cro-Magnon man kept better books than he did." He stepped off the sidewalk to get back in his car. He continued yelling at me over the shiny top of his Lincoln.

"My pictures are my pictures, Cooperman. They are mine! If you think I'm a liar, show me chapter and verse on paper. Where does it say that I have any of his pictures on loan? Show me that! In the meantime, just get off my back." Alex Favell unlocked the car, a badly timed gesture, got in and drove away. He tried to make the tires squeak to add the right note of contempt, but they were too good to play that sort of game. Class is class, Mr Favell.

Whenever I come up bruised in any way, I find myself driving to my mother's town house off Ontario Street. I have no theories about this, I simply point it out as a fact that came to mind as I parked my recovered

Olds beside Pa's oil stain in front of the house. I knew at the very least where Ma kept the aspirin. I got rid of the last of the plaster as soon as I was free of the driver's seat.

The town house wasn't really a house, it was a unit. It was attached on one side to all of the rest of these houses that weren't houses. These attached places shared the same street address. So, what looked like a house was a unit on a street that wasn't a street. I'll never get the hang of modern living. I let myself in with my key and found my mother seated in front of the television where I'd seen her last about four or five days ago.

"Is that you, Benny?"

"It's just me."

"I didn't think it was your father. He went to the club."

"No, it's just me."

"Well, you're quite a stranger. I haven't laid eyes on you since Friday night. Time certainly flies around here. How did your move go?"

"I'm unpacked and I don't hear the band from downstairs any more. It's an improvement."

"Your father can't see why you're paying out good money when the boys' room here is empty. But I know: independence is your middle name. You were always like that."

"Everybody needs a place of his own."

"Tell your father. I was reading that Englishwoman, the one who drowned herself. She says that a room of one's own is the most important thing."

"So there goes 'the boys' room.' "

"Oh, that was before I ran into Virginia...Virginia...Something. She's opened my eyes. I could become the oldest living feminist. I'll have to see if she wrote anything else. She was quite the crusader in her day."

After a battle with herself, Ma turned down the TV sound and got up. She was wearing a dressing gown. "I'll put on the kettle, if you can stay a few minutes, Benny?"

"I'm not doing anything for dinner, Ma. It might be nice to have dinner, just the three of us."

"It's too confusing having you to supper in the middle of the week. I think I'm into the weekend and it's only Wednesday. I'm too old to change my ways. Besides," she said as I followed her into the bright kitchen with the little painted plaster heads on the wall grinning at one another, "I've promised myself to make a chicken on Friday. I'll make a chicken soup with noodles and then roast the chicken. You know, the way you like it, with paprika."

"I can hardly wait. Ma, I think this place is going to work out okay. I'll be able to do a little cooking from time to time. Do you have any extra cookbooks around the house?"

"Cookbooks? Who has cookbooks? I've got the only cookbook I ever had in that drawer over there. The binding's gone. You can shuffle the pages like a pack of cards. *The Naomi Cookbook.* I've had it since before Sam was born. Everything else I learned from my mother."

"Did they have frozen filet steaks in those days?"

"Benny, you always ask too many questions. Maybe that's why I love you." She rolled her eyes upwards.

"I remember my mother telling me about her mother's kitchen in the old country. She said it was a back room with a dirt floor. If you wanted a roast cooked, you took it to the baker."

"What sort of place was it?" Ma lit a cigarette after she put out two cups on the round kitchen table.

"I guess it was pretty small. The only thing I know about it is the fact that her younger sister fell out an upstairs window. So, there was an upstairs. I guess it wasn't tiny after all. Isn't it funny the picture you make in your head about a place from the things people tell you?"

"Yeah, it's like having to revise the face of an old friend when you run into him again after ten years."

"Well, you should get marks for keeping her young looking for longer than she could herself." The water in the kettle had come to a boil. Ma took it off the stove and poured it directly into our cups. She took first privileges with the teabag. I got it next.

"Ma, you're always hinting that all my friends are women."

"I'm not hinting, I'm hoping, Benny. That neighbour of yours at the office, that Frank Bushmill. What kind of life is that? I mean I'm a woman and I don't see all that much in men."

"Ma, you can relax. There's nothing funny about your son. And Frank's a wonderful fellow. He's read even more than you have. And, if it will make you feel any better, let me tell you I'm going out tonight with a nice Jewish girl."

"Benny, I can only take so much."

"Ma, I'm not kidding. I've got a date for ten o'clock with a single unattached girl who is nuts about me. The only trouble is..."

"Ah! Now we come to it!"

"The only trouble is, she's loaded with money and is the daughter of a client. I don't think I can allow myself to become involved with a woman who is beautiful, desirable and filthy rich. It would be bad for my character."

Ma set down her teacup and looked at me. "Let your mother look after your character. What business is it of yours? Who is this bright child who is smart enough to love my Benny?"

"Anna Abraham."

"Anna Abraham?" she repeated back at me like she was trying to think which local family might have spawned an Anna Abraham. And then it came to her: "Anna Abraham!" She put the cigarette she had just set alight down in an ashtray and forgot about it until it had burned to the cork tip. "Anna Abraham! Benny, what are you teasing me, your old mother, about? Anna Abraham is the daughter of Jonah Abraham. She's an *Abraham*!" I nodded to show her I knew the basic facts myself. "She's worth at least twenty million," she said.

"We haven't set a date yet, Ma. We're just going to have a drink together."

"Don't bring her back here until I get new slipcovers!"

"I promise."

In half an hour my father's car came to rest beside mine, and the front door opened. A funny thing about my father: he never followed the sound of voices and came directly into the kitchen or wherever people were talking. He always did a tour of the dining-room, leaving a coat and jacket draped over the backs of the dining-room chairs. He was like a cat in that he never varied his routine. After he'd walked this domestic trapline and convinced himself that everything was secure, he would then feel it was safe to join in whatever was going on. He found us still in the kitchen.

"You're early," Ma observed.

"They've raised the stakes at the club. You can't get a game for under a dollar a line any more. It's too rich for my blood. Hello, Benny. What is this, Friday all of a sudden! This was a fast week." He leaned over and gave me a kiss. He smelled of talcum and the sauna at the club as usual. Funny, we still kiss each other, even the men in our family.

"He's not staying," my mother said. "He's got a heavy

date." I felt like a teenager and Pa just nodded. Ma was relishing our secret. She'd hold on to it for a few minutes of exchanging knowing glances with me before letting Pa into the inner circle. I stayed until Ma began to peel potatoes at the sink and then made my farewells.

As I drove through the neon jungle of Ontario Street past the fast-food outlets where fresh cream is a style and not a commodity, I tried to remember something Ma had said that got my mind working. Was it something about Pambos or lists or my employer, Jonah Abraham? I couldn't make the connection as I tried to keep my head in rush-hour traffic.

Chapter Seventeen

The lot behind the Beaumont Hotel was as crowded as it was the last time I'd given my licence number to the attendant. The old attendant was a snarly little man with missing fingers and blackened teeth. He complained of life in the Soviet Union without a trace of an accent. For my two bucks I got a parking place and an education whether I wanted it or not.

The Snug was the main lounge of the hotel. The trappings were intended to suggest the quaint cosy back room of an Irish pub, but the designer had totally failed at his task. The only authentically Irish thing about the place was a blown-up photograph of a wizened face grinning over a pint of dark stout. The rest of the décor was as Irish as *Abie's Irish Rose* or "Does Your Mother Come From Ireland?"

Anna Abraham was grinning at me when I caught sight of her sitting with her back to the wall at a small table towards the rear. It was a good location, about halfway between all of the ceiling-hung speakers, which were now filling the air with electrified guitar chords. I pulled out the chair opposite her and made myself uncomfortable. Anna was an uncomfortable woman, like a good book you hate to finish. She looked just enough like her old man to remind me that she was the boss's daughter. She was money and class and a million miles away from me and anything that I could ever more than dream of. But she was smiling at me across the table.

"Hi!" she said, and the other stuff didn't seem to matter.

"Hello. Do you drink Bloody Marys too?" I asked awkwardly.

"I leave those to my father, and I use what influence I have to get him to leave them alone as often as possible. He has turned mixing drinks into a fine art."

"Like building a picture collection?"

"I guess it taps the same instincts. I suppose to you he seems like a driven kind of compulsive type. Maybe outside the family he is, but from inside, he's the relaxed, laid-back Abraham. His brothers kid him about it. They carry their competitive edge with them over into private life."

"They didn't invent that."

"No, but in our family competition has been developed to a remarkable degree."

"Yes, I've been reading about you in a library book."

"Andrew Carnegie has a lot to answer for. What are you going to drink?"

"What are you having?"

"When I drink anything at all, I drink Black Bush. It's Irish."

"Sounds good. I'll try one." After I attracted the attention of the waiter, who turned out to be Wilfred Prewitt from my grade nine class, I ordered two Black Bush and he brought them without adornment to the table. "*L'chayim*," I said.

"*Slàinte*," she replied over the top of her lifted glass. We both sipped our Bush: I because I never gulp anything and she because that was the way to drink Bush. "Nice?" she asked.

"Nice," I replied. "Very nice."

Anna Abraham was wearing a soft grey turtleneck sweater with a necklace of lumpy glass beads. Her jacket, which was cut like a man's, was slung on the chair behind her.

"You're staring," she said.

"Just admiring the beads," I said, taking a slightly larger sip of my drink.

"They're African trade beads," she explained. "The sort people like Burton and Speke took out with them to Africa to buy the goodwill of the natives. I picked these up a few at a time in junk shops. If you know where to look, there are still quite a lot of them around."

"But they no longer bring a mandate to explore the interior, I guess."

"They're just beads nowadays. Their magic's all gone," she said, paused and then asked: "Why are you smiling?"

"I'm trying to reconcile the you sitting here drinking Irish whiskey and the girl who was making a pest of herself in my office this morning. I can't figure you out."

"I think I'm a little nuts where my father is concerned. I don't want anything to happen to him and I had to find out if you were trustworthy."

"His track record is that bad, eh?"

"Gosh, I could tell you some things, but I won't. For the most part he is pretty hard-headed, but when he's taken in, it's usually very painful for him. He hates to be wrong about judging character. It's not the money he loses, it's his self-confidence."

"Is that why you stick around? Just in case?"

"Oh, I keep busy. I like this town. I grew up here. I have a job. I'm a very responsible person."

"What is it you do, exactly?"

"I thought you'd researched us?"

"I couldn't get a line on you. Are you the black sheep?"

"When Mr Coldham did his research, I was all of seventeen and not very interesting. But I like the idea of being a black sheep. Although as a family we tend to run in that direction. Being the black sheep might make me blend into the background."

"I doubt if you'd ever do that."

"Why, thank you. How are you enjoying the drink?"

"It seems to have put me in front of a peat fire. Very mellow. You knew Arthur Tallon very well, called him 'Uncle Arthur'?"

"Did I miss a few pages or have you just changed the subject?" I had. I thought I'd better get down to work before the Irish whiskey tucked me up so comfortably that I'd lose my job. I had trouble looking into her amazing eyes without forgetting that this was an investigation.

"I just wanted to know more about him. I'm usually more subtle with witnesses. I must be losing my touch. What did he die of?"

"Oh, it was his heart. He had angina, whatever that is. He used to have attacks of it and go on a diet and plan to completely change his way of life. Of course he never did. His schemes only lasted as long as the pain, or maybe a week longer."

"Was there anything else wrong with him? Was his health generally good?"

"Well, he was a three packs a day man. But he only coughed for social reasons as far as I could see. You know, those polite warning coughs when someone is about to say too much or the wrong thing. He was tall, thin and wiry. Apart from his allergy, I don't think there was anything seriously wrong with his health."

"Allergy?"

"Penicillin. He was supposed to have had some very bad reactions and he wore one of those medical alert bracelets. In fact, I gave him one with his name engraved on it for his birthday. Must have been over six years ago. He was very fussy about personal jewellery.

He wore a ring on nearly every finger and changed them all the time. It was like his jewellery showed a chink in his very secure personal armour. It was his only personal extravagance. For instance, he didn't care what brand of cigarettes he smoked so long as they weren't menthols."

"And when you're not being the black sheep of the family, what was it you almost told me you did?"

"I was about to tell you I taught history at Secord University. I'm a sessional lecturer very much in the non-tenured stream. It's my second year. Strike three and out."

"What sort of history?"

"European. Some American. Eighteenth- and nineteenth-century."

"So, was Napoleon poisoned or not?"

"I don't teach that kind of history. Maybe there should be a place for it. If things keep going from bad to worse in the academy, they will add that sort of thing: who killed Napoleon, was Elizabeth I really a man, did Bacon or Walsingham write Shakespeare, who killed Christopher Marlowe and so on."

"But you wouldn't want to have anything to do with that sort of thing?"

"You don't really want to know."

"I really want to know."

"Well, history is full of so many important things, the collision of economic, social and political forces. There's so much to see, so much that is going on. When you settle for what happened to Napoleon after he'd been removed from the stage of history, it's like settling for warmed-over packaged soup when there's a great broth on the stove. It's like watching the ball after it's gone out of play. It doesn't mean anything."

"I'd like to know."

"Well, maybe I would too in a sort of way, but

knowing what happened wouldn't change anything. It's not relevant to anything except getting away with murder."

We were still talking half an hour later when we got up and left The Snug. She had been demonstrating that such amusements as retrying Richard III before the bar of justice or history was a mug's game. The results don't change anything. They titillate but add little to the collection of human knowledge. We walked across the parking lot to my car.

"...and suppose you did discover that *Hamlet* was written by Joe Smith from Smithfield, would it change a comma in the play? Would *Lear* be more or less tragic?"

"Shit!"

"You disagree?"

"No. Somebody's slashed my tires."

"They what?"

"Some son of a bitch slashed my tires while I was in there drinking with you!" Anna Abraham looked at me like four tires can be replaced for the price of a package of bubblegum. She couldn't follow my rage any more than I'd been following her talk about the dynamics of world conditions. Everything she mentioned as an example of what was an irrelevant sidelight looked like a good read to me. But, I don't pretend to be up on that sort of thing. What I do know something about is slashed tires. The Olds was sitting solidly on four rims and the parking attendant was gone for the night. I looked at the surrounding cars; mine was the only victim.

By now Anna was looking at the tires as well. She walked around the car with me and offered the sort of help you'd expect from a woman who doesn't care who killed the Little Princes in the Tower. "Don't worry, Benny. I've got my Jeep over there."

I didn't argue with her. I got into the Jeep and told her which direction to point it in. It wasn't hard for me to read a message into the slashed tires that was more significant than the price of another four tires. I knew whoever did it was trying to tell me something, but I got sidetracked in the related questions of whether my spare in the trunk and two summer tires in my parents' cellar would make the price any lower. I could just replace the front tires and forget about the back until next winter. The spare was as good as new, with less than a hundred miles on it.

"Have you any idea who did this, Benny?" Anna Abraham asked. I tried to get my mind working in this new direction.

"Somebody doesn't want me looking for Pambos Kiriakis's list," I offered. "Or maybe it's some irate husband getting even for some work I did for his now divorced wife. Some of these guys have long memories. Maybe I should go away for a trip or something until all of this blows over."

"I love your sense of humour, Benny." I looked over at her looking through the windshield at the dark streets running by on both sides of us and wondered what I'd said that was so funny.

"Somebody knows your car. Maybe he's been following you."

"I've had it three years. It's pretty well known around town. I once got shot at in that parking lot. I hope your old man knows what a bargain he's getting. Turn here." She'd driven up St Andrew Street and was about to pass Court when I pointed left. "You can drop me at the corner if you want."

"No, I want to see where a real private investigator lives." She made the turn from the wrong lane and slowed the car to a crawl.

"Be my guest," I said, or something like that. When

she got to the corner building with the schoolyard all around it on two sides, I told her to stop and I got out. "Thanks for the lift," I said. She turned off the motor.

"I thought we might have a nightcap," she said, getting out of the Jeep on the driver's side. Suddenly she was the daughter of the boss again and I felt peculiar.

"Hey, I just moved in. I'm out of everything."

"Which windows up there are yours?" Her dark hair fell back on her jacket as she tilted her head up to see the top floor.

"Mine are all on the other side. Thanks again for the ride home."

"What are you going to do about your car?"

"I'll think about that tomorrow."

"I've heard that before."

"That's because tomorrow is another day."

"Hey, Benny! Don't run away like that!" she said coming around the car to my door, where I was trying to distinguish my new keys from one another.

"It's kind of late isn't it?" I don't know where I was getting the words I was saying to her. The parts were mixed up. When I got the door open, I felt like a kid on a first date. Only I was supposed to be the guy asking to come in and she was supposed to tell me politely to go home to a cold shower. When this became clear, I asked her up and made instant coffee with water freshly boiled on the stove. She tried to make pleasant observations about the place and I thought that after she saw my stuff she would quickly make her excuses. I looked around the room; there wasn't a single object or picture that would have interested Anna Abraham for six seconds. The ashtrays were full. My dirty shirts were rolled into a ball by the door. The bed was unmade and the flattened boxes were still tied together with string and stacked where Pambos had left them. Now I could feel the memory of Pambos showing off his few rare coins and the folio of sketches by Canadian artists. Where was my pathetic collection?

"I see you're a chess-player," she said, noticing my board and the wooden box of pieces.

"Yeah, I like a game. But mostly I work out problems from the weekend papers. Do you play?"

She nodded. "Daddy taught me. I don't think I'm very good." I set up the board and brought in the mugs of instant. That was when the phone rang. I put the coffee down and lifted the phone to my ear.

"Hello?"

"Cooperman?"

"That's right. Who is this?"

"Cooperman, you're finished. You're dead meat unless you get out of town fast!"

"Who is this?"

"Never mind that. I know where you are and I know who's with you. If you don't want to see her hurt, you better drop this fucking investigation. I'm not shittin' you. You could both just disappear."

I tried to stall him, to get some clue to what he knew and how much of it pointed in a traceable direction. "Which investigation are you talking about? I've got a bunch of files I'm working on?" The answer was a click in my ear as he broke the connection.

Anna could see from my face that we were in trouble. "It was him, wasn't it? The slasher?" I nodded.

"He knows you're here. He's watching out there. He knew we were at the hotel and that we came back here. How long have we been here?"

"Not ten minutes. What are we going to do? Do you have a gun?"

"Anna, this is serious. It's not the movies. I have to get you home." All of the escape routes running through my head began at the City House, where there was a convenient back stairway. I hadn't been here at

Tacos Heaven long enough to have done any research. I felt as trapped as a fish on a line and about half as smart. Then I remembered that from the bathroom there was access to a fire escape. From there, unless the slasher had been busy again, we could get away in the Jeep. I explained this to Anna, who looked game to try. Sitting on the edge of my bed, she looked about half as tall as she had three minutes ago. She was playing with the black knight without realizing that she was holding it. I told her to collect her things, then opened the bathroom window.

Chapter Eighteen

T he noise of our feet on the steel slats of the fire escape echoed on the landing below and off the brick walls. A light over the locked garage box behind the restaurant sent slashes of light and shadow across us as we headed down the steps. Anna had slipped her hand in mine. I was glad it was there because it saved me from looking behind to see if she was keeping up. When in danger, I tend to save myself, yelling "Women and children first!" all the way to the nearest lifeboat.

When we got to the bottom, we were in a narrow alley between the main building and a low garage. Behind us stood the high wire fence of the schoolyard. The wire caught the light, cutting off all hope of seeing through into the yard. As a kid I'd tried climbing wire-mesh fences. I remembered that it wasn't easy. Then I thought of Anna. No, we had to avoid a climb. I told her to stand pat and wait for me to get back. As soon as I did it, I regretted the decision. Anna's heavy breathing beside me as we came out the window and down the steel stairs had been reassuring. A presence, a companion in adversity, something like that. But as I worked my way along the shadow of the wall of the building, I felt abandoned. I might as well be wearing a target on my chest, I thought, as I made my way towards the front of Tacos Heaven and the Jeep.

I could hear voices around the corner. I came closer to the angle of the building and looked around. It was like coming out of a movie and into the light. A party of four, two men and two women, were standing under the bright sign of the restaurant. Two well-to-do couples, the men in business suits, the women in dark dresses. They looked as though they were trying to make an occasion of it. The men were talking about where they'd left their cars, the women about Beatrice, who, they agreed, was not pulling her weight on the committee. Had they ever had to get out of their homes because of a threatening call? Had they ever had their tires slashed? I was feeling like a black-and-white movie that had blundered into one in Technicolor. What did I have to do with their world with its committees and Beatrices, or what did they have to do with me? I was watching them going into the humdrum pleasures of a leisurely leave-taking between old friends, when I felt a warm breath on the back of my neck. I pictured all of the major figures involved in this investigation, including Pambos Kiriakis, as I slowly turned to see the one face I'd forgotten all about.

"I told you to stay there!" I said in a stage whisper, my voice going hoarse from stress. She shook her head.

"A cat frightened me, so I followed you. Shall I go and get the car?"

"Ah, sure. I don't think he'll try anything with people outside the restaurant. Come on. We'll go together."

We walked out into the light arm in arm. The four under the sign didn't interrupt their conversations. During the time it took Anna to cross to her side of the Jeep and get the door open, the foursome under the Tacos Heaven sign said their "good-nights" and departed two by two. A second later the sign was switched off by someone anxious himself to be going home. Anna's car did not start on the first turn of the key. She shot me a look; I was glad it was her car and not mine. The motor caught the second time and we were

heading down Court Street at the speed limit. I let myself relax into the leathery seat and watched Anna handle the stick shift with expert timing.

"Where are we going?" I asked.

"I thought home. I mean Daddy's."

"The little place on the hill. It's after midnight. What
kind of reception will we get?"

"We'll be all right. Don't worry. Daddy's not the bear
you imagine."

"I wasn't thinking of him but of his hired hands."

"Don't worry. They know the car and there are elec-
tronic things that a real burglar wouldn't know about.
You're safe."

In the back of my mind was an idea that maybe we
should have dropped in at Niagara Regional first to
report the adventures of the night, but, when you got
down to making a list, there wasn't much to put on it,
unless you could put down each of my snow tires as
separate items. Slashed tires and a threatening phone
call don't add up to much more than misdemeanours.
My tires were worth more than fifty dollars, so at least
it wasn't a summary conviction offence. It was wilful
destruction of property. I had him—whoever "he"
might be—on that, whatever else turned up.

Anna drove up the hairpin turns of the escarpment
that led to that museum of modern art that Anna called
home. We'd covered the distance remarkably fast. I
guess it was the lack of traffic at the late hour, but I
had to give Anna high marks for her skill behind the
wheel. Of course, she probably drove the same route
three or four times a day. I was somehow trying to at-
tribute virtues to Anna, whether she wanted them or
not. I'd have to take a minute to figure all this out. In
the meantime, coming here made sense: it was safe,
it got Anna out of trouble and it was a well-defended
citadel. I added to that, it wasn't within a clear view of

any other building. The most frightening thing about that phone call was the caller's up-to-date information. He had seen Anna and me come back to Court Street. He had seen my car in the parking lot outside the Beaumont Hotel. He was keeping an eye on me and I didn't like that at all.

She slipped a card into an upright stand, the sort of thing you see outside automated parking lots in Toronto, and the big double gates swung open. Instead of driving up to the front door, she took a branch that led around to the rear of the mansion.

"We're here," she announced, removing the keys from the ignition and putting them into a leather handbag.

"I'll come in and phone for a taxi," I said.

"No you won't. You're spending the night. What's the use of having a place this size if you can't cope with unexpected guests."

"But, officially I'm not a guest. I work for the firm, remember?"

"Don't be silly. Come on." She got out and led the way through the dark to an illuminated doorbell. She put a key into the nearby lock and we were in an unfamiliar hallway that was much more the family side of the house, without the monumental and artistic touches of the front rooms. Here the guided tours never penetrated. In five minutes I had a bedroom assigned, pyjamas laid out for me, my own bathroom, and a toothbrush still in its plastic wrapper. Anna brought me another shot of Black Bush and she led the way to a small study with a fireplace and a wall of books. The fire wasn't lit. That gave me the feeling that I was in a real house and not a movie set. Little things like unlit fires and coffee stains on the kitchen table give me the reassuring notion that even rich people live according to the same natural laws as the rest of us. A coffee stain is the same for everybody, rich and poor alike, and it will stay on the table top until a hand with a rag in it washes it away.

"Are you tired," Anna asked.

"Yeah, I guess I'm pretty beat." I sipped on the Irish and so did she. I watched her and remembered the way she'd looked in my office earlier. She'd been so suspicious of me and the investigation. "Do you really think your old man took that list?"

"What happened to your devious and subtle method, Benny?"

"You may call me 'Mr Cooperman.' Did he take it?"

"I don't know. I worry that he did. But it wouldn't have been like Daddy to do such a thing. What I want to know is if he didn't take it, who did, and what does he mean to do with it."

"If it's blackmail, the people whose names are on the list won't have to wait very long to hear from the thief. It's unlikely that he'll sit on it. There seems to have been a brisk trade going on in Tallon's uncatalogued paintings. I know who's behind that now, but it still is a different answer to the question you raise."

"I suppose you can't tell me about that."

"It's your old man who's paying me. He should be the first to know. But I'm not even sure I'll tell him until I know the whole story. When you start handing out parcels of information you give them a life of their own. The approved practice is to give a full report when you have all the facts and not give briefings from time to time along the way."

"And you always go by the book?" she asked, throwing back her head in that way women have.

"No. If I went by the book I wouldn't be sitting here. I'd be back in town looking for the guy who slashed my tires and made that threatening call. I'd probably have reported it to Niagara Regional."

"Will you?"

"In the morning." Ever since the incident of the phone call and our flight from my place, Anna Abraham had become quiet and rather withdrawn. In the bar she had been friendly and curious. Now she only seemed to be going through the motions of being the polite hostess. I'd had to bank the coals of some very unprofessional feelings. They probably didn't go with sharing the boss's roof anyway. As we got up and she walked me back to my room, we started talking about her job again. She told me about her classes and the number of essays she wasn't looking forward to marking.

"Starting next Wednesday, I've got to unscramble thirty papers on the American Civil War. It's hard charting a course through those long-dead battles, trying to find trends in leadership and trust, the politics of generalship and so on." She was leaning against the doorframe. "You know the one about Lincoln offering to send all his generals a case of whatever it was that Grant was drinking."

"No, I missed that. What I always wanted to know was did the people investigating the Lincoln murder ever discover whether there was a second gun."

Anna laughed. "See you in the morning," she said. It had been an awkward moment for both of us, but I'd managed to get through it without betraying my boss or embarrassing either Anna or me. I was dead tired anyway. I didn't even get a chance to enjoy the luxury of my surroundings. I was asleep as soon as my head hit the fancy pillow.

Chapter Nineteen

B reakfast came on a tray. I think it was the first
time that had happened since I had measles or
whooping cough. Not only were there things
like croissants and jam along with excellent coffee, there
was even a carnation standing up in a tall vase. I wondered whether the flower was supposed to go with my
jacket. I knew it wouldn't pass on St Andrew Street,
so I left it in the vase. But it was a nice thought, one
that suggested the isolation between this house and the
city I lived in. In Grantham only a mortician would
wear a flower in his lapel for everyday wear. A politi-
cian would sport one only during an election campaign.

After eating my way through the little curls of fur-
rowed butter and rolls, all the way to the Royal Danish
pattern on the china in fact, I dealt with my teeth and
headed for the shower in a bathroom that overwhelmed
me with white terrycloth. The shower stall was huge,
with jets of water coming at me from at least three directions. The shampoo came in a plastic bottle. When I
squirted a blob of shiny blue shampoo into my palm,
it squirted right back into the bottle the moment I
released pressure on the container, rejecting me and
all I stood for. It knew a fake when one came along.
On the same rack as I found the shampoo, I discovered
a conditioner and a special rinse all in the same matching plastic bottles. I don't think I ever did so much reading in the shower before in my whole life.

When I came out of the bathroom, my clothes had

been brushed and my shoes polished. Surely goodness and mercy shall follow me, I muttered as I wondered where the elves were hiding.

The first familiar face I saw belonged to Vince, whom I hadn't seen since my first visit to see Abraham. He knocked softly at my door and gave me the Toronto paper and a note from our boss. I put that away in my unadorned jacket and asked if I could call a taxi. Vince winced slightly. He told me that a car was ready to take me to town whenever I was ready to go.

Back in the real world, where coffee comes with cream in plastic containers and where the counter of the United Cigar Store is real because I'm leaning on it, I made a few calls from the pay telephone. First, I dealt with the car. The Motor League would tow it and take it to the garage where new tires would be added if, as I thought, the others were past repair. I telephoned the garage and warned them what was coming and asked if I could collect the car before eleven o'clock. I got an argument and after a few hot exchanges, I told them I'd pick it up around noon. Then I had words with Staff Sergeant Chris Savas about the recent harassment I had undergone. He gave me his sympathy and suggested I go back to school and become a teacher and thus get out of his hair for ever. I told him I had no taste for the work. The hours were too rigid for the likes of me.

"Benny, we've had a few calls about you in the last couple of days."

"Yeah?"

"Yeah. Citizens making inquiries about your status."

"Uh-huh. Any complaints?"

"Nothing specific. But the tone is usually critical even if there are no charges. I took one of the calls myself. Staziak got the second one. They just want us to know that you are making a nuisance of yourself and that certain bigger-than-average tax payers are just making friendly inquiries."

"Why are you telling me all this, Chris? I know you aren't going to tell me who called. But I can guess."

"I'm just tellin' you. There are more ways than one to slash your tires. I hope they weren't new."

"The front ones had less than five thousand miles on them."

"That's rough. I don't think I've got a thousand miles left in my front tires. You should have taken my car."

"Thanks, I'll remember next time," I said. "Chris, what's happening with Pambos? Did the post-mortem tell you anything?"

"It might have, but it sure as hell isn't going to tell you anything. Back off, Cooperman. I mean that."

"Has Mattie Lent turned up? The girlfriend?"

"Where did you...? Damn it, Benny!"

"Okay. Forget it. I was just asking *en passant*, as they say. But I'm willing to put down good money that says she hasn't come forward."

"Think we'll find her in a ditch, eh? Well, we'll get her in time. What do you know about it anyway?"

"Me? Nothing. I'm looking for a list that got lost, remember? I leave murder to the homicide fellows. Where do I get off telling the cops what to do?"

"Benny, put down the goddamned fiddle and talk straight. What do you know about Mathilde Lent?"

"Chris, I don't *know* a damned thing and what I suspect isn't of much interest. But I promise, if I run into anything like a hard fact, I'll send it your way. Pambos was a good friend and I want to see his killer caught as much as you do."

"Yeah."

"Maybe Phin Lawder and that crazy sister of his did him in. They still own part of the Stephenson House. It's been in their family for generations."

"Yeah, well, the blood isn't what it once was, Benny. She's in a home and Phin isn't capable of much more than pulling a cork these days. We checked him out for the night of the murder. He was drinking with two leading citizens and your pal Kogan, the panhandler, back of Gilmore's Hardware. Dead end."

"Have you got a line on his ex?"

"Oh, she's not anywhere near this. Linda's not even living in town as far as I know. They made a clean break a few years ago."

"But you're checking every avenue that might unmask the killer, right?"

"Cooperman. You go right to hell and get off my back!"

After hanging up on Niagara Regional's finest, and he is, I rejoined my cold coffee on the green marble counter. I was about to complain that they were out of croissants and that there were no flowers on the counter, when Bill Palmer and Barney Reynolds came in and took a booth. They gave me a friendly greeting, so I took my cold coffee in their direction. After the usual complaints from Barney about the paper, the town and society in general, I got to ask Bill a few more questions that I was wondering about. "Any breaks in the Kiriakis murder?"

"Nothing. The cops aren't saying a thing. I got to talk to Ted Lansky in the Coroner's office. He said there wasn't anything special about what killed him. He was stabbed and the knife that did the job was still in the wound. Nice and tidy, he says."

"Tidy for him," said Barney. "He doesn't have to try to get a new lead on it for tomorrow morning."

"Barney," Bill said, "neither do you."

"Yeah, well, I could be, if I wasn't trying to rewrite the stuff for *City and Vicinity*. They tell me to edit this stuff that comes in from the boondocks. *Edit* it, for

God's sake, I bloody well have to *translate* it!" We commiserated with Barney for a few minutes while he told us about how he'd been undermined by yet another journalism school graduate. "Still wet behind the ears and he's telling me where to put my hyphens!" When this familiar line began to grow tedious, I changed the subject back to where I wanted it.

"Bill, Pambos didn't have any family other than his former wife, is that right?"

"Yup. He lost one brother in Cyprus the way I told you, and the other one was killed off by the mob up around Malham. The famous Malham torso case, remember? Geez! Now they're all dead, all three of them, dead under fifty. That's bad luck!"

"Is it?" I wondered out loud. "The first died in a political scrum. According to you, the Brits set up the Greeks and the Turks were waiting for them. That sounds like dirty pool to me. I can understand the second brother going anti-social after that. What had authority ever done for him?"

"You're digging too deep, Benny, and too long ago. Cyprus is over and done with."

"The hell it is!" said Barney. "You send me out there, and I'll send back some stories that would send these kids back to school. They never saw a shot fired in anger except at a hockey game." Bill ignored Barney for the moment and shook his head in the affirmative. He'd weighed what I'd said while Barney went on about what he'd done in Stanleyville back in the 1960s.

"Yeah. You could be right. If I lost a brother to politics, I might not end up a choirboy. But what about Pambos? There wasn't anything bent about him. He was a sweet guy..."

"Who was hung up on paintings, tin soldiers and Napoleon," I concluded his thought for him.

"Aw, Benny, you can't use that against him."

"I'm not even trying to. What I mean is that we all react in our own way. One brother fell in with bad company, the other had a thing about improving himself, becoming a success, collecting things."

"He had a great collection of old toys, Benny," Barney added. "You ever see all those trick banks and stuff?" From here on the conversation got away from what was on my mind and closer to what was on Barney's. For the fiftieth time we heard how Barney rowed across the Congo from Brazzaville to Léopoldville, now Kinshasa, with an exclusive interview. We both congratulated Barney and then we got up to leave the United. Bill let Barney walk ahead of him towards the cashier. He turned back to me.

"You know, Benny, I was over there and covered that Guenyeli business. I mean, I ploughed through all that British red tape trying to find out what really happened. In the end I got as clear a picture of what happened as anybody. Hell, I was a bloody expert on the incident. That's what they called shootings in the street and bombs going off: *incidents*." He took the cigarette I gave him when he discovered that his package was empty. We both lit our cigarettes from his butane lighter. "It was a major story. Nine Greeks were killed. All that. And the British were sitting on it even tighter than usual. But finally, I got to the boy whose brain-child the whole operation was. He was a major who'd been in Palestine and then went on half-pay until the emergency in Cyprus started to heat up. Of course, I was never able to use his name, but I was able to write a few good stories about it."

"Yes," I said, thinking he was about to get lost in his nostalgia.

"Well, when I first knew Pambos, he was very interested in all of the things I'd found out about the incident. He badgered me all the time about the details.

In the end, I think he knew as much about it as Tim Bell or me. The point I'm making is," he said, "you're right about how that event got to both the surviving brothers in their own way. In a way, Pambos tried to collect it. Funny, isn't it?"

"Uh-huh. Who's Bell?"

"Oh, Bell was the galloping major. See you."

I watched him join Barney at the cashier. He bought a package of cigarettes, while I wondered why all majors were galloping majors. I didn't get anywhere with the thought, but I'm still working on it.

Half an hour later, I was standing on the doorstep of Dirk and Gertrude Bouts's house on Queen Street again. When she came to the door, she peered through a crack. "Mrs Bouts?" I said, with a false lift in my voice. "Remember me, I'm Benny Cooperman." She opened the door an inch wider.

"Yes, Mr Cooperman. I remember you very well." She stopped there so that I'd have to pick up the momentum.

"I wanted to thank you for all your help." She swallowed the bait and allowed the door to swing open the rest of the way. "Yes," I went on, "you were a big help."

"Then they know who killed him?" she said with a kind of hope or relief. "Come into the living-room." I followed her to the big, bright room with the baby lying on the blanket in his playpen and minding his own business. I greeted Willum by name and got a smile from his mother for my memory. We both sat down, with a corner of the playpen between us.

"Not exactly," I said, answering her earlier question. "The police are still looking for the killer."

"Then, why...?" She was suspicious again.

"Please take it easy, Mrs Bouts. They'll get the murderer in time. The Niagara Regional Police are among the best in the country. Like the Mounties, they get their man or woman."

Gertrude Bouts flinched slightly at my choice of a moment for equal recognition of the sexes. "Do they think that a woman is involved, Mr Cooperman?"

"Oh, yes. They know that Mattie Lent was involved with Pambos. They don't know to what degree she was mixed up in his death, but they'll sort that out. The fact that she's gone missing is suggestive, don't you think?"

"Not necessarily," she said, drawing the words out slowly as she slipped on a sweater that was lying on the chair. "There are many reasons why a young girl moves on. They don't all kill people."

"Of course. In fact a few of them get killed themselves." I got a smile for my pains.

"Exactly, exactly," she said, playing with the hem of her skirt. "Oh, but that's a terrible thought. I won't be able to sleep tonight. Would you like some tea or coffee?" she asked smoothly, looking like she was going to get up. I smiled and followed her into the kitchen, which was yellow and cluttered.

"Mrs Bouts, may I take you into my confidence?"

"But of course, if you want to."

"Well, I am not a great believer in the story of Mattie's disappearance."

"No!" She forgot that the water was overflowing the kettle as she stood at the sink. "Why would you say that?"

"Because I think you know where she is."

"No! Don't say that even as a joke. I know nothing about her."

"I think you know everything about her." She looked at me with steady eyes. She no longer was going to make tea or coffee. And we'd never determined which it was she'd intended to make. She stood there and I knew I had to make my next words count. "When I came here yesterday, you told me a lot about Mattie."

"That's right. We were friends."

"But you told me things that only Mattie would have known. You told me about the town in Austria where she came from, what valley it's in..."

"That's right. It's a well-known valley for skiing."

"For someone who hasn't been there, you seem to know a great deal about it. I thought something was wrong when I talked to you last. You appeared to be worried, but you hadn't really done anything about Mattie."

"What could I do? I didn't know anything about Mr Kiriakis. You told me he was dead. And that was only yesterday."

"You could have gone to the police after I left. But you didn't. Why wouldn't you report Mattie missing if you were friends?"

"But she's hardly missing yet! It's only a few days."

"If Willum went missing, you wouldn't wait days or minutes before reporting it. You'd be on the phone in seconds. No, there's only one reason why you didn't report Mattie missing."

"I don't want to listen to this."

"You didn't report her missing because she isn't missing, Mrs Bouts. You know where she is."

"Me?"

"And there's something else. Mrs Bouts, you told me all about Mattie's home in Schruns. Have you ever been there?"

"Why, no, I just heard Mattie talk about it. And I saw her pictures."

"Black-and-white pictures, Mrs Bouts, but you described the village houses and church to me in colour."

"Mattie must have..."

"You told me about the white and green houses, the

green dome of the church. The pictures upstairs, even the postcards, are in black and white." Gertrude Bouts put her fingers in her mouth and didn't seem to notice she was doing it. She made a throaty noise but I couldn't make out any words. "No, no, I think there's a simple explanation here, Mrs Bouts, something that explains everything. And you know what it is as well as I do." She shook her head from side to side. "The reason you know so much about Mattie, Mrs Bouts, is because *you* are Mattie Lent. It's the only way it makes sense."

"Me? You're being ridiculous! What are you saying? I have my feelings, Mr Cooperman."

"You and Mattie Lent are the same person. That's why you didn't want the police looking for Mattie."

"I have finished talking to you. I have nothing further to say."

"I know, I know. I'm just going. But I want you to know that I understand. I'm not blaming you. You invented Gertrude Bouts because you were living with Dirk as his wife. You want to protect your parents at home in Austria, so you pretend that you, Mattie, are the tenant of the Bouts. To anyone on Queen Street, you're the wife of Dirk and the mother of Willum, and to the folks at home, you're still Mattie, up on the second floor. It seemed an innocent enough deception at first. Who could be hurt by it? You only did it out of the most generous motives, to prevent your parents, who, I understand, are both elderly and ailing, from being hurt in their old-fashioned ways. Where's the harm? And then when your sister, Greta, came for a visit, you got away with it neatly. I haven't called Greta at the UN, but I could if I have to. Did you tell her that Gertrude Bouts was in hospital? How did you explain her absence downstairs to your sister?"

"I am not opening my mouth."

"That's right, Mattie. Don't say anything. You see, I'm not here to give you away. I only want to know what Mattie knows about Pambos Kiriakis's death and anything else about him that might shed some light in that direction."

"I see."

"I'm not in the pay of the police. I have no direct line to the Kirchplatz in Schruns. I only want some information that might help find your friend Pambos's murderer. You owe that to him, Mattie."

"But if you come, others will come. I'll never have any peace."

"They may come, but they won't come through me. Others may catch on to your Austrian accent under your excellent imitation of Dirk's Dutch. But Dutch and Austrian aren't the same and your voice helped give you away. You'll have to watch that."

"Will you go if I tell you?"

"Cross my heart." She sat down on a sturdy kitchen chair and I found its mate.

"All right. I won't tell you about myself, only Pambos." I nodded my agreement to her rules and she went on. "I met him first when I came to Canada, when my English was very bad. I was taken to his restaurant. He was kind to me and gave me the name of someone who helped me with my English. I didn't see him again until after three years. By then I was living with Dirk, but it was all fighting from morning to night. Pambos was at the hotel and he gave me advice, but I could see he was lonely, so I became his little *Schätzchen*. Dirk was away then, even more than now. We had a lot of fun, Pambos and me. He *knows* so much. I mean, he knew so much. But, I began to get worried."

"In what way?"

"Well, in the first place, Dirk wanted to get serious. In the second, I got tired of Pambos's stories. He had a mind like a ski slope. There were many trails, but always the same trails. It was either his paintings or Napoleon. Or Cyprus! He could go on with his newspaper friend about Cyprus until after three in the morning. I might as well be in bed with Dirk. You know? In the end, I didn't come back any more. Dirk and I had Willum and now Dirk spends all his time in Hamilton again. I don't know what I'm going to do."

"Are you saying that you haven't seen Pambos for a long time?"

"Not since before I was pregnant. We didn't have a fight, we just wanted different things. He was always kind to me. He was a good man, Pambos Kiriakis." She paused here, thought a moment about what she was going to add and then said: "But he was for *me*, you understand," and she pointed to herself, "a very boring man, Mr Cooperman. With one friend he would talk about how Napoleon could have invaded England near Dover because of the way the cliffs gave way to beaches a few miles away. Or he would go on for hours about one painter and another. He was very partial to a painter named Lamb, I remember. He tried to buy pictures from the painter, but he wasn't painting any more. Pambos lent him some money to have his television set fixed. He was a dear man, Mr Cooperman, but for me he was not fun. I respected him, I was grateful to him for *sooo* much he did, but in the end, not even the love-making was enough."

"How much of this does Dirk know?"

"Oh, he knows nothing about Pambos. *Nothing!*"

"Okay, we'll try to keep it like that. What about the other little deception?"

"Well, he agreed that for the sake of my parents..."

"I see. How long were you going to keep this game going?"

"My mother has only a few more months to live."

"I'm sorry." That seemed to stop things for a while.

"Have you heard from the police?"

"A Sergeant Savas called yesterday. I said Mattie was out. He said he'd call back." I wondered how long she would have been able to keep up the fiction of being Gertrude Bouts once the police came looking in earnest for Mattie Lent. If they began by asking for passports and other papers, she might have cracked after thirty seconds.

"Do you know anything about his wife?" I asked.

"I think that it was over and done with a long time ago. When he spoke about her, he was always kind. I didn't get the feeling that he avoided talking about her. It wasn't a big issue."

"I wonder if she felt the same," I said, thinking out loud.

"Well, you can ask her."

"I can, I guess. All I know is that she's living in Montreal. I suppose I could ask the police if..."

Mattie nodded impatiently, so I stopped nattering. "She is here in Grantham."

"What?"

"I called her when I heard that Pambos was dead. I didn't want her to read about it in the paper. I thought it was something I could do. She said she would try to come for the funeral. I just got off the telephone with her. She phoned me from the police station. She was being questioned by them, and then she is going to the hotel."

"Which hotel?"

"Why, the Stephenson, naturally. She is probably the new part-owner. It's only natural that she should stay there."

"So natural that I couldn't think of it." I got up and showed signs that I was about to make tracks. Mattie sat, a bit stunned by the fact that she had survived an ordeal that had given her more bad nights than the deception was worth. In the end, she got up and showed me to the door.

"You know, Mr Cooperman," she said, holding the door wide, "I'm glad you came here today. I feel a lot better."

"Thanks for the information," I said and started down the sidewalk. She watched me go for a few seconds. I was almost down to the *Beacon* when she went in and closed the door.

Chapter Twenty

"They took the beam and the central control panel."

"If they're gonna get in, they're gonna get in."

"As soon as I saw the signs, I knew it was the kiss-off for the TV and the VCR, but they even took a vice off my workbench. I mean, I thought they didn't bother with heavy stuff like that?"

"Yeah, you expect antiques and expensive light stuff like that. Now, Louise, she once lost a coat. It wasn't all fur, but with a fur collar. I can understand that."

"Yeah, but a heavy vice. It musta weighed fifty pounds!"

I was sitting on the sidelines waiting for my car. It was high on the hoist and two mechanics were fitting new tires. I hadn't intended to supervise the work, but they had told me it would be ready around noon and I believed them. Both wore greasy white coveralls and caps without a peak in front. One was tall and skinny, with a face full of vertical lines. The other was short and skinny with a bushy red beard that didn't belong. Their conversation was punctuated by the whirr of the airgun from time to time as they cemented the nuts in place until the final trumpet. It was no good telling them that I might have to fix a flat myself on the highway some time. They didn't follow the argument. What's the sense of leaving the nuts loose when they could be tight?

By the time I drove away, I knew all about a burglary

and the security system that made it possible. I was wondering why they stole the vice. Maybe they needed one. It could be as simple as that. I wondered what I was going to do next. I tried to think when I'd eaten last. Ah, yes, breakfast in bed. That reminded me of the note I'd put in my pocket from the great man himself. I took it out and worried away at the flap with my little red pocket knife.

> Dear Mr Cooperman,
>
> *I recognize that looking after Anna was not part of our bargain, but I appreciate it just the same.*
>
> Yrs,
> J.A.

A pink fifty-dollar bill fluttered from the envelope to my lap. I found myself suddenly very hot at Jonah Abraham. If the fifty wasn't part of my fee, then it must have been a tip. I don't like tips.

At the Diana Sweets I ordered a chopped egg salad sandwich on untoasted white bread with a glass of milk and a vanilla sundae. This was the kind of food I could understand: simple, readily available, difficult to ruin. It was part of my very conservative character, I guess, to keep returning to the things that matter, what Frank Bushmill calls the immutable basics. I thought about all the things in the world I couldn't live without while I finished the first half of the diagonally cut sandwich. I liked the way they worked pimento olives into the egg salad. A very nice touch, I always thought, whenever I'd been away from them for a long period. The egg salad sandwich was one of my immutable basics. A place of my own is another. The third is buying a girl a drink because I think well of her and not because her old man is paying my salary. I could already feel the white bread making a knot in my stomach. I reminded myself to buy more antacid tablets next time I was near a drugstore.

The Stephenson House hadn't changed since the death of Pambos Kiriakis. It still presented an ivy-covered brick front to the visitors arriving from the main gateway. Under the ivy, you could see where later additions to the original central heap had been made down the years. From the front, you got no idea that the back end plunged down the bank of the Eleven Mile Creek to pick up three extra storeys. The creek here was at its swiftest, but the view was uniformly dismal. The meanderings and curves had been straightened out over a hundred years ago when it was made to serve as a chief part of the Welland Canal. More recently, it had lost a tiny island when engineers had further smoothed the watercourse to accommodate an increased runoff from hydro-electric projects some miles upstream. The hotel had taken over part of an old brewery. The bricks had lent authenticity to the new dining-room with huge out-of-period windows that looked up the manicured slopes of Oak Park towards the TV station. Part of the land was used for the additional parking that success had made necessary. As I got out of the car, parked between clearly drawn white lines on the fresh asphalt, I saw no signs of mourning. No crêpe on the door to frighten away tourists or conventioneers. In fact it was business as usual with a big smile right up to the moment I asked the receptionist whether Mrs Kiriakis was in. His smile disappeared and a suitable dour expression was substituted. "That was terrible about Mr Kiriakis," he said. "Just terrible. Will you call 311 on the house phone, please. Have a good day."

I hadn't felt low when I came in, but that receptionist scuttled my morale. I walked over to the beige-coloured house phone and was buzzed up to Room 311, but there was no reply. I wondered about the receptionist. Was he born wishing people a good day, did he learn it in school along with the height of Niagara Falls and the date of the Battle of Hastings? Was it something for which he got a commendation in hotel arts in some place of higher learning? I wasn't really curious, but it made me sad as I replaced the phone and decided to have a look in the restaurant and bar on my way out.

She was in the bar. I hadn't seen Linda for maybe six or seven years, but she hadn't changed all that much. Linda was never a raving beauty, and she'd held her own on that. In her late forties she was still striking, almost handsome, in her tailored green suit. It wasn't a Toronto suit. It looked more like New York or at least Montreal. I walked around the long way, so she'd have a moment to recognize me. The smile wasn't as automatic as that of the receptionist. It was more of an organic outgrowth of a real emotion. And when it came to her face, it belonged there.

"Benny, how are you?" she said, taking my hand. "Are you alone? Please, sit down." I did that and we exchanged small talk, trying to postpone the inevitable pause and what came after that.

"Oh, he was always fair to me, Benny. I never wanted for anything ever. We kept in touch about important things. He knew how to make me laugh. That's what I'm going to miss most, I think. He knew what made me happy even when he knew it wasn't him any more. Most people write him off as a jumped-up kid, just off the boat and with more ambition than Alexander the Great. He was that all right, but that doesn't even begin to sum him up. What am I going on about, Benny, you knew him. You know how thoughtful he was."

I agreed and we talked about Pambos's fun and his tenaciousness. He'd go a long way to match the right present to the right party. "I don't want to hold a wake

right here in the bar, Benny, but I'm going to miss him."
Linda signalled to a waiter who had been hovering near
my elbow. "What'll you have, Benny?" I ordered a rye
and ginger ale without thinking too much about it, and
before he got away, Linda handed her own drink back
to the waiter. "This doesn't have any sting left, Karl.
Could you get me another?"

"Yes, Mrs Kiriakis."

"See, they all remember me from the old days. When
we were young and happy and you could wipe off a
stain with spit."

"How long are you going to be in town?"

"I don't care. Two weeks, two months, two years. I
don't know. I've got a share of this albatross around
my neck. Want to buy a very chic hotel, Benny? I didn't
think so. It'll all work out," she said, and then looked
at me with the eyes of a ten-year-old. "Won't it?" The
waiter put down the drinks and cleared empty glasses
that had been piling up before I'd arrived.

"When did you talk to him last?" I asked, and then
worried that it would seem too much like I was working on the case. But Linda only knew me as a divorce
investigator from the days when I could make a living
by following people to lovers' lane or to the Black Duck
Motel out old Number Eight.

"I last talked to Pambos about two weeks ago. It was
my birthday and he called up my apartment in Montreal. He never forgot my birthday, not Pambos. He was
the most thoughtful man in the world. I just couldn't
stand to live with him, that's all. There's no crime in
that."

"Was he worried about anything?"

"Oh, he was always worried about something. Let's
see, let's see, he told me about a friend of his who'd
died. And then..."

"Arthur Tallon?"

"That's right, the art dealer. And then we just talked about the happy times: the trip to Bermuda, our cottage on the Lake of Bays, skiing in Arizona, the month in England. All that."

"And that's all?"

"It was just to say happy birthday, really. The rest was to fill up the three minutes. He could be very charming on the phone. He could almost make me forget how much I hated married life. If I let that guy near me for a minute, he'd sweet-talk me back into bed with him and right away I'd be picking up his socks and shorts all over again. Life's too short to spend it picking up anybody's socks and shorts all the time, right?"

"What if they belong to Mr Right?"

"Mr Right picks up his own socks and he doesn't wear shorts."

"Have you talked to the police yet?"

"Yes, I talked to a Sergeant Savas. He knew Pambos, so that made it better. There's so much about a death that's maddening: the way people are always handling you, like you're not all there, the professional manner, you know what I mean? Savas was human and I liked that."

"He's a good cop and he liked Pambos. He'll find out who did this."

"You're not drinking. Come on, Benny. Help me through the next half-hour, will you?"

I drank a big sip from my glass and settled down for a long siege. Linda had never been particularly friendly to me in the past, but she'd accepted me as one of the many people in Pambos's background, one of the yardsticks that reminded him of how high he'd climbed. Maybe I'm just imagining that I was important to him. I tried to remember his kindness to me just three days ago. Linda was talking when I looked up. I could hear her voice, and I caught the drift. She was talking about their favourite holidays. "We travelled very well together for a couple who got on so badly at home," she said, adding, "although we had a monumental fight in the railway station in Milan and another in the middle of Omonia Square in Athens. He had a terrible bump of direction and was always charging off south when he wanted to go east." I nodded and sipped. She sipped and had her glass changed at regular intervals. "I'll never forget the time, though, when he left me in London to shop while he went on one of his historical expeditions to the south. That was our last trip to England, the summer we separated, July '85. He called it a farewell present. He was gone two days down in Kent, while I had the run of the shops along Oxford Street. And you know what? I missed him and his twisted sense of direction and was very happy to see him back at the hotel again." Linda went on in this vein for the next hour, then I urged her to go back to her room for a rest. She held her drinks well, but she'd consumed more than enough for both of us. She took my suggestion without argument and I walked her to the elevator. "I'll be here for a few weeks, Benny. Please come back and see me, won't you?" I said I would and I watched the double doors close.

When I got back to my office, I put the car in Pa's old space at the bottom of the lane and walked up the slope to St Andrew Street. I scouted the front door before going in. I saw no new desperate characters lurking about along with all the usual desperate characters. My old friend Kogan was on his corner and waved a greeting in my direction through the one-way traffic. Dr Bushmill had a full waiting room, judging by the sound of conversation coming through the frosted glass of his door. My own door was unbreached, a good thing for a change. As I get older, I think I like surprises, even pleasant ones, less and less.

I scooped up my junk mail from the obscene pile it made inside my door and carried it to my desk. The answering service had two calls for me that looked interesting: one from Paddy Miles of Arthur Tallon's gallery and the other from Peter MacCulloch of Secord University. I tried the gallery number and got nowhere. I lit a cigarette and put my feet up before trying the second number. The junk mail again failed to lure me into a world of imitation Dutch clocks and appliances that run from the lighter in my car. The secretary at Secord got me MacCulloch's secretary, who in turn, after a routine cross-examination, got me Peter Mac-Culloch.

"Ah, Mr Cooperman! Glad you could get back to me so quickly," he said and I wondered what he was trying to pull. "Look, I've been going over my inventories again. You know the art collection belonging to the university?"

"Yes."

"Well, I've found the most extraordinary thing!"

"Well, I'm glad you decided to share it with me."

"In going through the lists very carefully, you understand, I came across two paintings that were on loan from Arthur Tallon's gallery that had got mixed in with the university's own collection."

"No!" I don't think I gave a very good performance, but MacCulloch wasn't interested in my believing him. His problems ended when he told me.

"Yes, isn't that an amazing coincidence?"

"Extraordinary," I allowed. "How about your own personal collection? I bet you had a couple of surprises there too?"

"Boy, news really travels fast in a small town, doesn't it? Yes. You could have knocked me over with a feather."

"Amazing, as you say yourself. And to think I'd just been to see you a couple of days ago about that very matter. Well, it's very public-spirited of you to come forward like this, Mr MacCulloch. I'll bet there are a few others who will take up their own inventories and make similar discoveries. But I'll remember that you were the first. What exactly did you find?"

"Ah, yes, I found three Lamb landscapes, a portrait of a woman and two oil sketches on birch panels."

"Well, that's quite a find. Congratulations. Have you told Paddy Miles about it?"

"I just got off the phone with him a moment before you called."

"Good," I said. "That will make my life a lot easier from now on, Mr MacCulloch. Thank you very much for giving me this preview of the news."

"Oh, not at all, Mr Cooperman. Not at all. Always glad to help out."

When I got off the phone, I wondered how he could have just got off the phone, when I'd got no answer from the gallery at the time he claimed to have been talking to Paddy Miles. Either my telephone or MacCulloch was lying. And by now I was getting to know MacCulloch very well. I tried the number at the gallery again. The line was still not answering. And I was getting a little uncomfortable sitting behind my desk, feeling smug about Peter MacCulloch.

Chapter Twenty-One

T he sign attached to the Contemporary Gallery's front door said "CLOSED." Further inspection informed me that a *vernissage* was scheduled for Thursday night. That was only a few hours away. I didn't know what a *vernissage* was, so I decided to ask. I probably would have tried the door anyway. I was glad to find the door unlocked.

The door opened into a hallway with walls painted a flat white and linoleum flooring and stairs leading in two stages to a second floor. A rectangular window over the door washed the steps with outside light. I followed the steps to the top and found myself outside a second closed door. But this one had light shining through the crack at the bottom. I knocked and waited, wondering how prepared I was for previewing a *vernissage*, still having no idea whether it was a French orgy or a routine stock-taking. I couldn't guess which. My ignorance in this area was unfathomed.

Paddy Miles opened the door and, after a moment of trying to place the face, invited me inside. "Mr Cooperman, as I live and breathe! Welcome aboard!" He retreated into the large room and I advanced. On the white walls I could see about sixty pictures, most of them simply framed, and all belonging to the period I'd been seeing a lot of these last few days. At a glance I saw more Lambs and Milnes than I'd ever seen in one place before. One wall was still empty and a pile of canvases was leaning against it. Martin Lyster was standing

on a ladder with a hammer in one hand and a mouth
full of nails. Paddy and Martin both looked surprised
to see me.

"I know you're closed, but I wanted to see how things
were going," I said lamely.

"You mean you have some questions for me, Mr
Cooperman. We're both on the same side, remember."

"That's right, I forgot." The gallery was badly provided with places to sit down. There was a grey pouffe
thing in the middle of the room; fine for admiring the
collection from, but far away from the two other people in the gallery.

"May I get you a drink?" Paddy Miles asked and then,
as an afterthought, introduced me to Martin Lyster.
Lyster smiled at me, enjoying the redundancy. I was
busy declining the offer of a drink. "I only have some
plonk that I bought for tonight. I hope you're planning
to come?"

"That depends on what it is," I admitted, flatfooted.

"Why, it's an opening. 'Another opening, another
show.' What did you think it was?"

"That word on the door..."

"Oh, *vernissage*!" he laughed, and Martin joined in.
"It's very pretentious of me to keep on using Arthur's
pet words, but there it is. It's French for a varnishing.
The painter's friends used to get a special preview of
a show while the artist varnished his canvases. That
was in the old days, of course. Now it just means 'opening' or perhaps 'sneak preview.' Arthur loved all that
French cant that litters the trade. I suppose it's too late
to change now. Arthur is still very much with us, isn't
he, Martin?"

Martin, who was about to swat a nail from a distance
that was too far away to be rewarding, gave up the attempt in order to answer. "The place is spooked, and
that's the truth. Only I don't think Paddy'd want the

news to leak out. It wouldn't be good for business."

"You'll be blackmailing me next, Martin." Martin went back to hanging pictures. Paddy turned to me. "How is the investigation going on?"

"It's always slow at the beginning," I said, letting him think that I'd investigated so many cases of art-related crimes that I had seen patterns and had developed graphs and statistics. "I scared Peter MacCulloch into discovering that he has a cache of your paintings at home and at the university."

"Good! I'm glad you're getting results. Any others?"

"Not so far, but I wouldn't be surprised to hear from some people before long."

"Well, here I was about to make a speech about how unlikely it was that you'd be able to uncover anything, and here you are, reeking with results. That's excellent work!"

"I'm pretty sure that Alex Favell has a change of heart coming. Mary MacCulloch has been doing some picture-dealing on her own hook through Hump Slaughter."

"Mary? I can hardly credit that! Can you, Martin? I am prepared to believe anything about Slaughter. I don't think he has a straight bone in his body. He might take advantage of Mary."

"Is this all right?" called Martin. He was holding a landscape with a lot of purple sky up on the wall. Paddy cocked his head and nodded.

"Martin's my half-brother. Did you know that? Same mother, different fathers." I indicated that this was news to me, but as information, I didn't know what to do with it. Was it good or bad for my current problems? I suppose it accounted for the long, lean look of both the gallery manager and the book-finder. I thought that I'd collect my information and then get on my way. I tried a round of questions and collected a blast from

Paddy Miles for my trouble.

"Now look, Mr Cooperman. What I said at Alex Favell's office still holds." As he spoke, he was checking through a list of pictures still unhung, with more attention to detail than the job warranted. "Find the list that Kiriakis told you about and if it's genuine I'll genuflect in any direction you prescribe. I'll dance in the streets, I'll shout from the housetops, I'll wash and iron your shirts, if you want. But the damned thing has to be genuine. When Kiriakis said he had it, I thought it was too good to be true. And it still is." He moved away from a Group of Seven painting of a pine tree *in extremis* and began cracking his knuckles one by one, with the precision of long habit. I watched, hypnotized. "Oh, you didn't know Arthur, Mr Cooperman. He was a genius, wasn't he Martin?" He didn't wait for a reply. "He was clever like a genius and maddening like a genius. In the ten years I worked for him, he left me two written communications. *Two*. That's all. And now this list! You see what I mean?"

"I've been hearing all over town he was crazy in his way," I said. "There are people, Mr Miles, who might take advantage of a character like that."

" '*Might*,' you say? It happened all the time. He'd pay Wally Lamb two or three times for the same canvas that came from a prepaid commissioned lot in the first place. He nearly drove everybody crazy. Like the times he'd take off and leave town without a word. He could be gone for weeks. Oh, if I was not preparing for this opening tonight, I could give you chapter and verse about his 'lovable' eccentricities." Paddy moved to the pouffe end of the gallery, waving his wineglass grandly. I followed, surveying the pictures.

"Lucky he had you around to look after things when he went through the keyhole."

"He'd sometimes invite a hundred people up here

without telling Paddy," Martin added from his perch on the ladder.

Miles made a mime gesture to indicate that the point had been made, and I nodded agreement.

"I'd have been carted away to the booby-bin if Martin hadn't shown up."

I was about to return towards the door, when another thought hit me. "Mr Miles, how exactly did Mr Tallon die?" The question hit Paddy Miles with an irrelevant clunk. He shrugged. I sat down on the pouffe.

"That was at least quick," he said. "Heart."

"I heard he was in the General."

"He was sitting where you are, finishing up a plate of spaghetti. It was his second helping. Suddenly, he had one of his heart attacks. He had angina, you know. Very bad. He went pale, had a hard time breathing, said he had a shooting pain in his arm. I used to be a medical student. Dropped out to sculpt in my fourth year. So, I knew I had to get him to the hospital at once." Paddy Miles entered into the spirit of his tale; I felt quite caught up in it. "But," he said, letting his hands fall helplessly to his sides, "he was DOA."

"Just one of those things," I said.

"He was a wonderful human being," Miles said, then gestured towards a blown-up photograph near the door to the private or office part of the gallery. "That's him. It's an enlargement of a snap from a canoe trip. That was five or six years ago."

I looked. He looked healthy enough in the picture. There were lines on his face, but his body was lean and fit. His arms were sinewy and strong. "He doesn't appear to be about to blow away."

"He knew the north," Paddy Miles said. "Loved it up there. Even went sketching in the Barren Lands."

"That bracelet he's wearing doesn't quite go with the paddle and knapsack." Martin laughed from his wall.

Miles gave him a stern glance.

"There wasn't anything effeminate about Arthur, Mr Cooperman. You're reading a lot into a bracelet."

"At this stage, Mr Miles, I'm not reading at all—just sounding out my words." Miles appeared to be trying to read something written on the wall behind me for a few seconds and then he smiled. At the same moment, or nearly, Martin began driving another nail into the wall. The conversation was over. After a few years in this business you get to recognize punctuation like that.

I walked along Church Street and cut across Market Square to King, where a small coffee shop much frequented by the legal profession runs an emergency tea-and-bun service for refugees from the County Court House. I ordered a cup of tea and vaguely looked around to see who was there. I'd often been able to get free legal advice both at the counter and at the chipped vinyl tables. But today the profession must have been off burying a QC or chasing ambulances. The place was deserted. It was too early for the high-school kids too. That meant the telephone was free and the noise level was such that I would be able to hear both sides of the conversation I was planning to have.

"Hello?"

"Ella, it's me." There was a pause at the other end of the line. I could feel my self-image deflating like a discarded birthday balloon. "Benny Cooperman," I added.

"Oh, that 'me.' What can I do for you?"

"How would I look up information about a British Army officer?"

"What century?"

"The present. He was active around 1955-60."

"Living or dead?"

"I don't know."

"Well," Ella seemed to add about three additional "ls" as she drew out the word to give her a moment to think. "Well, in the last act of *The Importance of Being Earnest*, Jack Worthing consults something called the *Army Lists* to discover his father's name."

"What's that got to do with anything?" I should never quarrel with other people's thought processes. Knowing how peculiar my own are, I should allow free rein to the ways and means Ella Beames has of placing misplaced information. "I mean, Ella, are the *Army Lists* still published?"

"I'll have to check and I'll call you back. Who is it you're interested in?"

"He was a major in Cyprus during the troubles there. His name is, or was, Timothy Bell. That's all I know about him except that he served in Palestine before going off on half-pay. He went active again in the fifties to do his bit in Cyprus."

"I've got that down. I'll call you. Are you at your office?"

"No, Ella, but I will be in an hour's time."

"I'll try you there. Anything else?"

"That's it and thanks." She hung up and I went back to my tea. There was little heat in the metal pot, and I spilled most of the remaining tea into the saucer and onto the table. This pot, like all commercial teapots I've encountered, dripped everywhere. Where was the inventor of the dripless metal teapot? I pondered this while sipping the tepid stuff. As I paid up and left, a bunch of teenagers with designer hair came in in a clump and took possession of half of the tables. Generally I'm not in a hurry to greet middle age, but I was happy, just then, to be out of my early years. I might be sorry later, but I didn't think I could wrestle with the rigid rules of being uniformly unconventional.

An hour later, good as my word, I was sitting in my

place of business. Some ideas had started percolating
in my head and I made a couple of calls to find things
out. One of these was to Bill Palmer at the *Beacon*.

"Palmer here." He had a tone in his voice that told
me that he had a pencil poised above a pad of paper.
But that's the romantic in me. Such props are probably outlawed in a modern newspaper office.

"Bill, it's Benny Cooperman."

"Oh, hi, Benny. What's up?"

"Bill, I'm just playing a hunch and it may not lead
anywhere, but it would help for me to know as much
as I can find out about Major Tim Bell of the British
Security Police in Cyprus."

"Tim Bell! The Ghost of Christmas Past? He's been
dead for—let me see, nearly three years. It was in the
London *Times*."

"I want to know whatever you know about him."

"Can I call you back or meet over a drink?"

"Sure, what about at the Harding House in, say, half
an hour?"

"Hey, you must want this pretty bad. I'll try to get
away from here for a few minutes. See you then."

I still wasn't sure what kind of bee it was that was
buzzing around inside my hat, and I didn't know what
it had to do with what happened to Pambos last Tuesday night. All I knew was that I had an itch at the back
of my knees and that it seemed to ease off when I began thinking in this direction. It was now an hour and
a quarter since I'd talked to Ella at the library. She was
late. I began to imagine her research interrupted by a
couple of hoods in black balaclavas. Ella put up quite
a struggle, but in the end they stuffed her still-fighting
frame into an unmarked vw van and headed off out
of town. I was trying to think what to do to get her out
of their clutches, when the phone rang. It was Ella. I
didn't ask her how she'd escaped from the sinister van

heading for the international border, not because I'd escaped from my own daydream, but because Anna Abraham was suddenly back in my office.

"Hello," I said to Ella, while smiling at Anna. "I'm glad to hear from you so soon." With my hand over the phone I told Anna that this was important and to sit down. But she didn't. She began pacing my office and examining everything in sight, including the bald manikins.

"Benny," Ella said, "the library's no good on a thing like this. I had to go to my personal network of experts."

"Like who?"

"Never mind. Suffice it to say that he's a retired military man living a few miles out of town."

"Niagara-on-the-Lake?" I heard Ella breathe in a gulp of air. "I thought so. What did the Brigadier have to tell you?"

"I'm not admitting anything, Benny. I've always protected my sources."

"Okay, I won't quiz you about him."

"Well, your major was retired with the rank of lieutenant-colonel from the Royal North Surrey Regiment when he died in September 1985. My source also checked his scrapbook of obits from the *Times*. Col. Bell was living in Walmer, near Deal, England, when he died of a massive heart attack."

"Damn it! Are you sure about that date?"

"Oh yes, I got everything down straight. September 12, 1985."

"Well, thanks anyway. I was looking for another date."

"Sorry."

"Well, thanks, Ella. I owe you."

"Yes, and if I ever asked you to pay up, where would I be?"

"Out of my debt, Ella. Thanks again."

Anna was staring at me when I got clear of the phone.

"I thought you worked scientifically, like Sherlock Holmes."

"I work any way I can. Books are easier and neater than real life. I had a theory and it just blew up in my face. So now I have to get another one. I'm only human. I'm sorry to see the first theory go. There was a sort of neatness to it."

The word "neatness" sparked a nerve, and I remembered the fifty-dollar tip Anna's old man had sent me. It had been bothering my sense of the neatness of our professional relationship. I knew that the feeling would stay with me until I gave it back. I wasn't suddenly against money and the free enterprise system, I was simply trying to keep complications to a minimum. With Anna looking on, I addressed an envelope to her father, slipped in the pretty pink bill, wrapped in a sheet of my office stationery, and sealed it.

"What's that all about?" Anna asked as I pasted on a stamp. It's a smart girl who can read upside-down.

"Just unfinished business," I said.

She was back to wearing jeans and a blue denim jacket. But the blouse underneath was silky and white. To me, it clashed with the motorcycle-look, but what do I know about fashions today? I haven't learned a thing since Pa retired and closed the store downstairs. "Can I buy you a beer?" I asked her, and she looked like I asked to borrow her toothbrush. "It's the drink of the people," I said. "You might find it amusing."

"Oh, shut up and get off my back," she said. "Shall we?" She opened the door and I followed.

Chapter Twenty-Two

The Harding House is a Grantham institution. It should have a brass plaque outside telling the world that this is the pub where Ned Evans planned his productions of *A Midsummer Night's Dream* and *Richard III* over several gallons of draught beer. If the owner is ever tempted to tear down this watering place in order to put up another glass-fronted six-storey box, the city fathers would come running. They'd chain themselves to those venerable doors and shout to the bulldozers outside, "You shall not pass!" At night I could sleep secure in the knowledge that the good conservatives of Grantham conserve the best of the past before running to the shoddy, the untried and the novel.

From my chair at one of those historic round tables, I could see the door that Bill Palmer would use coming into the pub. It was a minor distraction from my view of Jonah Abraham's lovely daughter who shared my table. At first I thought she was wearing no make-up, but closer inspection showed that it was there, but there with a subtle hand. The waiter in a blue apron hovered near and dropped four draughts and made change from his apron before dancing away to deliver more glasses and bottles in the more sedate of the two beverage rooms. This, the "Ladies and Escorts," was relatively quiet, the people well-behaved and temperate. On the "Gents" side of the partition fights sometimes broke out, the language was colourful and the consumption up to the limit of the busy plumbing. Anna made a brave show of downing her first draught in one gulp. Her cheeks turned a pretty pink and she tried to smile at me over the rim of her glass. "I think that gesture is restricted to fine wines," I said.

"Now who's the snob?" She put her glass down and then began making patterns with the wet rings on the red table top. "Have you found that list for Daddy yet, Benny?" she said, changing her tack before we got into that familiar wrangle again. I put a hand over hers.

"Look, Anna, we're only going to fight if you keep trying to pump me for information. I'll tell your father what I've learned as soon as I have things figured out. That might take a few more days, it may take a few more weeks. Some cases go on for months. This one won't. You can tell him that at least. Did you tell him about the parking lot last night?"

"Of course."

"And he said stay clear of me, right?"

"He... How did you know?"

"Maybe I've got the makings of a father myself. Maybe I was listening on the clothesline."

"I can't stay long, I've got to go home to change."

"You're going out?" As soon as I'd asked the question, I guessed the answer, but I let her give me her version.

"Yes, I'm going out. I do occasionally do my social duty, you know." She looked like she wanted to tease me more but I put a spike in her cannon.

"Have you been back there since he died?"

"No. You think you know everything. Will you be there?"

"I wouldn't miss it. I'll even put on my good suit for the occasion."

"Good. It'll be nice to see you dressed up." It was a disarming smile and I was responding to it when Bill

Palmer came through the door on the "Gents" side looking for me. "What's the matter?" I didn't know my face was so responsive.

"It's just a man looking for me. He's been digging up information I thought was going to be useful half an hour ago. Now, it's just information, but I have to see him anyway."

Anna got up and tried to peer through to the men's side. "Before I go, I should give you this." She dug into a pocket and brought out an envelope with my name on it. "Daddy wanted me to give it to you." She passed it over. "Another payday so soon," she said. I ignored the remark. I was learning how to talk to Anna Abraham.

"I'll look for you tonight," I said. On her way out, Anna paused at the door, looking back into the "Gents" to see if she could see who it was I was going to talk to next. Palmer must have blended into the crowd. From Anna's expression I could see that she was leaving the pub disappointed. Even in personal defeat, however, her passage across the room gave delight: patrons lifted their faces from a contemplation of their draught beer. A moment later and she had found the fresh air on James Street. I left a few coins on the round table top and made my way next door.

Palmer was in a narrow passage near the service centre. He was sitting closer to the smell of chips and the sound of beer being opened and poured, but away from the din in the main part of the room. There were already two amber glasses at his table.

"Well," he said. He was using a trick I thought was my own: you raise your eyebrows, cluck your tongue, say "well" in a certain tone and the confession of guilt follows automatically. I found myself about to explain, then recognized the position and enjoyed the joke of having the tables turned on me by another pro.

"Were you able to dig up your files?" I asked.

"I found a few things. I haven't been through this stuff in a few years. Not since..."

"Kiriakis was bugging you about Guenyeli."

"Right. He was pretty obsessed with it. You know what he was like."

"Did you ever actually meet Bell? I know you talked to him, but..."

"Meet him? Sure. I even went sailing with him a few times while I was trying to get information. He kept a dinghy in Kyrenia. That's a little harbour on the north coast, a few miles from Nicosia. Tim was crazy about boats, claimed to be a typical Englishman in that." Bill handed me a sheaf of paper in a faded green file folder. Inside were a dozen pages of onionskin paper. I only glanced at them. I thanked him but he made no sign of hurrying off back to the paper. "He went out to Palestine with the Royal North Surreys. He was regular army, Sandhurst and all that. They bumped him up to a higher rank before he retired. He never won any big decorations, just the regular ones most officers get when they've actually been in the field. It's all in there."

"What was he like?"

"Oh, Tim was a 'matey' sort; liked his pint in private and whisky and soda in public, liked the water, knew a hell of a lot about the island—archaeological stuff. He was the man to see if you were planning a trip. He knew the good roads and the churches to look at. Not that we were doing much sightseeing in those days. I didn't see much of him after my pieces began to appear. Never much liked him."

"He was living in Walmer, near Deal, when he died. Where's that?"

"Close to Dover."

"Ah, the white cliffs and all that?"

"I guess so. I once got a letter from him from there.

He talked about how he and another retired major would walk out to the local of an evening. He said that they'd become characters: both of the same age, both ex-army, both with the same sort of regimental moustaches and both called Tim. 'Tim and Sir Tim' they called them as they wound their way home after an evening's booze-up."

"Sounds cozy. I suspect they were both unmarried or widowed, right?"

"One of each, I think. But I don't know which was which. It was a sad letter. The only one he ever wrote me. He was upset because his pal had just died."

"Heart attack after passing the port?"

"Nothing so traditional: hit and run on the road a half-mile from the pub."

"Poor old fellow. Here's to him. Here's to both of them." I lifted my glass of beer, then both of us set our glasses down without sipping. I guess we both remembered Guenyeli at the same moment.

It's funny thinking of people and the things they do. I've sat in dozens of courtrooms trying to reconcile the face in the prisoner's dock with the crimes that have been committed. I read a mystery once about a policeman who tried to sum up faces from history and decide whether they belonged on the bench or in the dock. It seems to me it's even harder than that. We are all so full of worn-out ideas about villainy. When you look at pictures of Eichmann in his glass booth in Jerusalem, what do you see? All I see is the ordinariness of the face. The sort of face you see on the street every day. If Guenyeli was an evil act—and I haven't heard the army's side of the story: maybe it was an important strategic act that helped shorten the emergency, I don't know—it was executed by Tim Bell, who spent his last years in quiet retirement. Nobody ever branded him a killer. No clubs were closed to him.

He got his pint every evening with his old friend and an obit in the *Times* when his time came. If a neighbour tapped him on the shoulder in that pub and said, "Excuse me, aren't you the chap who arranged the affair at Guenyeli?" would Bell have kept his mouth shut, changed tables, or quoted the man in the glass booth: "I was just following orders"?

Bill Palmer must have been thinking about Bell too. Neither of us said anything for a long time. When he began making motions to leave, I promised to take good care of his file and return it in a day or two. "Take your time," he said. "All of the people concerned are dead now. It's all water over the falls."

It was his saying that they were dead that did it. It clicked into place and I understood. Bill must have thought I'd had my limit. In fact I nearly knocked over an empty glass with my elbow. "Bill, when did Sir Tim get hit by that car?"

"What? Why it was in July of 1985."

"That's great! That's wonderful!"

"Well, I bet he didn't think so!"

After Bill left to return to his word-processor at the *Beacon*, I opened the fat envelope Anna had given me from Jonah. There were two letters inside: the first was a brief note from Davies, Dickens, Fowler and Butler (signed per Michael Bodkin) stating that George Tallon was executor in the estate of his brother Arthur; the second was neatly typed under the letterhead of Consolidated Galvin. It read:

To the Director of Medical Records
Grantham General Hospital

Dear Miss Rilski,

I would like to authorize Benjamin Cooperman, a licensed private investigator of this city, to have access to all medical and health records relating to the death of my brother, Arthur Tallon, who died on 29 February of this year. As Arthur's next of kin and as his executor, I am asking you to aid Mr Cooperman in his research into this matter.

Yours sincerely,
George F. Tallon

Encl.

I vaguely remembered asking Abraham to get me access to Tallon's medical file. Now, I didn't know what to do with it. I put the letters back into the envelope and buried the evidence in my inside breast pocket, next to my heart, and hoped that something would occur to me.

I counted the change in my pocket. There wasn't enough for what I had in mind, so I complimented the waiter on his service and exchanged a two-dollar bill for eight quarters. He made me pay for this courtesy by forcing me to listen to a diatribe levelled at his employer behind the bar. With no sign of burning ears, the bartender kept moving around in his cramped kingdom, filling glasses of amber draught beer and opening imported and domestic bottles. Not a movement was wasted as he danced along the invisible duckboards.

Back out on James Street, the world looked bright and artificial after the pub. I collected the car and drove to Papertown to make two phone calls. The first could have been made from my office, but I was too excited about the idea behind it to wait until I was back in my own neighbourhood. I placed the call from a pay phone across the street from the Kesagami-Copeland Paper Mills through the overseas operator. She took the details of my credit card and passed me on. The English operator assisted me in getting the officer in charge at the police station in Deal, Kent. It didn't take long. I talked to the desk sergeant for nearly ten minutes, as our voices bounced from dish to satellite and back again. Harry Armstrong's local knowledge was nearly inexhaustible.

My second call was both cheaper and shorter. I dialled the number of the paper mill and asked to speak to Alex Favell. It seemed more than a month since I'd first talked to him and not three days. Let's see, that was after I'd driven Mary MacCulloch to the golf club and allowed myself to drink while on duty. This time my approach was more cautious. Favell or somebody— it could be any of the people I'd run into since Monday—was cooking up trouble for me, just enough to interfere with the free and open way in which I've been able to operate in this town. He might be arranging for me to buy my second set of tires in two days. He might be having a word with a friendly alderman, or maybe the mayor himself. Savas warned me that he'd had complaints about me and my unprofessional manners and practices. Gilbert and Sullivan were right about policemen. Poor Savas is always getting it in the neck about me. All he had to do to put a permanent wrench in my spokes was to send a nasty note to the Registrar of Private Investigators, care of the Provincial Police. Pa would like that, of course. I could then find a real career, like helping my cousin Melvyn search titles and serve summonses and subpoenas. I think I'd rather set sail in a rowboat and hire on to assist Harry Armstrong in Kent.

"Hello?" It was Alex Favell at last.

"Mr Favell, it's Benny Cooperman again. I'd like to talk to you." It was just five o'clock. I was hoping to irritate him enough to expand my knowledge of the puzzle. I wasn't sure how he might do it, but I hoped that I would be ready for him.

"You! Cooperman. I have nothing further to say to you. Why don't you try to get honest employment, Mr Cooperman? Why don't you get off my back? I can't talk. I've an appointment and I'm just leaving. I've no time for you. Goodbye!" The phone went dead with a loud click in my ear. The voice that had suddenly vanished from the other end recalled to me that earlier meeting. I could see his face, the bald dome several inches above my own head. He worried me. People who live at the edge of their tempers worry me. Favell either lived a very restricted life or he was angry a good deal of his time.

And there he was. Just as I'd hoped, right on time. I'd made my call from a booth with a good view of the front door of the executive entrance of the paper mill. He came out puffing like he'd just run up three flights of stairs and the ladder of success. His Lincoln was in the most preferred parking space. It came with a sa-lute and bow from the parking attendant. It was either a bow or he was making sure it was Favell who was driving off in the familiar car.

It wasn't hard following Favell's Lincoln from Davis Road to the highway. He was a steady driver; it almost seemed that he was a chauffeur driving on somebody else's instructions: "Forty-five miles an hour, James, and please raise the temperature to sixty-five. Vents open, please." I kept well to the rear, letting some rush-hour Fords and GMs come between us. He turned off at the tunnel road and I followed him under the Welland Canal and up again into the light on the other side. Af-ter another mile, he took the right lane that took him smoothly to Highway 406 heading north. I was still be-hind him as he raised his speed to the limit when he went over the Glendale Avenue bridge. Now the six-lane road dipped into the ravine of the old canal where it entered Grantham through a back door. Quickly we curved around the backs of the stores along St Andrew Street, then found ourselves already well up Ontario and crossing the old canal near Welland Vale. Here, Favell abandoned the 406 and returned to Ontario Street for the drive through the industrial confusion before reaching the QEW, the Toronto highway. I couldn't figure out why he chose the crowded two-lane road at rush-hour over the six-lane freeway, until he pulled into a service station for a fill-up. I took a right turn at the first opportunity and found myself at a family restaurant offering coffee with artificial cream and no doubt pancakes and waffles with artificial maple syrup. I didn't have time to order either of these, but I did pick up a fresh pack of Player's Medium. I was back in the car with my motor running when the Lincoln went by me with its windshield freshly washed and the fuel supply restored.

Favell took a left turn at the Embassy, a hotel and pub that featured the same country music that sometimes played the City House. As I came around the corner, I recognized some of the names on the crooked sign. Favell took the road over the old canal bridges into Port Richmond with its views of lighthouses and piers. The boats in the marina were tucked under canvas where they would stay for another few weeks before the summer would claim them. Marie's Lobster Restaurant had its sign illuminated already. I read the notice that said the place would be closed on Good Friday. I guess that was coming up on the morrow. I was glad I wasn't in Dublin. Frank Bushmill had often told me what a fearsome place Dublin is on Good Friday. "A man could starve to death," he'd said. "Everything's closed up tighter than a Kerryman at a wake." Favell turned from Canal Street into Lock and went up the hill. Traffic was thinner here, so I didn't get too close. I was glad of that, because in a moment his brakes lit up and the car came to rest at the curb near the intersection of Lock and Main. I slipped over to the curb as well and turned off the motor.

In my rear-view mirror, I could see the harbour below me and part of the remaining section of Lock One of the old canal. In the fading light it looked rather forlorn and neglected. Ahead of me, Favell was looking up and down the street to see if he'd been followed. I was getting more and more interested all the time. So were the seagulls, which slid down to the sidewalk looking for crumbs, acting like they were pigeons. Favell walked up the hill another four or five houses and then turned in to a pebble-dashed bungalow with green trim around the windows and a screen door that went back to those pre-war days when everything cost five cents and there was no sales tax. I pulled out a sketching pad and a hat from the back seat of the Olds and got out. Working the stiffness out of my legs, I walked down to the waterfront. I sat on an ancient bollard from where I could see what was going on up the hill and attract little attention. The streets were as bare as the marina was of aluminum masts riding at anchor. A character reeled out of the beverage room in the Mansion House at the end of Canal Street. He ignored me and the rest of creation until he came to rest in some bushes behind an abandoned freight shed. Here he urinated loudly against the galvanized siding. Nobody noticed him either.

Favell was inside the house up the street for forty-five minutes by my watch and three lame attempts to render the yacht club across the harbour. When the door opened and he came down the steps, I was ready to follow him again, and I would have, except for the fact that the woman in the silk dressing gown who followed him out onto the porch waving goodbye was

Mary MacCulloch. Favell got into his car and drove off, Mary watched him go and returned to the house. I stayed put. I smoked a row of cigarettes, waiting with my eyes fixed most of the time on the quiet bungalow up the hill.

Opposite me, a coal barge was unloading across the slate grey water. Gulls were grabbing at something dead in the corner of the harbour where garbage collected. I didn't want to see what it was. For the first time I noticed a tiny wooden hut on the top of the old lock. It must have been a shelter or summer lock-keeper's hut —a stone house across the road was the restored residence of the lock-keeper. The shelter was a simple structure with tidy lines and I became fond of it at once. I tried a sketch and then another. It helped to pass the time. My old art teacher, the one I had a handful of lessons from when I was in high school, was also an expert on the canal. He knew where each of the old locks had been, and what the land looked like before the roads were relocated to accommodate four successive Welland Canals. He knew where there were tunnels under abandoned locks and bridges with grown-over roads running under them. Some of these places made great swimming holes when summer heat lowered standards of hygiene and raised the need to cool off. Nowadays the kids swim in public swimming pools, and the old weir and the place we called "The Showers" are left to birdwatchers and hikers.

I was on the point of calling it a day here in Port Richmond. If I wanted to attend the *vernissage* at the Contemporary Gallery, I should be making plans to have a shower and change. I didn't know what people wore to things like that. I had one suit that had to do for all fancy social occasions. I put away the sketchbook and took a last friendly look at the shelter by the lock and got up, unexpectedly stiff, from the bollard. I was about to cross Canal Street, when a dark Volvo parked near Marie's Restaurant. Paddy Miles got out. I felt a little peculiar seeing him, since his shindig at the gallery was the most recent thought in my head. It was almost as though my thought had drawn him into the picture.

I stayed with my feet on the curb, for all the world an admirer of the fine line of restaurants and stores that faced the harbour. Today they were pubs, bookstores and eateries; a hundred years ago they were ship chandlers and hotels for homesick sailors. Miles walked up the hill and turned in to the bungalow I'd been watching. He was carrying a narrow brown paper bag in his hand, the sort men take when they go calling on women they are not married to. I crossed the street and kept the line of parked cars between me and Paddy Miles as he rang the doorbell. After a few seconds, through a windshield decorated with plastic religious symbols and two parking tickets, I saw a startled Mary MacCulloch open the front door. Miles waved the paper bag, Mary grinned and both went inside. I unlocked my own car and made myself comfortable in the front seat.

For half an hour I played with some chess problems in a book I kept in the glove compartment. There is a lot of waiting around in this business. That's why I liked watching private eyes in the movies. They never have to wait for anything. And TV is just as good. From the opening credits to the last commercial or the fade-out, the hero is on the run and never even has trouble finding a parking space. In real life, investigators tend to put on weight because of all the sitting around and waiting we do. The chess problems helped me pass the time, and I never remembered the solutions from one long wait to the next. "Black to move and mate in three." I tried it out in my head, while beginning to work down the second row of cigarettes in my pack. Just past the thirty-minute mark, which made this a short wait, the door opened on the front porch and Paddy Miles came out. He wasn't exactly running, but he was going at a fair clip for a man having just made a social call. Then I remembered that he had his gallery opening to get to. He walked down the street, missing the chance to catch me by looking straight ahead of him as he went, and got in the Volvo at Marie's. He drove off in the only really useful direction: back to Grantham.

For a moment I thought of following him, but as I replaced the chess book, I knew I could catch him again if I wanted him. The more interesting prospect was right on the street. I climbed out of the car and locked it, then walked up the front steps and rang the doorbell of Mary MacCulloch's little hideaway.

There must be thousands of houses like this one in the Grantham area. It was tiny by any standard, but with the pebble-dashed stucco exterior and the brave little front window, it looked like somebody's dream of independence and enterprise. I liked the echo of my feet on the wooden porch as I put in the minutes waiting for Mary to come to the door. I rang again. No answer. It wasn't as if she had miles of corridors to hurry through and stairs to run down: it was a bungalow. The bell was in working order, I could practically hear it echo from across the street. I tried again, and still there was no response from inside. I must have tried the bell seven or eight times before I started getting those old radio program worries that come with unanswered doorbells. I thought of earlier this week, finding Pambos. That's when I decided to try the door. It was practically broad daylight, so I couldn't be charged with Breaking and Entering. I don't think so, anyway. Besides, I knew the occupant. And what was I going to steal? I was just doing my job. Mary was one of my suspects and I thought of a whole horror movie of things that might have happened to her while I was trying to get black to mate in three moves. The door came open in my hand to a little pressure. My stomach was beginning to feel vulnerable. I closed the door behind me and walked along the cheaply decked out corridor towards the light coming from the back of the house. The feeling at the back of my knees and below my rib-cage signalled trouble. So why was I still walking down the hall towards the kitchen?

Chapter Twenty-Three

S he was sitting at the kitchen table wearing a pink T-shirt two sizes too small and bikini panties with a Sony FM Walkman clipped to her hip. There was a lot of Mary MacCulloch showing. The silk dressing gown covered convention and little else. There was a drink on the table in front of her. Most of it had disappeared into the woman now moving in time with the rock music that spilled out of her headset. She was having a ball all by herself. She didn't even look up when I came into the room.

"Mrs MacCulloch? Mary? Are you okay?" She looked up with a happy smile on her face. For a moment her forehead creased as she plumbed her memory for my name, and then the grin returned.

"Benny! How the hell are you?" she said, shaking my hand formally. "Come in and join the faculty wives. We're very, very informal tonight. Let me get rid of the earphones." She removed the headset and placed the Walkman on the white vinyl table top. "What did you say?" The music spillover from the headset stopped abruptly as she clicked off the radio. "Tell me," she asked, "could you use a drink? You look cold. Like a man who could use a little stimulation." The bottle Paddy Miles had brought was standing half-empty on the table. She pulled down a tumbler from a shelf above her without having to get up, and filled it with about three ounces more rye than I consume in as many weeks.

"Didn't that old charmer Paddy Miles have a drink with you? I just saw him leaving."

"Sure he did," Mary said. "We even drank a toast. What was it? What the hell was it? 'To...' What was it to? Ah, I remember," she said, lifting high her glass once more, "'Here's to crime!' That's what he said. Here's to crime, Benny." I lifted my glass and joined in.

"To crime," I said, but I didn't drink from my glass yet. Something wasn't right here. Paddy Miles had brought the bottle, he and Mary had consumed most of it, and now there was no sign that he had been there at all. Why would he clear away his glass, wash it up and return it to its shelf?

"Benny, drink up!" she admonished me from her side of the table, while trying to pile her hair back on top of her head with her free hand. It wasn't working, but she didn't seem to notice. "Benny, what's another toast? Give us a good one."

"Here's to Wallace Lamb," I offered and it didn't even make Mary blink. She seemed in a world of her own. If it included me, it was at a distance. She looked at me like I was sitting across a ballroom. Something was funny about the set-up.

On the table in front of Mary I found a scrap of note-paper. It had been torn neatly both above and below the writing, which read: *Ending it all*.

"Do you like sushi, Benny?"

"Sushi? What's sushi?" She was leaning with both elbows on the table and her head wobbled towards the middle of the table. "Mary, where did you get this scrap of paper? Is this your handwriting?"

"Lemme see." I handed it to her and she held it up very close to her face. "Paddy asked me to make tags for a bunch of the pictures he's got in tonight's show. He said he likes the way I write. I used to do calligraphy, you know. I bet you never even knew that, and

you're supposed to be some kind of detective or something." She looked at the paper again. "Ending it all,"
she said. "Very melodramatic. He took the rest of them
with him. I must have written out twenty of them. Do
you like sushi?"

"Let me smell your glass." I reached over and took
it from her.

"Hey! I was using that!" I took a sniff. I got the smell
of the rye first, but my second sniff took in something
faintly chemical, like the glass had been disinfected in
a strong solution of caustic.

"Do you have any sleeping pills here?" I had to repeat
the question.

"Sure. You're not bad looking, Benny. Did you know
that? In your oh-so-quiet way." I reached over and took
her hand, not because I had suddenly seen the beauty of her mind and body, but because, by holding it
tightly, I could get a better share of her attention.

"Where are they? The sleeping pills?" She regarded
me with strange eyes, like I was changing the subject
unreasonably. "Where are the damned sleeping pills,
Mary?"

"Bedroom, of course." I got up and rushed through
the bungalow looking for the bedroom. I didn't have
to run far through this oddly furnished love-nest with
its second-hand furniture and framed prints. The phial of pills looked empty even from across the room. It
lay on its side with the top and a cotton wad next to
it. I checked and I was right. The cotton ball smelled
a little like the caustic scent of the rye Mary was sipping. I came back to the kitchen. Mary's head was now
resting on her arm flung across the table.

"Mary, where's the telephone?" Again, I had to repeat
the question.

She looked at me like I'd just reappeared in her life
after thirty years' absence. "Fr-front room, Benny. Don't

phone and tell anybody I'm here. That's the big secret. Shhhh!" I didn't wait to hear more, but returned along the corridor to the front room with its brushed plush easy chairs and couch. The telephone was where you'd expect to find the television set. I dialled the number for the Emergency Service. Behind me I could hear Mary going on about the sushi bars in Toronto and the lack of them in Grantham. It was only then, while waiting to be connected with the ambulance service, that I remembered what sushi was. I'd never had any, but I had a picture of people sitting around a bar eating raw fish off wooden rafts passing for platters. Once I got the dispatcher I discovered that I didn't know the street number. I had to dash to the porch to read it off the front of the house. I thought I should be able to behave like a tried professional, but I found myself sweating and giving unnecessary details over the phone. At least I repeated the important information:

"Hurry, it's a drug overdose!" I was assured that the vehicle's status was now active. I hope he meant it was on its way. I hung up and returned to the kitchen. Mary was quiet, with her head buried in her crossed arms on the table. I slapped her face twice before she opened her eyes slightly.

"Hey! Quit that!"

"Mary, I want to talk to you. I need to know all about you. Mary! Wake up! Don't go to sleep while I'm talking!" She stirred, then closed her eyes again. I swatted her again until her eyes came open again with irritation showing.

"It's raw fish-sh-sh," she said. "Sing a song of sixpence, a belly full of rye. Raw tuna's best. You ever looked a monkfish in the eye?"

"Mary, try to get up!" I lifted her to her feet. I tried to wrap the dressing gown around her so that I could concentrate on business. "Come on, Mary. We'll go for a walk." I tried to take a step with her and we fell over in a pile on the linoleum.

"Hey, buster! What's the big idea?" I tried to unscramble myself from her and got to my knees. She was out again. I couldn't get her off the floor. I tried, but I had to face facts. I tried slapping again, but it wasn't reaching her. She curled up into a fetal position on her side. I got to my feet and tried to imagine what thinking clearly might be like. I went back to the bedroom and pocketed the phial that had contained the pills. I collected some clothes into the suitcase under the bed and went back to where I'd left her. I shouted at her, calling her name loudly, but it made no dent in her unconsciousness. I gave up and sat down in one of the straight-backed kitchen chairs. I could hear the sound of the ambulance coming in the distance. That made me feel better.

The boys in white got Mary MacCulloch into their ambulance. I remember her hunched shoulders as they lifted her to the stretcher. They were able to rouse her slightly. An eye blinked and I crossed my fingers as they slammed the double doors and hurried off in the direction of the General. I took a brief look around the house without turning up much of interest. It was clear that bills weren't paid from there. There were no stacks of last year's Christmas cards in the back of a drawer. For the most part, the closets were empty. Alex Favell had made sure that if anybody could link him to this place it would have to be the forensic experts in Toronto. I tucked the bottle of open rye under my arm and pocketed the suicide note. I even checked to see that the stove and the lights were out before I locked the door and headed for the car.

The waiting room at the General is not a place I like to spend much time in. In spite of efforts to take the institutional curse off the place, it remained, under the curtains and the assortment of recent magazines, exactly what it was. Across from me a middle-aged couple sat as close together as the seats would allow. She was staring a hole in the wall; he worked a set of amber worry beads between his large worn thumbs. A fourteen-year-old kid sat bolt upright every time an intern or orderly walked by the glass windows that looked out into the corridor of the Emergency Department. I'd already started distorting time; hospitals do that to me. When I arrived, I handed in the empty pill phial and gave the nurse on duty my health insurance number. When they thought that Mary was my wife, I let them go on thinking it. I could clear up any misunderstanding later on. I sat in a seat watching the old couple and the teenager. It probably calmed me to be a watcher instead of a waiter like them. It suited my personality. I went through to my last cigarette in spite of the intimidating signs that warned of the evils of smoking. I read all the posters. Even as a smoker, I agreed with the message. I'd been promising to give up the filthy habit as soon as things calmed down and I could give it the attention it deserved. But I still resented the superior moral tone the posters took. Why couldn't they find a way to say what they had to say without sounding smug and self-righteous?

"Are you Mr Cooperman?" I got to my feet and found myself face to face with a good-looking Chinese in operating room greens. A surgical mask hung around his neck, and his hair was still covered by a green cap. I guess by standing up, I acknowledged his identification. He went on. "I'm Dr Leung," he said. "I just left your wife and I want to tell you that we think she's going to be all right. She's a very lucky woman, you know."

"She's going to be all right?" I know he'd just said that, but sometimes you just have to say the things that pop into your head without editing or polishing them.

"You're Dr Young?" I was still trying to take hold.

"Not Young, Leung. Kiu Leung," he said patiently. "If you'd delayed another half-hour, I don't think we could be so certain of recovery. I could have been giving you some very bad news. You understand?" I nodded gravely, which seemed to be what was required of me. Did he think that we were playing games with those pills and one went off by accident or what? "We had to pump her out thoroughly. She's going to feel like hell for a couple of days. We'll be admitting her and there will be more information later tonight, if you'd like to check in. You can see her now, if you want, but they'll be moving her to a room very soon."

I never seem to take in more than about forty percent of what a doctor tells me. If I concentrate on getting the name, I lose his message. If I get the message, I can never locate the doctor again. I should always leave my office with a wire taped to my liver so that everything will be recorded and nothing will be lost. Even while I was thinking this, I was missing something Dr Leung was saying. "Now, Mr Cooperman, I'd like to get the details of how this accident happened. Who prescribed these pills in the first place? The combination of the drugs and the alcohol gave us a very hard time in there."

"Well, I'm not sure I know about all that. But could I get back to you when I've got the details fixed in my own head? Right now, I have to get in touch with the police. Can I use your phone?" He pulled at his chin, trying to decide whether or not to quiz me further on this or to return to his patient. He indicated a phone inside the nurses' station and I helped myself. When I looked up again, Dr Kiu Leung had gone through one of the doors back into the wonderful world of medicine and the thousand-and-one stories that unfold every day in a general hospital. I called Savas.

I could say I went up to the Medical Records Department to kill time while waiting for Savas to arrive, but the results deserve a better place in the record than that. And it didn't hurt when I saw that the clerk on duty was Alison Simmers. She read the letters from George Tallon and his lawyer, then disappeared into the office of her supervisor after asking me if I had seen my brother, Sam, recently. I confessed that it had been some weeks. While she was gone I realized that it was really several months since I'd been to Toronto to see him. By the time she returned, I was quite homesick for my older brother and feeling guilty about not getting to Toronto more often.

Alison brought me the file and showed me where I could sit down while looking through the forms. Basically, there were three of these: the Emergency Report, an Itemized Clothing List and Admission Form. Tallon had arrived by stretcher from an ambulance, had been treated in Emerge by Dr Kiu Leung, of recent acquaintance, but had died before he could be properly admitted. I tried to read about all the work the resuscitation team had tried on him, but I couldn't make out much of it. It looked like they tried everything in the book. The clothing list included the following items of interest. The printed words were accompanied by numbers and check marks in ballpoint pen:

VALUABLES

✓ rings	*3*	handbag	
✓ watch	*Seiko*	medical alert	
✓ money	*$187.56*	✓ keys	*3*
✓ wallet - credit cards *2*		✓ other	*gold piece foreign coin*

This list was used with unconscious, very ill and confused patients. I saw further down the page that Tallon did not have a prosthesis listed—no eye, wig, dentures-upper/lower, or cane. Alison explained to me that Tallon couldn't have come in DOA, or the file would never have been made up. "If they aren't viable when they get to Emerge, there's no Emergency Report. We just log those cases. They don't get numbers except their order in the log." She leaned in closer and read over my shoulder. "This was a routine cardiac infarction, a heart attack. See, there was no autopsy ordered and it wasn't referred to the coroner. But I see they took some tissue samples, which they'll probably still have around. When did this happen? Oh, the end of February. Oh, yes, we'll still have them at the Tissue Centre."

I thanked Alison and asked after her sisters. That too helped to pass the time. My thoughts began to stray to the patient now in Dr Leung's care on the floor below.

Twenty minutes after I started bringing Chris Savas up to date on what had been going on, there was a uniformed guard reading *Sports Illustrated* outside Mary MacCulloch's door. Savas suggested that we both leave in his car for the destination he had in mind. I left the Olds in the hospital parking lot with an old parking ticket under the windshield wiper. Chris gave me a long-suffering glance and cleared the family belongings off the front seat for me. He headed in the direction of the Contemporary Gallery on Church Street.

"I've had a belly-full of this case," he told me. "Why don't these people leave crime to the people whose business it really is?" I grunted agreement and kept my eye on the road. I'm a terrible passenger. Chris went on soliloquizing and I kept grunting approval when it suited me and kept silent when, as he sometimes does, he went overboard. "Knocking off one another and then trying to start a fresh page by faking a suicide! Jeez! And I can't even *look* at some of the pictures this is all about. What's wrong with *September Morn* all of a sudden? Don't tell me I'm short of couth. I got couth I never used yet." He drove down Queenston Road and took the turn to the right onto Church Street where the last horse trough in town still sits at the point of a tiny green park. We drove past the synagogue at the corner of Calvin, passed Welland and headed up the slight rise where King Street begins. As we got closer to the gallery, we began to see parked cars under the streetlights. Grantham is a town that rolls up its streets after six at night, but tonight, somebody had a licence to run a major party. Every big car in town was parked in a row on both sides of a usually abandoned Church Street. There were two stretch limos looking expensively sinister.

"Pull up here, Chris." I saw a spot, but missed the fire hydrant. I avoided making further suggestions and Chris got parked by himself, but a block and a half from where we were going. As I got out I could see well-dressed people still moving in the direction of the unimpressive brick arch and the door to the second floor.

"We may throw a monkey-wrench into this fancy shindig," Savas said. We continued down the street to the door. "How does he get people to come to look at that stuff, Benny?"

"It's like olives, Chris. You have to get used to them."

"Don't try to tell a Cypriot about olives, Benny. I won't tell you about gazing through keyholes and taking dirty pictures and you stay off my case, okay?" Savas was just filling in the time by letting off nervous energy. I was thinking about how his big, brave front was a great piece of theatre, when I spotted a familiar dark Volvo.

"That's Paddy Miles's car," I said. "I'll be right back." I walked past Chris, who went on ahead of me, and went over to examine the car more thoroughly. I had a moment of doubt, but I dismissed it when I saw that the back seat had a stack of paintings with their edges protected with cardboard corners. The colour of the car was right too. I reached into my pocket for a familiar shape, while planting myself at the front end of the car.

Chris had meanwhile interrupted his own progress. A police cruiser had pulled alongside the parked cars. The roof lights were still and unflashing. The two occupants watched Chris make his way off the sidewalk and through a narrow space between two top-of-the-line imported Japanese sedans. He was large enough so that it was a difficult squeeze. As he moved to them, the window was rolled down on the driver's side. I finished doing the little job that the Volvo inspired, and walked along the outside of the line of cars with the cruiser double-parked in front of the gallery entrance. By this time Chris was in conversation with the two uniformed men in the cruiser. As I caught up, I recognized my old friends Kyle and Bedrosian. I was surprised that they were still partners. I first met them a few years ago when they were still apple-cheeked and bright-eyed, new to the force and dedicated to taking a reported Breaking and Entering suspect into custody. I remember that night very well. I was the suspect. I was surprised that Kyle and Bedrosian hadn't either left the force for greener fields or risen to become deputy chiefs by this time. It just shows how wrong you can be. As I hove alongside, Savas was finishing his instructions. "...and stay close. Keep the front door in view at all times and try not to be seen by people going into the gallery. Leave the car up the street and keep your eyes peeled from across the street. We'll be inside and we'll yell if we get in trouble."

"We?" asked Bedrosian, leaning out the window and looking at me. Savas shot me a quick look too, but put his face close to Bedrosian's and said, somewhat louder than necessary:

"Go to hell, Bedrosian! He's a goddamned key witness!" Bedrosian pulled his head back into the cruiser faster than he had done lately. There are lots of things cops learn to do to heads hanging out car windows. I was glad I wasn't tuned into Bedrosian's imagination. Savas and I turned and went up to the gallery entrance, while the car slowly moved off to hunt for a place to park.

Chapter Twenty-Four

U pstairs, on the gallery floor, the room had been transformed from a few hours earlier. The walls, where I could see them, were familiar but the room was so full of well-dressed people that it was difficult to see whether Martin Lyster had finished the job he'd started or not. Everybody was standing in groups of twos and threes, stuck like photographer's models on the green summer grass of a fancy shoot. This party looked impressive, except the drinks were, in keeping with tradition, the worst wine available. "Plonk" Miles called it, and that's the way it hit the stomach. But I didn't see anybody actually drinking any of it. This was a wine to hold while engaging in conversation. It held very well without losing any points for bitterness, mustiness or letting its high tannin content embarrass anyone.

Looking around for familiar faces, I took a stand beside a table which only had a tray with cheese cubes and crackers on it. Maybe I was foolish to hope for cold cuts, but, judging from the gownage and tailoring, to say nothing of the blue hair in evidence, I should have thought I'd find more than those cheese cubes. Alex Favell was deep in conversation with a large woman with upswept wings to her glasses. He kept looking towards the door over the woman's red velvet shoulder. She was talking, he was nodding vaguely, like he wasn't listening. I know the feeling.

"Mr Cooperman! Good to see you." It was my boss

with his daughter on his arm.

"Hello, Benny," Anna said. "Are you improving your-self or still working?"

"Oh, I forgot for a moment that you two know one another," Jonah said. "Have you been here long?"

"Just arrived. Hello, Anna." Once again, I was ren-dered speechless by Anna Abraham. It was a power she had, even when those smouldering eyes were turned on the paintings, or when she was doing her best to make me throw her out the door. She was dressed rather more informally than most of the older people at the gallery. She was in a bluish grey outfit with generous lapels, puff sleeves and a Chinese green turtle-neck top. The skirt was cut fashionably short. Right away I began wondering if the top was full or just a dicky. Her earrings were jade pieces with intri-cate carving I couldn't quite see clearly at this distance. She smiled at me and I tried to make polite conversa-tion with her old man.

"I think there's been some movement in the last few hours, Mr Abraham."

"You mean you have it? The list, I mean?"

"Oh, the list. Um, yes, I've been thinking about that."

"Thinking? I hope your efforts are more substantial than that."

"You'll see what I mean in a few minutes. Will you excuse me?" I tried to say it the way they do in the mo-vies. I think my cigarette should have been newly light-ed for the full effect; mine was a small nub of a butt between my stained fingers. I spotted our host greet-ing guests at the top of the stairs. I went through the talking throng in his direction.

"Madeleine! How wonderful to see you! Martin," he called as though his half-brother was standing at his side, "get Madeleine a glass of wine!" He disengaged himself from the comfortable-looking Madeleine and went on working the crowd. From a distance I could see him place a *bon mot* in the ear of one silver-haired man in a business suit. He looked like he would feel undressed without his cheque book in his inside breast pocket. Over his shoulder, I saw Peter MacCulloch come in alone. Favell was watching too, but made no move. Miles continued working the crowd with skill and the right word for every guest. He caught my eye at last. "Ah, Mr Cooperman! You are very welcome! You were saying that you'd never been to one of our *vernissages* before. What do you think?"

"Feels like a nice party, Mr Miles." Before I could put in another word, he was off shouting the name "Tilly" at the top of his voice. Tilly was a lustrous blonde in a pale pink diaphanous thing that had been imported to Grantham for the occasion. I got this news by circulating and keeping my ears open. I also heard that I wasn't the only one to think that Wally Lamb had gone to where all good painters go when they die. Being dead was a good cover story for dealers, since dead artists are artists you can be sure about. They fetch a higher price at sales and auctions than live ones. And in a sense poor old Wally was as far away from the arts scene there at the Contemporary Gallery as his girlfriend Ivy was. I caught up to Paddy Miles again. Savas was behind me now. It seemed like a good time. Several of the guests had butted their cigarettes among the cheese and crackers. I was being disillusioned on all fronts, like I'd been living in a cave for the last five years.

"Mr Miles," I said, taking Paddy by the arm, "I'd like you to meet someone I don't think you know. This is Staff Sergeant Savas of the Niagara Regional Police." The smile came automatically to Paddy's face and his hand shot out at once.

"Any friend of Chief Carr..." he said, letting the name

drop loudly. "I hope you will enjoy yourself, Sergeant."

"Sergeant Savas is investigating the suicide of a friend of yours, Mr Miles." Paddy put on a grave expression. It came out of the same box the rest of his expressions came from. What we got was deep concern such as he might feel for the fall of the dollar on the international market or the overthrow of a Middle Eastern government by a bunch of army colonels. "You'd better prepare yourself for a shock," I said.

"I see," said Paddy Miles, running a thumb along the top edge of his glass. "Well, you'd better tell me then. That's all I need tonight: a shock. Well, the wine wasn't doing it. You'd better tell me."

"It's Mary MacCulloch," I said as simply as I could.

"Oh, no! Mary? I don't believe it! That's a cruel joke. I mean, well, it's impossible!"

"Steady on," said Chris. "Would you like to sit down?"

We found the pouffe that had looked so isolated earlier in the day. One end was free and Paddy Miles sat down hard. Neither of us said anything and he just looked at the floor and shook his head.

"I know things may have been looking bad for her, but to take her life! I just can't..." He looked up at Chris waiting for him to tell him what else he knew.

"Can you give me some idea what her motive for suicide might have been?" Savas asked. I could see how subtle he could be with people. It was a new side of the old bugger. I kept learning from him.

"Well, I don't know," he said. "She was distracted, I guess, about all this pressure."

"Pressure?"

"Mr Cooperman, here, has been on her tail pushing pretty hard all week, even before Mr Kiriakis was killed."

Savas gave me a dirty look. "Pushing, was he? I want to learn all I can about that."

"Well, there's not very much to say, except that he's pushy. He frightens people, intimidates them. If I was the nervous type and had him pushing me like that, I might take an overdose too."

"Well, you know, Mr Miles, these investigators are licensed by the province. We don't regulate them locally. Most of them have very little police training. Right now, there's not much we can do about it." Savas repeated the dirty look, and I fell to the bottom of the birdcage of my chosen profession.

"Luckily," Miles went on, "I'm not easily scared. I'm not the type to scare easily. Poor Mary. Now, if you'll excuse me, I should say a word to..."

"Just a moment, Mr Miles," I said. Miles shot a look at Savas to show that he shared Savas's own sensitivity at having me around. They exchanged a glance at my expense, while I tried to keep my big, dirty feet from breaking anything valuable on the floor. "With your permission, could I ask you one more question?"

"Yes, but please make it a short one. I have guests."

"How did you know that Mary MacCulloch took an overdose?" Eyebrows shot up on at least two faces. Miles tried on an uncertain smile.

"Did I say she'd OD'd? Well, I guess she didn't strike me as the type to cut her throat or shoot herself. She's gentle, the no-fuss, no-muss type. She's not going to jump off the roof, now, is she?" He looked to Savas for confirmation of his natural guess. I'd caught him out in one of those traps that TV thrives on and courts of law have very little patience with. But, I had more. "Would you say she was a jumper, Mr Cooperman?"

"Not off hand. I see you've given the matter some thought. And of course the roof of the house in Port Richmond is too low. Not dependable enough. But you know the house. I was forgetting. I saw you going into it and coming out late this afternoon."

"Like hell you did! I haven't been near there. You're not going to get a rise out of me that way."

"You know the house though?"

"What house? I don't know what you're talking about. Sergeant?" Savas tried to calm him down. He took a big swallow from his glass. "Look," he said once he caught his breath, "you're telling me that Mary killed herself. I find the whole idea terribly upsetting. She was a good friend going back several years. And I don't care how she did it. If she'd hit herself over the head with an axe, it's still suicide, and it's a good friend dead."

"You *must* admit to being at her house in Port Richmond just before it got dark tonight?"

"Not even to convenience you, Mr Cooperman. You can't place me anywhere near that house. Not today, not ever."

"I guess your brother will say you were here in the gallery all afternoon."

"You saw me here yourself." He looked at Savas, seeming to indicate that this was a demonstration of how to handle my type in the future. "I don't think he can put me anywhere near Port Richmond late this afternoon."

Savas nodded to Miles: we have to indulge these cranks and amateurs, you understand, he seemed to be saying.

"Mr Miles, what if I wasn't the only witness? What if there is someone else who can put you at the scene of the crime? What then?"

"Cooperman, watch it. Sergeant, are you going to let him go on like this? What do you mean, 'scene of the crime'? What 'crime'? And 'witness' to what?"

At this point somebody interrupted, asking Paddy to direct him to the "Men's Room" he called it. Miles gave him directions and told him to lock the door,

because it was a unisex facility. When he got back to
me and Chris, the dramatic momentum had been lost.
He'd had a second to think and rally his defences.

"We've got another witness," I said, to bring him back
to the story at hand.

"You're bluffing. You can't scare me. Now, if you'll
excuse me...?" He got up, crossed the room and shook
hands with a familiar-looking middle-aged man.

"Sergeant," Paddy Miles called. Savas shot me a fast
look and we walked over. "Chet, I want you to meet
Sergeant Savas of the Niagara Regional Police and Mr
Cooperman from town, here. Chet Bryant, the crown
prosecutor." Miles looked self-satisfied at the juxtapo-
sition of the justice team. Bryant bowed his head slightly over the hands he was shaking and said something
inconsequential. He looked well fed and comfortable.
His face reflected a mine of inside lore about the workings of the law. Maybe he knew about murders that
were never brought into court, or cases of plea-
bargaining that would make three heads curl. There
was a look of agreeable genteel corruption about the
hang of his jowls and suit. We all mumbled something
and Bryant was only removed from us by the appearance of Mrs Bryant at the edge of the company. She
was near enough to smile, but far enough away not to
be drawn into the introductions.

"This show seems a great success already, Paddy,"
Bryant said, clapping him on the arm, before moving
off. "I think my wife is looking at something beyond
the reach of a poor public official." He expected the
laugh he got, and then he was gone. Miles looked at
me, still showing no emotion, still not sweating.

"I'm calling your bluff, Mr Cooperman. I think the
next move is up to you."

"We know everything, Paddy. It's all over." My voice
surprised me. It was less sharp than I thought it would

be. It was quiet and relaxed. "You thought Mary's death would cover your tracks, didn't you? One good suicide to cover both murders."

"*Both* murders?" Savas and Miles said it like a chorus in Gilbert and Sullivan.

"Yes, *both*. You are all forgetting Arthur Tallon. Tallon was murdered just as Kiriakis was. They're both connected. But Mary didn't kill Tallon and she didn't kill Kiriakis, in spite of that silly clue you planted: the button in Kiriakis's hand. And one more thing," I said, catching my breath and watching Paddy Miles's face trying to deal with this theory of mine. "Mary didn't kill herself either. She's a little light-headed at the moment, but in the morning after a good breakfast she's going to talk her head off. She's that other witness I mentioned. You're it, Paddy."

Before he could say anything, Chris Savas moved in and put the arm of the law on him. "He's right, Mr Miles. Let's go outside. We'll go over to the station and see if we can get your side of things."

"You must be having me on. You can't be serious. I've got two hundred guests here!"

"You'd better come along all the same," Savas said. Miles looked at Savas and then back at me again. His mouth contorted in a sneer.

"I'll be damned if I'll listen to any more of this!"

In a flash, Paddy Miles made his move. A table overturned, sending blocks of cheese, crackers and cigarette butts flying. A woman screamed. Paddy Miles was halfway to the door before I was fully aware that he wasn't standing there glaring at us.

"Hey! Stop that man!" Savas shouted. "Miles, stop! You won't get far!" But Miles was out the door and on the stairs. Savas worked his way through the crowd with a little more consideration than Miles had. I caught up to him on the top step. "He won't get far," he said partly to himself and partly to me.

"You're right," I said. "He won't get far with a flat tire."
Savas looked at me suspiciously. My little red pocket-
knife felt warm in my pocket.

Chapter Twenty-Five

Kyle and Bedrosian picked up Paddy Miles crying over the right front bumper of his Volvo. They said they didn't have any trouble with him. He went as quiet as a lamb with them to Niagara Regional's Church Street headquarters, while the party at the gallery continued. Savas whispered something to Peter MacCulloch, who then began looking for his light raincoat in a pile of coats that had collected on a small table under the few hooks by the door. When he'd rescued his own from the rest, he quietly left the party with a solemn expression darkening his face as he made for the stairs. Behind him, Alex Favell watched his back. He looked confused both by the fact that Mary was missing and that her husband was leaving so early. He was unlikely to ask me what was going on, and as I turned back into the crowd, still talking about Paddy's sudden rush out the door, I wondered whether I'd tell him. It was one of those things you never know until you see what you've done. Me, I'd just as soon see Favell squirm on in ignorance, but my character isn't pure. Maybe I'd have told him the truth, just to see how he'd take it.

Martin Lyster had taken charge of the gallery. He moved through the crowd with skill and charm, occasionally writing something down on the back of an envelope and placing one of those little red dots in a bottom corner of a picture that had just found a new owner. By the time I left, there was a benday explosion of red dots, the walls looked like they'd broken out in measles. The Lambs were snapped up fast. I wondered whether Wally and his Ivy would ever see any of the money. Probably not. Probably not.

On my own way out, Jonah Abraham caught up with me on the stairs. Anna was a few steps behind him. "What was that all about?" he wanted to know. I tried to put him off with a smile, but he wouldn't buy that.

"Okay," I said, stopping on the landing where the stairs turned. "It looks like this thing is winding down."

"Then I want to know about it!" he said sharply. Anna had now caught up to him.

"So do I!" she added, as though I had to be told.

"Savas, that's Staff Sergeant Chris Savas, has a suspect in custody. He has enough on him to hold him for the night anyway. I suggested to him that we try to meet someplace later on. He doesn't like the idea, but I wouldn't be surprised if he would accept an invitation from you if you asked him up to your place for a drink after he got off duty."

"He'd never come, Mr Cooperman, especially if we were going to ask him questions about the case."

"That's right, but he might just come to listen. I know Chris and he's one of those cops who knows that listening is the way to learn things."

"Are we going to be listening to you?" Anna asked with a wicked smile.

"Partly, but not completely. That's why I want to invite some other people to come up to your place tonight, Mr Abraham, if you don't mind."

"Won't it be rather late when Sergeant Savas gets finished?"

"It will be close to midnight, I suspect. He's been on duty at least since four this afternoon. So his shift should end at midnight."

"Who are these others?"

"I'll tell you all about it while you give me a lift to my car."

"Your car?"

"Yes, I left it at the General Hospital."

Jonah Abraham looked at me like I'd asked him to take me to Winnipeg for a corned beef sandwich. Anna took his arm and after a pause he nodded. We continued down the stairs and out into the night, which had turned chilly.

An hour and a half later, we were sitting in a room at the Abraham mansion. We were holding drinks and making polite conversation in what was a strange setting for most of us. Bill Palmer had had a few of Abraham's prize Bloody Marys, while Linda Kiriakis was still sipping her first. MacCulloch had arrived a few minutes after Alex Favell had left his rubbers in the hall. It had started raining on the drive up the escarpment, one of those fine, misty spring rains, heavy with the smells of local industry. I'd once complained about that smell to an advertising man who worked in Alex Favell's agency. He said it was the perfume of money. I wondered while I was waiting for Savas to come and make our group complete whether the smell ever gets too strong for the money to be worth it. I'd thought of asking Mattie Lent to join us, but there wasn't a good reason, and I'd promised to keep her out of it as well as I could. I did invite Wallace Lamb to join us. I wasn't sure what he could tell us, or whether Ivy would let him, but they both came when Abraham sent a car to fetch them. Anna was amazed that Lamb was still alive and so was Alex Favell. Martin Lyster came as soon as he was able to close up the gallery and check on what he could do for Paddy.

"Well," Jonah Abraham said, as soon as Chris Savas had taken off his wet raincoat and had been handed a Bloody Mary, "if everybody's comfortable, Mr

Cooperman, why don't you get started?"

"Good idea," I said and immediately wondered where I should start. I told them that there had been an attempt on the life of Mary MacCulloch and that she was still in the General, but that Dr Leung had told me that he was sure that she would be all right. Favell breathed a raspy sigh at the news. He glanced over at MacCulloch, who was looking at one of the many pictures by Milne and Lamb that decorated the walls of the room.

"You see," I said, trying to get closer to the meat of the subject, "Paddy Miles not only tried to kill Mary MacCulloch, but he tried to blame other crimes on her as well. If he had succeeded in killing her, he would have silenced a witness who could connect him to other wrongdoing."

"You mean that bum cheque he gave Wally," Ivy said, collecting glances from everybody in the room.

"Hush, precious," Wally Lamb said to Ivy, patting her ample arm on the couch next to him. "Listen to the man."

"You're not being very specific, Mr Cooperman. What wrongdoing?" asked my employer and host, ignoring Ivy.

"Paddy Miles had been selling paintings from Arthur Tallon's collection at scandalously low prices to Mary. She would take them to Hump Slaughter's auction house where they would fetch a healthy profit, which she in turn would share with Miles."

"How do you know this?" asked Peter MacCulloch in an overbearing tone on the edge of rudeness but lacking that last inch of malice that hinted he was half-afraid I had an answer. "Where's your proof?"

"I overheard Mary talking, arguing, really, with Slaughter yesterday afternoon. They were worried that the other partner was going to give the game away. There wasn't much trust between them. I doubt if

Hump ever knew that Miles was knowingly lending a hand. He may have thought he was just trying to clear out Tallon's stuff without realizing the market value of the paintings."

"That seems hardly likely," said Alex Favell. "If Hump auctioned the paintings, then he would collect the money. If he split the profit with Mrs MacCulloch, it would leave out the third partner. Are you suggesting that Paddy Miles took half of Mary's share? That seems illogical to me."

"I think you imagine that Mary was involved in this simply for the money. I think it's a safer bet to say she was in it for the adventure and the thrill of putting one over. She was a wealthy woman. There's no sign that she needed the extra cash. To her, crime was a prank, a way of kicking up her heels at society. There were other things we needn't go into here that suggest that she was trying to be as unconventional as she could be and get away with it. She's not a hard case in any way."

Favell was looking at the pattern on the rug. Savas gave me a good look at his scowl. His views on middle-class crime were on record. Anna was getting bored by these preliminaries, she was restlessly moving from one perch to another. "So," she said, "you're going to forget all about her?"

"Look, Anna, I'm not an avenging angel; I'm a poor working stiff. All this stuff is up to the cops and then the Crown." She pouted and allowed herself to slip deeper into her chair. "Let me try to deal with everything that happened in an orderly way. If I get it twisted up, it's because it's a complex business."

"Start with that dud cheque," Ivy offered, leaning forward on the couch. "Paddy Miles gave Wally here a cheque and it bounced. I took it to the bank as soon as it arrived and it was no good!"

"Shut up, precious," Wally Lamb said. "Keep still and listen." He put a hand on Ivy's knee and she moved closer to the painter.

"A moment ago, Benny, you said there were other crimes that Miles was trying to pin on Mary MacCulloch. Is that a good starting place?"

"Yeah, Bill, I'll try it that way." I should have known that it would be a veteran journalist who'd help me find a hard line through this. He had taken out a pipe and was busy packing tobacco into it. I watched him as I talked, it was relaxing entertainment.

"We all know that Pambos Kiriakis was murdered," I went on, keeping an eye on Bill Palmer's fingers as he tamped down the shag from his oilskin pouch. "Few are aware that Arthur Tallon was murdered as well."

"Tallon! What are you talking about?" There was a general sensation when I said that. Martin Lyster merely expressed it for the company. "We all know he died of a heart attack. I mean, I was there! He had a bloody heart attack. No two ways about it."

"The symptoms of a heart attack are well known. Anything that appears to have the same shooting pains and so on is often labelled a heart attack when really it is something else. In this case, a dose of penicillin."

"That's impossible!" Anna said, slightly raising herself on her elbows. "Everybody knew Arthur was allergic to penicillin. He wore a bracelet." She encircled her left wrist with the fingers of her right hand in case the reference was obscure.

"I know," I said. "But the bracelet had been removed from the body when it arrived at the General. I checked the list in the Medical Records Department while I was waiting for news of Mary MacCulloch's condition. The medical team that worked on Tallon had no hint that he was allergic to the drug, because he wasn't wearing the medical alert bracelet Anna had given him. Without that, the people in Emerge had no way of knowing that this wasn't a heart attack."

"But who would do such a thing?" asked Anna.

"Someone desperate enough. Someone in a corner," I said. "You see, Arthur Tallon was such an eccentric, he was a walking opportunity for the rip-off artists of this town..."

"Now, Cooperman, see here...!" I tried to calm Mac-Culloch with a gesture and by going on quickly.

"But he wasn't as dumb as he looked. He began to catch on to some of the things going on around him. When his suspicion of Paddy Miles was discovered, his days were numbered." I reached into my trouser pocket and found the medical alert bracelet. I handed it to Anna. "Is this the bracelet you gave Tallon?" She looked at it and nodded in the affirmative at once.

"Yes," she said, "but how did you get it?"

"The night I stumbled across Pambos Kiriakis's body at the hotel, I found this bracelet hidden in a cold cup of coffee. Pambos had hidden it from his murderer, which leads me to think that the person guilty of killing Tallon also killed Pambos Kiriakis."

The people in the room weighed the possibility and came up with the same conclusion I'd come to. The proof wasn't strong, but the logic had a certain compulsion to it. They looked like they wanted me to go on, so I did. "The question arises, how did the bracelet get into Pambos's possession? Well, we know that he hired me to look for a list of Lambs on loan from Tallon's collection at the time of Tallon's death. Clearly, he was curious about Tallon's affairs. In Alex Favell's office, Paddy suggested to me that he was hoping to get a free painting from the estate by locating the ones listed on the missing piece of paper. That could be one reason for Pambos's interest. It also could have been blackmail."

"Blackmail?" This from Mrs Kiriakis, without much outrage. She was simply caught off guard.

"I'm not suggesting that Pambos was demanding money from the person who had been stealing from Tallon's collection. I think he may have been demanding that the stolen property be returned or he would take certain steps. If the medical alert bracelet had come into Pambos's possession, it would make a substantial threat to Miles. After all it had Tallon's name on it."

"This is a high-wire act, Mr Cooperman," Alex Favell volunteered. "None of this is getting us anywhere. Theories are all very well, but they get short shrift in a courtroom." He looked to the others for support, and, not finding as much as he'd hoped for, contented himself with draining the melt-waters from his empty Bloody Mary.

"You're right, of course," I said. "But there's somebody here who might be able to stiffen part of the theory." I turned to Martin Lyster, who began untwisting his long legs as soon as he felt my eye on him. "Martin, you used to work off and on at the gallery. Is that right?"

I could see that Martin wasn't anxious to put Paddy in more trouble than he was already in, but he could see no harm in my first question. He nodded in the affirmative carefully.

"Good, now the morning after Pambos was killed you told me that you'd fixed up the problem between yourself and your book-loving friend in Boulder, Colorado. Is that right?" Eyebrows went up, wondering how we'd got from Tallon's gallery to Colorado.

"That's right."

"You said you'd told Pambos that it was all fixed?"

"Yes. What's this in aid of, Benny?"

"I'll get to that. When did you tell Pambos that, Martin?"

"It must have been that night in his office. When you were there."

"Are you saying you telephoned Colorado from Pambos's office?"

Martin tried to look relaxed by interlocking the large fingers of his hands over his jacket. "Well, I may have done it the following morning. What's the difference?"

"And when did you tell Pambos?"

"It must have been after that."

"On the day he died?"

"Yes, I guess so. He came to the gallery looking for Paddy. I told him then."

"What happened after that?"

"Nothing. Paddy came back and he took Pambos into the office to talk privately. I didn't hear what they said, Benny. I didn't put my ear to the door."

"Of course you didn't. Now, you were a witness to Tallon's heart attack at the gallery?"

"That's right."

"Was Tallon wearing this medical alert bracelet when he became ill?" I held it out to him, and he moved his hand towards it, but without taking it from me.

"Benny, I don't want to say any more about it."

"That's right, Martin. I'm sure we all sympathize with your loyalty to Paddy." Here I looked over at Savas. I'd been avoiding eye contact ever since I confessed to having found the bracelet in Pambos's office at the hotel. He was wearing his usual scowl with a difference. There was a focus to it and I was it.

"Chris, I've placed Pambos at the gallery in conversation with Paddy on the morning of the murder. If the bracelet was there at the time, Pambos had access to it. We know it was in his possession that evening. I think that's enough to check the tissue samples taken from Tallon at the time of his death. I'm suggesting that you look for an overdose of penicillin."

Savas sat deep in his end of a leather couch, with his arms folded expectantly. They seemed to be challenging me to make more incriminating disclosures. If he wasn't going to buy what I'd just said about Tallon's murder, then I was going to hear more about removing that bracelet from the spilled coffee on Pambos's desk. I hoped that I still had his curiosity aroused. He'd want to see how this story all tied up together. Then he'd bring out his handcuffs for me. I decided that I probably deserved it anyway.

"With Tallon safely dead," I went on, "Miles had thought that he could operate more easily. While pretending to be administering the estate, Miles could go on to broader and broader crimes, without any inventory to rein him in. Then along comes Pambos and threatens to blow the whistle on more than even he suspected. Kiriakis only knew about a few Lambs on loan being held and not returned by ... by several of our leading citizens. But Miles couldn't afford to have anybody snooping around for any reason at all. When Pambos threatened to go public and perhaps cause an investigation into either the disposal of the collection or the death of Tallon or both, Miles had to act fast. He went to see Pambos last Tuesday night and killed him with his own antique paper-knife. He put a button from Mary MacCulloch's jacket in Pambos's hand, hoping that that would throw the blame in her direction. But the NRP aren't taken in by such desperate tricks."

"So Tallon first thought he'd blow the whistle on Miles and then Pambos tried the same thing?" Bill asked, although it came out as a statement of fact.

"That's right. Tallon may have been eccentric, but he wasn't retarded. He may have been a chaotic administrator, but he knew his pictures when he saw them, and when they went missing, he began to ask questions."

"And what about Tallon's list? The list Kiriakis got you to look for?"

"That's right, Mr Abraham, it all started with that list. Pambos came to me and told me he thought that it had been stolen by one of the people whose names appeared on it. He thought that it might be Alex Favell or Peter MacCulloch or you. The fact is, there was no list."

"What?" This from most of the people present.

"There was no list," I repeated.

"But why did Kiriakis...?" Jonah began.

"You mean he was *bluffing*?" demanded Favell, showing an unfeeling animus towards the late Charalambous Kiriakis.

"There never was such a list. None of your names were ever given *in writing* to Pambos. Names passed in conversation are hearsay. Pambos only had his memory of a conversation with Tallon. In court that's less than nothing. So he needed the list. He just needed a hook to get me involved. He hoped that I would uncover the rest of the plot, while looking for the invisible list. After all, Pambos couldn't start throwing accusations around about what he suspected but couldn't prove. He needed me to take the heat, to act as a sort of lightning rod."

Favell and MacCulloch were exchanging words that I couldn't hear. It was one of the few times I'd seen them speak. They'd both been outwitted by their own guilt. Linda Kiriakis was smiling to herself. When I caught her at it, she turned to me:

"Funny," she said, "it's too bad Pambos didn't live to see you crack this case open. I think he would have got a kick out of the way all the grubs and worms started wiggling once you lifted up the stone."

"It was an expensive rock for Pambos, Linda," I said.

"But maybe he would have approved the results even though it cost him his life. I wouldn't be surprised if his generalship of this whole business is as impressive as some of the battles fought by his hero Napoleon."

Chapter Twenty-Six

I t was an hour later. Chris Savas, Bill Palmer, Anna Abraham and I were sitting looking at placemats in a hamburger place at Turner's Corners. The placemats offered all sorts of information for no extra charge. Mine showed the whirling planets dramatically orbiting the sun with all their spots, rings and moons neatly labelled. Anna's showed a variety of mixed drinks and what sort of glasses they are served in. I didn't see the mats in front of Savas and Palmer clearly. We all ordered hamburgers and coffee. They were hot and tasty when they came, and now, half-eaten and getting cold, they made the hour seem even later than it was. We had been talking about the case, of course. Everybody was praising the late, great Charalambous Kiriakis. Partly because I remembered Pambos as a friend and partly because he was my employer of record in the first instance, I kept my mouth shut. Tributes were heard from Savas and from Bill, who was probably going to write up the case for the *Beacon*. Anna and I kept quiet. She hadn't known Pambos well, had never known his late-night sessions with Napoleon.

"What are you being so quiet for?" Savas demanded, taking another sip from his coffee cup. I shrugged.

"He was a wonderful little guy," I said. "The day before he was murdered, he helped me unpack all my worldly goods. Without him, Miles would have got away with murder."

"You say it, but you don't say it like you believe it,"

Chris said.

"Aw, he's just tired, aren't you, Benny?" said Bill, with his eye on Anna.

"Yeah, I'm tired. I'll be glad to see my bed."

"Wait a minute!" Chris said. "You've still got some explaining to do."

"Like what?"

"Like where you got the idea that you can lift things from the scene of a murder investigation and get away with it. Like why you didn't come forward with that goddamned medical alert bracelet before tonight. Like how you found out that the bracelet wasn't with Tallon's other stuff when he arrived at the General."

"Yeah, Benny, you've been scant with the details," Bill said.

"Okay, okay! I plead guilty to having slipped that bracelet into my pocket. But I did it when I heard Anna's father coming back into the office. For all I knew it was the criminal returning to the scene of his crime. And since nobody puts a medical alert bracelet into a coffee cup for fun, I got the idea that it was something important to Pambos, something he didn't want the murderer to find. After that, it just slipped my mind. I didn't come across it again until I changed my pants. And by that time, Chris, you'd warned me to stay clear of this business." It was as lame an excuse as I'd ever heard, but I had to go with it because I couldn't think of anything smarter.

"Oh, great!" Savas groaned. "It's all my fault!" Anna and Bill smiled and Chris dropped the matter of my culpability. "So, what about the hospital? Having removed evidence from the crime scene, you went on to break Regulation 865 of the Public Hospital Act which regulates access to medical records."

"Come on, Chris! I saw the records because I had authorization from Tallon's brother. I had it in writing yet. Don't give me a hard time."

"You must have turned on the charm. I've drunk a lot of hospital coffee waiting around trying to see records."

"Well you didn't go to school with Alison Simmers. She's a clerk in Medical Records and was once sweet on my brother."

"You sure it was your brother?" Anna wanted to know.

"She had blonde braids and an elephant bell. She was irresistible in grade five." Anna shared a look with Bill Palmer.

"Well, Benny," Chris said, "if you get out of this case a free man, I'll be surprised. What with withholding evidence and slashing tires..."

"That was just poetic justice. He slashed mine!"

"You got proof for that too, Benny?"

"What do you have to do to get the waiter's attention?" I said.

"Try setting the napkin on fire," Bill suggested. It proved unnecessary, and with fresh coffee all round, we got along better. Bill was looking at me funny. "Tell us, Benny. There's something on your mind that you're not saying."

"What are you, a mind-reader all of a sudden? I told you everything."

"You told us almost everything. There's something else."

"Bill, get off my back. What have you been smoking?"

"You're right," Chris said. "I can see it in his eyes. Come on, Benny. What are you holding back?"

"It has nothing to do with any of this."

"Spill it," Chris insisted, and I felt some pressure on my arm from the Abraham connection.

"It has to do with Pambos, right?" Bill guessed.

"It doesn't have anything to do with why he was

killed. It's something extra, something that doesn't lead anywhere."

"Come on!"

"Christ, Chris, I liked the guy! I saw him lying in his own blood! He brought me into this in the first place. I don't want to..."

"It has to do with Guenyeli, I'll bet," Bill Palmer said. Nobody said anything after that. Anna was waiting for a translation, while Chris was searching his memory for that familiar name.

"What's Guenyeli?" Anna asked at length.

"It's a village in Cyprus," Chris said slowly, as though the place was gradually coming into focus. "A Turkish village on the road from Nicosia to Kyrenia." After that, he looked at me, still puzzled like the others, and so I told them.

"Pambos had a brother who was killed by the Turks outside that village back in the 1950s. Michael, his name was. The British picked him up with a bunch of young Greeks and let them off in the fields behind Guenyeli. The Turks were waiting for them with knives and axes and clubs. Nine were killed. Bill, here, covered it for the *Times of Cyprus*. Later, here in Canada, another of Pambos's brothers was killed. This one had got in with the mob. He had always rebelled against authority, the injustice of it all, and came to a bad end. Now Pambos was more subtle. He set about trying to find out who was behind the massacre at Guenyeli. Bill here told him after a lot of prodding.

"On his trip to England with Linda, Pambos went down to Kent, where the British officer who had ordered the Guenyeli massacre was then living in retirement near the coast. Maybe you noticed, Bill, what an expert he was on the coast between Dover and Deal? He was talking about possible landing places for Napoleon. He tracked Tim Bell, the officer in charge, to a house in Walmer and he watched the local pub. One night he caught up to the old man and killed him, probably with a tire iron, and left the body by the side of the road so that it would be taken for a hit-and-run case."

"That's terrible!" Anna said, surprising herself when the words in her mind could be heard by the rest of us. "He did that? In cold blood?"

"Yes, he did that," I said. "But he missed his mark."

"Uh?"

"He killed Tim Bell's longstanding drinking crony, another retired officer, another old-timer, another Timothy, as it happened. Bell hadn't gone drinking that night. He killed the wrong man. Then Pambos drove back to London and continued his visiting of museums and castles with his wife."

"I guess you know what you're talking about?" Chris asked without much steel in his voice.

"Oh, yes. I talked to Linda and Bill, here. I got curious enough to make a phone call to the police at Deal. The pub's the Thompsons Bell. The Dover Road from the village is quiet at that time of night. Closing time. The two Tims were familiar old brothers-in-arms as they wandered back along that road. Lieutenant-Colonel Tim Bell was sick with the flu the night of the murder. He died two months later."

"Kiriakis behaved like he was a one-man Nuremberg," Savas said at last. "Even if it was his brother. You can't take the law..." He didn't finish. He knew we knew.

"Funny, to think of Pambos being both a victim and a murderer," Bill said. "And there's no connection. Nothing. Just his passion for getting involved, I guess. The same way he got involved with Napoleon on St Helena and fussed about the paintings that hadn't been returned to Tallon's collection."

"To be too busy is some danger," Anna said, and I thought of Wally Lamb who'd said the same thing. I guessed it was a quotation from somewhere. It fitted Pambos like a cap.

The very last piece of news I put on the table was the fact that Alex Favell had caught up to me on the doormat, while putting on his rubbers. He announced without looking away from his feet that some pictures had been found at home that weren't his. He wondered whether they might belong to the Tallon estate. I suggested that he get in touch with George Tallon about it. Favell nodded like he wouldn't have been able to come to that conclusion on his own. He thanked me and still without looking me in the eye, rushed out into the night with a clear conscience.

I didn't bother telling them that after Jonah Abraham had waved the rest of us good-night, he went back into the house where, I suddenly remembered, Wally Lamb and Ivy were still sitting and drinking Bloody Marys. Something good may come of that too, I thought.

Chris and Bill went off in Chris's car and I started to drive Anna back through the city to her father's house on the hill. Neither of us said anything for a long time. The lights on the highway dulled the powers of speech. Anna snuggled up to my side of the car, making me glad I wasn't a "four-on-the-floor" purist. Beyond the oncoming headlights, a purplish glow hung over Grantham. For a minute I thought of my old room at the City House, the last of the United Cigar Store on St Andrew Street and Ella Beames's coming retirement. I thought of the death sentence Pambos had pronounced on Tacos Heaven. I'd have to wait and see how accurate he was in his prophecy. "I still like him, Anna," I said. "Is that wrong?"

"I don't know," she said. "I don't know. You like what you remember of the man. That doesn't mean you approve of what he did." We were quiet again as I came through the shoulders of a cut that led to the edge of the escarpment. After a while she said:

"He made a terrible hash of it, didn't he? Killing the wrong man. You can't justify that."

"No." We were coming down under the purple haze and into the valley of the old canal. "It's almost worse because there was no human contact in it. No fight, no argument, no falling out."

"An execution, that's what it was."

"He may have thought so. But where were the judge and jury?"

"Maybe it was Paddy Miles."

"You believe in a complicated universe, Anna." The Olds left the highway and came up to St Andrew Street and its eastbound traffic. "If Major Bell had had his day in court, what would he have said?"

"'I was trying to shorten the fighting; I was only following orders; I was doing my duty.' I don't know."

"Were they both exceeding their authority? Both Paddy and Pambos?"

"Yes, I think they were. But it's never easy, is it?"

"No, Anna, you're right there." It had started to rain again as I turned off St Andrew into Court Street. We were heading into April and there was no avoiding it.

ALSO BY HOWARD ENGEL

The Suicide Murders
The Ransom Game
Murder on Location
Murder Sees the Light
A City Called July